PRAISE FOR THE *NEW YORK TIMES* BESTSELLING SCUMBLE RIVER SERIES

Murder of the Cat's Meow

"Swanson serves up another romance-sweetened tale of murder in the endearingly zany town of Scumble River."
— *Chicago Tribune*

"Well-crafted.... From normal to nutty, the folks of Scumble River will tickle the fancy of cozy fans."
— *Publishers Weekly*

Murder of a Creped Suzette

"Another great book by this master of the small-town mystery." — *CrimeSpree Magazine*

"A Swanson novel is always going to have tongue-in-cheek humor, complex motives, and unique murders. The latest cleverly crafted tale is another entertaining mystery." — *Romantic Times*

Murder of a Bookstore Babe

"In the latest installment in her cozy Scumble River series, Swanson serves up another irresistible slice of romance-spiced mystery." — *Chicago Tribune*

"As always, Skye Denison and Scumble River provide a reliable, enjoyable mystery. Reading about Scumble River is as comfortable as being in your own hometown." — *The Mystery Reader*

Murder of a Wedding Belle

"The latest carefully crafted installment in Swanson's Scumble River series features a charming heroine who is equally skilled at juggling detection and romance."
— *Chicago Tribune*

continued ...

Also by Denise Swanson

SCUMBLE RIVER MYSTERIES
Murder of the Cat's Meow
Murder of a Creped Suzette
Murder of a Bookstore Babe
Murder of a Wedding Belle
Murder of a Royal Pain
Murder of a Chocolate-Covered Cherry
Murder of a Botoxed Blonde
Murder of a Real Bad Boy
Murder of a Smart Cookie
Murder of a Pink Elephant
Murder of a Barbie and Ken
Murder of a Snake in the Grass
Murder of a Sleeping Beauty
Murder of a Sweet Old Lady
Murder of a Small-Town Honey
"Not a Monster of a Chance," short story in
And the Dying Is Easy
"Dead Blondes Tell No Tales," novella in
Drop-Dead Blonde

DEVEREAUX'S DIME STORE MYSTERIES
Nickeled-and-Dimed to Death
Little Shop of Homicide

Murder of a Stacked Librarian

A Scumble River Mystery

Denise Swanson

AN OBSIDIAN MYSTERY

OBSIDIAN
Published by the Penguin Group
Penguin Group (USA) Inc., 375 Hudson Street,
New York, New York 10014, USA

USA | Canada | UK | Ireland | Australia | New Zealand | India | South Africa | China

Penguin Books Ltd., Registered Offices: 80 Strand, London WC2R 0RL, England
For more information about the Penguin Group visit penguin.com.

First published by Obsidian, an imprint of New American Library,
a division of Penguin Group (USA) Inc.

First Printing, September 2013

ISBN 978-0-451-41650-6

Printed in the United States of America
10 9 8 7 6 5 4 3 2 1

ALWAYS LEARNING   PEARSON

In memory of Sally Fellows, an inspirational teacher, thoughtful mystery reviewer, and true friend

Author's Note

In July of 2000, when the first book in my Scumble River series, *Murder of a Small-Town Honey*, was published, it was written in "real time." It was the year 2000 in Skye's life as well as mine, but after several books in a series, time becomes a problem. It takes me from seven months to a year to write a book, and then it is usually another year from the time I turn that book in to my editor until the reader sees it on a bookstore shelf. This can make the timeline confusing. Different authors handle this matter in different ways. After a great deal of deliberation, I decided that Skye and her friends and family would age more slowly than those of us who don't live in Scumble River. So to catch everyone up, the following is when the books take place:

Murder of a Small-Town Honey— August 2000
Murder of a Sweet Old Lady— March 2001
Murder of a Sleeping Beauty— April 2002
Murder of a Snake in the Grass— August 2002
Murder of a Barbie and Ken— November 2002
Murder of a Pink Elephant— February 2003
Murder of a Smart Cookie— June 2003
Murder of a Real Bad Boy— September 2003
Murder of a Botoxed Blonde— November 2003
Murder of a Chocolate-Covered Cherry— April 2004
Murder of a Royal Pain— October 2004
Murder of a Wedding Belle— June 2005
Murder of a Bookstore Babe— September 2005
Murder of a Creped Suzette— October 2005
Murder of the Cat's Meow— March 2006
Murder of a Stacked Librarian— December 2006

And this is when the Scumble River short story and novella take place:

Scumble River is not a real town. The characters and events portrayed in these pages are entirely fictional, and any resemblance to living persons is pure coincidence.

CHAPTER 1

By the Book

Skye Denison adjusted the stack of books in front of her, making sure that she was completely concealed behind their brightly colored spines. It was the morning of December 23, exactly a week before her wedding, and she was hiding out in the Scumble River Public Library.

She was supposed to be working on writing her vows, but in truth, things had gotten out of hand and she was avoiding all the people who were stressing her out. She'd known from the minute she set the date that her mother would drive her crazy, but she hadn't anticipated that others would join May on that trip. As it turned out, the entire town had an opinion. From the flowers for the church to the menu at the reception, people stopped Skye wherever she went to lobby for their favorite selection.

Didn't they realize that all the choices had been made months ago and it was far too late for Skye to change her mind now? Unless she just called off the whole shebang and went back to her nice, boring, regular life. Surely Wally wouldn't mind delaying their marriage another year, or two, or ten. He was a patient guy and didn't deserve the psycho bride she was becoming.

Skye's fiancé, Wally Boyd, the town's chief of police, had been strangely exempt from all the hoopla. It might have been his age—he was forty-three—or the fact that he had been married once before, or because he was male, but no one was making helpful suggestions to him about the decor or the food or telling him what not to wear.

Sighing, Skye closed *The Everything Wedding Vows Book: Anything and Everything You Could Possibly Say at the Altar—and Then Some* and added it to her camouflage pile. Next up was *Yes! I Will! I Do!: Your Step-by-Step Guide to Creating a Wedding Ceremony as Unique as You Are*. She examined the pale pink cover, then flipped it open to the index. As she ran her finger down the column, looking for the chapter on vows, a loud voice drew her attention to the circulation desk.

Chip Nicolet, the owner of the new health club, Guns and Poses, had backed librarian Yvonne Osborn against the counter and appeared to be enthralled with the beautiful woman's many assets. The muscular man's expression reminded Skye of her cat, Bingo, just before the Fancy Feast was spooned into his bowl—hunger, impatience, and entitlement all mixed together in a quivering mass of desire.

Yvonne had been substituting for Scumble River's regular library director since June, and during that time, Skye had noticed that although the temporary librarian had the hourglass figure of a Playboy Bunny, her outlook on life was more like Margaret Thatcher's than one of Hugh Hefner's average cottontails. Apparently, Chip hadn't gotten the memo on that, because he was staring at Yvonne's considerable bustline and nearly drooling.

Happy for a distraction from her wedding woes, but more than a bit alarmed at the man's belligerent attitude, Skye pushed aside a pillar of books and leaned forward to hear the conversation. She felt a twinge of conscience at blatantly eavesdropping, but anything was better than thinking about the big day looming on her horizon like a dentist appointment for a root canal. Why, oh, why hadn't she eloped like her brother and his new wife had?

Skye saw that Yvonne was trying to shush Chip, but evidently the health club owner had never heard of the "whisper in the library" rule because he boomed, "Come on. Say you'll go out with me."

"No." Yvonne's expression was adamant. "Now move aside and let me do my job."

"I promise you, you'll have a good time," Chip persisted, edging closer.

"I seriously doubt it." Yvonne took a deep breath, causing her chest to expand and Chip to stare. "Is there a book I can help you find?"

"A book?" Chip looked confused.

"You know, those items lined up on the shelves." Yvonne pointed to the crowded bookcases around the room. "The reason you came into the library."

"I know what a book is. What? Do you think I'm an idiot?" Chip snarled. "I just didn't realize anyone still read them."

"Yes. Many people whose attention span is longer than a television commercial still read books."

"I'll make a mental note of that," Chip jeered.

"That might be difficult for you to do since your pencil is obviously out of lead." Yvonne's voice was cool. "And since it doesn't appear you're here for any of the library's usual services, is there something else I can help you with? Perhaps directions to the bathroom?"

"What?" Chip wrinkled his brow. "Why do you think I need to go to the can?"

"Frankly"—Yvonne placed her palms on Chip's well-developed pecs and pushed, but he didn't budge—"I don't think about you at all."

"Well, you should." His gaze dropped to her curvy bottom. "A hottie like you should be hooking up with someone like me, not acting like a nun. Who are you saving it for?"

"Myself." Yvonne finally managed to step to the side

and wiggle past him. "I've found that I'm much better company than most men."

The library was divided into two main rooms, and Yvonne pushed a cart toward the section where Skye was sitting. A few wooden chairs and tables shared the cramped space with jam-packed bookshelves and racks stuffed with magazines. Yvonne stopped a few feet from Skye and started reshelving novels, pointedly ignoring the man who had followed her.

When Chip moved in front of Yvonne and put his palm on her shoulder, Skye's initial twinge of alarm grew stronger, and she dug her cell phone out of her tote bag, ready to call for help.

"Go out with me tonight. There's a new spot in Kankakee that's supposed to really rock," Chip wheedled.

"No." Yvonne glanced down at the wet spot where his fingers had rested and said, "If you're perspiring this much standing still, I'd hate to see you dancing."

"If you ain't sweating, you ain't doing it right," Chip boasted. He smoothed a hand over his shaved head. "If you don't want to go to a club, we could grab a pizza and go to my place."

"No." Yvonne reached around him and slid a hard-back into place, straightening the spine before adding, "Thank you, but I have other plans."

"Babe, you don't know what you're missing." Chip flexed his right arm, making his biceps bulge. Although it was winter, he had on a short-sleeved black T-shirt, formfitting jeans, and leather trainers.

"I know exactly what I'm missing," Yvonne assured him, narrowing her baby blue eyes. "Just because I don't want to date a Neanderthal like you doesn't mean I'm living a life of chastity."

As Yvonne reached around him again, Chip's hands spanned her tiny waist and pulled her against him. "Don't call me a Neanderthal."

"Would you prefer that I call you a caveman?" Yvonne stood perfectly still, seeming unwilling to give him the satisfaction of struggling. "Or perhaps *Homo sapiens neanderthalensis*?"

As Chip's face turned the color of the Scumble River fire engine, Skye rose to her feet to intervene, but before she could move toward the out-of-control jerk, Chip roared and leaped backward, clutching his groin. Skye's attention had been on the health club owner, but when she turned to look at Yvonne, she saw the librarian tucking a pink palm-size stun gun into her blazer pocket.

Chip stared at Yvonne for a couple of seconds, then threatened in a shrill voice, "You'll be sorry for that, bitch. You may look like Jessica Rabbit, but just remember, she was easy to erase." He hobbled out of the library, muttering about women who didn't know their place.

Yvonne met Skye's concerned gaze and shrugged. "He's not the first man to confuse how I appear with who I am."

"I'm sure he isn't," Skye sympathized. She'd learned long ago that being a round woman in a world obsessed with sticklike supermodels wasn't easy either. "Are you afraid he might retaliate?"

"Not a chance. One thing my ex-husband and his business partner taught me was how to take care of myself." Yvonne patted her pocket. "And I have some little friends to help."

"Where did you get that Taser?" Skye asked. "I've never seen one so small."

"Online. Best ninety dollars I ever spent." Yvonne handed the gadget to Skye. "Since you're the psych consultant for the police department, you should convince the city to buy you one. I can give you the details."

"Thanks." Skye examined the tiny device, then returned it to its owner. "I doubt the mayor would approve the expense. He thinks my services are pretty useless."

"Even though he's your uncle?" Yvonne asked. Then, without waiting for Skye's answer, she added, half to herself, "Of course, he actually thinks the entire PD is pretty useless."

Skye opened her mouth to ask what Yvonne meant, but the librarian spoke again before Skye could form the question. "How about requesting the weapon from the school district? As the school psychologist, you probably deal with some fairly violent adolescents."

"True." Skye's eyebrows shot up. "But I'd never Taser one of them." She added under her breath, "Maybe one of their parents, but not the kids."

"Everyone needs to be prepared for the consequences of their actions." Yvonne crossed her arms. "Especially teenagers."

"Right." Skye decided it was time to end the conversation and pulled a book from the pile toward her. "I better get back to writing my vows or I'll be ad-libbing next Saturday."

"Yes, you'd better." Yvonne headed toward the small office wedged into a corner of the library, but said over her shoulder, "I hear your wedding is the social event of the season around here. You don't want to ruin it by being unprepared."

Skye shivered. It was probably just bridal jitters, but she had a bad feeling that something would mar her big day. She only hoped that all of her carefully laid plans didn't unravel like a poorly sewn bridal gown.

CHAPTER 2

A Book in the Hand

Skye stared at her to-do list. Why, oh, why had she thought it would be a good idea to get married the week after Christmas? Not only did she still have holiday gifts to buy and wrap—she also had a million and one last-minute details to attend to for the wedding.

Okay, she knew why she had agreed to the date. As a school employee, she had only two choices if she wanted any significant time off—winter break or summer vacation. Last spring, her mother had insisted summer was too soon to plan a large wedding, and her fiancé had said he wasn't waiting until the next June rolled around. So, December 30 had been a compromise. When she had made the decision, it had seemed the obvious solution. Now, faced with the reality, Skye realized she should have just said no.

At least Wally was handling the honeymoon arrangements, and his father, Carson, was taking care of the rehearsal dinner. Both men had wanted to surprise her, so she had no idea what was going on with either event. And she didn't care. She'd be happy as long as the honeymoon was somewhere warm and private, which Wally had assured her it was, and the dinner was nearby so that no one had to worry about getting home safely, which her future father-in-law had guaranteed.

Telling herself that she was lucky to have the week prior to the wedding off from work, Skye left the library and set out on her errands. Right now, the most urgent matter was buying the rest of her family's Christmas presents.

Since Scumble River was located seventy-five miles south of Chicago, shopping was limited unless you were willing to drive to either Joliet's or Kankakee's malls. Considering it was two days until Christmas, the last thing Skye wanted to do was try to negotiate the kind of madness those retail outlets were currently experiencing.

Which left the Gift Box in Clay Center. The sprawling shop sold everything from wine to jewelry to gourmet food and was the only place within a half hour where she could get the items she wanted.

Fifteen minutes later, Skye was wondering if she'd made the right decision in avoiding the malls. The Gift Box's parking lot was jammed and she'd already circled it twice without finding an empty spot. Finally, she saw brake lights a few cars down and eased into position. Turning on her signal, she gripped the steering wheel of her '57 Bel Air and prepared to do battle for the space. It was almost a letdown when no one else noticed the opening, and she pulled in without having to fight to the death for the slot.

As she expected from the crowded parking lot, the place was packed. Accepting that this would be neither quick nor easy, Skye examined her options. Most of the gifts she needed were little stocking stuffers. She'd given in and ordered the big presents online. Despite her best efforts to remain a technophobe, she was becoming fairly adept at the computer. Now if she could just figure out all the options on her cell phone — or at least remember to keep it charged . . .

Squeezing through the congested aisles, she headed

for the baby section first. Her brother, Vince, and his wife, Loretta, were expecting their first child on January 9, and Skye wanted to get something for the newest member of the family. Loretta and Vince had decided not to reveal the infant's sex before the birth, so the gift needed to be appropriate for either a boy or a girl.

This area was less crowded than the rest of the store, and Skye took her time studying the assorted items. Everything was darling and it was difficult to choose, but she finally selected a layette set packaged in a pale yellow box shaped like a house. A sign hanging on the window of the door with a satin bow read WELCOME HOME BABY! The mailbox said SPECIAL DELIVERY. And the roof lifted off to reveal a long-sleeve yellow nightgown, nightcap and pair of booties—all with white trim accented with tiny black polka dots.

Skye had picked up a shopping basket by the door, and she slipped the layette set into it before making her way to the shelves displaying gifts for men. Because her fiancé was the son of a Texas oil millionaire, or maybe billionaire, and could buy himself whatever he wanted, finding a present for him was difficult if not downright impossible.

She had ultimately decided on a subscription to the Beer of the Month Club. Unlike her male relatives who would drink whatever was on sale, Wally was picky about his beer, so she knew he'd enjoy the monthly assortment of lagers, ales, and ambers from different U.S. microbreweries. But she wanted to get him something more. Something that wouldn't be consumed and tossed out with the recyclables. Something permanent.

Almost immediately, she spotted a shelf of Ford Thunderbird collectibles. Wally's father had given him a sky blue T-bird for his fortieth birthday, and Wally was extremely fond of that car. An item with the Thunderbird emblem would be the perfect Christmas present.

Skye bit her lip as she scanned the possibilities, torn between a stainless-steel card case and a Ford Thunderbird fiftieth-anniversary watch. The case was more within her price range—about thirty bucks—but she liked the watch more. Shrugging—what was another hundred dollars on her credit card?—she tucked the watch into her basket and moved on to the jewelry counter.

She'd planned to buy a scarf slide for her mother. May had recently begun wearing scarves, but found it difficult to tie them correctly. When the silk rectangles and squares inevitably came undone, she grew frustrated, and if May was frustrated, she tended to share that experience with everyone around her.

The area in front of the glass cabinet was mobbed, but Skye scooted into a space vacated by a large man clutching a foil-wrapped box. She immediately spotted what she wanted and plucked a gold tube with an intricate knot design from the display. She checked the price—twenty-two dollars, well within her budget.

Before she could ease away from the case and allow someone else to take her spot, the person behind her said, "Skye, what are you doing here?"

Skye turned and recognized the speaker as Anthony Anserello, a nice-looking young man with sandy hair, sincere brown eyes, and a shy smile. He worked part-time for the PD and part-time for his father, who owned an appliance-repair business.

"Hi, Anthony." Skye made room for him beside her. "Probably the same thing you are."

"Last-minute Christmas presents?" he asked, edging into the space she'd created.

"Yep." Skye extended the package containing the scarf ring. "I'm getting this for Mom." Once he'd admired the gift, she put it in her basket and asked, "Who are you shopping for?" When he didn't respond right away and his cheeks turned red, she teased gently, "Someone special? Or maybe more than one someone special?"

"Just one," he answered quickly. "Judy. She gets back tomorrow."

Judy Martin was the director of the Scumble River Library and had been away on sabbatical studying at the University of North Carolina for the past six months. In her midtwenties, Judy was young to be running a library on her own, but the salary was too low to attract a more seasoned librarian. The Scumble River school district had similar difficulties attracting experienced applicants.

"I bet you can't wait." Skye smiled at Anthony. "Are you meeting Judy at the airport?"

"Uh-huh," he mumbled, then added, "I'm not the only one who will be glad to see her."

"Oh?" Skye knew that the young librarian was popular among her patrons and staff, but was Anthony referring to something else?

When he didn't continue, Skye prodded, "Who else is anxious for Judy to come back to town?"

"Probably everyone who uses the library." Anthony frowned. "Ms. Osborn has been so mean about stuff. I've heard a lot of grumbling."

"Really?" Skye was puzzled. As far as she'd noticed, the library had been running smoothly. "Like what?" Heavens, what in the world was there to complain about? Well, now that she thought about it, probably the same things people complained about when they were unhappy with the schools: issues the employees had little control over and the administrators were never going to change.

"Judy looks the other way when the kids get a little rowdy," Anthony said, shoving his baseball cap to the back of his head. "And she lets the overdue fines slide if it's just a day or two."

"And Yvonne doesn't?"

"No." Anthony wrinkled his forehead. "She enforces every little rule."

"You can't blame her for that," Skye admonished. "It's hard filling in for someone who's as well liked and respected as Judy."

"Yeah. Judy's great." Anthony tapped his fingers on

the glass countertop. "But did you see the rant about Ms. Osborn in the *Star*?"

"No." For the past several weeks, Skye had been too busy to read the local newspaper.

"It was in that column where people can call in anonymously, whine into an answering machine, and the editor decides which of their complaints to write up."

"Uh-huh."

"Well, someone said that Ms. Osborn better mind her own business or she'd regret it."

CHAPTER 3

Lost and Foundering

Sunday was a whirlwind of activity. Skye started her day with nine o'clock Mass, then hurried home to wrap her presents for the Leofanti party. Her mother's family celebrated on Christmas Eve with a huge potluck and gift exchange, while her father's side picked a Saturday in early December for their more sedate get-together.

Skye had decided to forgo sending cards and decorating the house this year, but she'd drawn the line at skipping the tree—which had turned out to be a smart decision. Whenever she took a moment to inhale the fresh pine scent and enjoy the twinkling lights, she regained a small piece of her sanity. And she needed every little bit she could recapture.

Although it was both the weekend and a holiday, Wally was on duty at the police station. Theoretically, as the chief he worked eight to four Monday through Friday, but with such a small force, he often ended up covering for an officer who was sick or had a family emergency. With only six full-timers, it took just one case of the flu or a vacation to create a staffing problem. The two part-timers were supposed to fill in the gaps, but they often weren't able to take the shift since they both had other jobs.

Skye had been counting on Wally's help with last-minute wedding tasks, and she was not happy about his absence. In her opinion, he should have ordered someone else to come in to the PD. She wasn't sure if he'd agreed to work because he was too nice a guy to force one of his officers to give up a holiday they were originally scheduled to have off, or if he just didn't want to be around during the eleventh-hour bridal madness. Probably a little bit of both.

Either way, she was once again coping with all the chores alone. So as soon as she finished wrapping the presents and had cleaned up the scraps of paper and bits of ribbon that littered the sunroom floor, she moved into the kitchen to begin her next project. Opening the Tiffany blue leather organizer, a gift from Wally's father, she flipped to the GUEST tab and started phoning people who hadn't yet responded to the wedding invitations. Of the nearly two hundred invitations that had been sent, thirty-seven recipients had disregarded the request to RSVP.

Skye would have been happy to assume they weren't attending, but the wedding planner at the Country Mansion restaurant where the reception was being held had insisted that Skye contact the slackers. Thirty-six calls and three hours later, she stared at the remaining name on her list. Should she or shouldn't she? In most cases, it was her policy to let sleeping Dooziers lie.

The Dooziers were hard to explain to anyone not from Scumble River. They had their own little kingdom on the water's edge, and as with so many imperial dynasties, the crowned heads did as they darn well pleased. They felt that rules didn't apply to them, whoever wasn't a part of the royal clan deserved what they got, and they were entitled to whatever tribute they could grab. Their philosophy was render unto the Dooziers the things that were the Dooziers'. And in their mind, everything that wasn't nailed down belonged to the Dooziers.

Strangely enough, Earl, the monarch of Doozierland,

had adopted Skye. She wasn't sure if it was because he saw her as the ambassador between his realm and the rest of the world—a role she had often had to assume within the school system—or because he'd saved her life on more than one occasion. Whatever his reason for taking a shine to her, she had felt obligated to invite him and his family to her wedding.

Doing so had infuriated Skye's mother. May had begged her not to include the Dooziers, claiming that they would ruin everything, but Skye had stood firm. They were her friends and they'd be hurt if they didn't receive an invitation. Besides, Skye figured the family would show up anyway, and forewarned was forearmed.

Of course, they hadn't sent back their RSVP and she had to decide whether it was worth the hassle to call them. Any conversation with Earl had more land mines than the perimeters of the DMZ in Korea. Did it really matter if she didn't know if one family was coming or not? Unfortunately, she was forced to conclude that it did, because the Doozier party could consist of any-where between two—Earl and his wife—and the whole tribe.

Sighing, Skye dialed the last number she had for them, a disposable cell. Like so many others, the Dooziers didn't have a landline. However, unlike most people, their reason had more to do with keeping off the government grid and less to do with a fondness for modern technology.

Skye wasn't sure how the Dooziers obtained their electricity, but she would bet her engagement ring that it wasn't from Commonwealth Edison—at least not with the power company's knowledge. And she knew for a fact that they didn't use Waste Management to collect their garbage, because if they did, their trash wouldn't be decorating their front yards and backyards.

After a half dozen rings, Skye was ready to hang up when Earl's groggy voice buzzed in her ear. "Miz Skye, issen that you?"

"Yes, Earl, it's me all right," Skye assured him. "How are you doing?"

"Well, I was fine when I was a-sleepin'," Earl drawled, "but now that I'm awake, I'm not so good."

"I'm sorry to disturb you, Earl." Skye glanced at the kitchen clock. It was a few minutes before three. "Aren't you feeling well?"

"I'm okay, but that crazy biddy that rents the property next door woke us all up at five this mornin' complainin' about old Blue."

"Blue?" Skye asked, unsure whether Blue was one of Earl's animals or one of his kin.

"Youse know, my bluetick coonhound."

"Right." Skye vaguely remembered the animal. "What did he do?" Earl's house was on several acres and separated from his nearest neighbor by a section of trees, so she doubted the dog's offense was something as simple as barking.

"He musta got outa the pen, 'cause she claims he was over to her place humpin' her daughter's fancy pooch." Earl snickered. "Blue's like his daddy; he likes a good f—"

"I'm sure he does," Skye interrupted, not wanting to discuss the sex life of Earl's dog—or for that matter any other member of the Doozier family.

But before she could change the subject, Earl added, "She's got the fella on the other side of her land shittin' a brick, too. That female really needs to back off afore I—"

"I'm sure she does," Skye said, cutting Earl off again. "I'll let you get back to sleep. I just called to see if you're coming to my wedding."

"Sure I is, Miz Skye," Earl answered. "Me and Glenda and the kids wouldn't miss it fer anything."

"Great." Skye put a check after their name on her list. "How many of you are coming?"

"Let's see, now." Earl paused. "Me, Glenda, MeMa, Junior, Bambi, and Cletus, so that's six." He hesitated, then added, "I's sorry that Elvis and his wife and kid can't make it. They's got to go to her pa's barn raisin'. And now that Elvira's workin' in the city, she don't come home much anymore."

"Uh-huh." Skye made a note. "Six it is." Then, before Earl could continue the conversation, Skye said, "So, I'll see you next Saturday. Bye."

Hanging up the phone, Skye briefly felt sorry for Earl's neighbor, but she was soon distracted by her wedding to-do list. Next up was the caterer. The woman had told Skye that although she wouldn't be answering the phone on Sunday or Monday, Skye should leave a message with the final head count.

Once that call was made, Skye checked to see what else she needed to accomplish before going to her parents' house at five thirty. Due to the holiday, she couldn't contact any of the other venders to confirm the details, so she decided to make the zuppa Inglese for the party.

It was a testament to May's frantic state of mind that she had assigned a crucial component of the meal to her daughter. The zuppa Inglese was the Leofanti family's traditional Christmas dessert—like a trifle, but richer and more calorie-laden. Skye had baked the pound cake the day before, so all she had to do was whip up the vanilla pudding, and while it chilled, blend the rum and apricot jam. After she'd layered the cake, pudding, and rum mixture into a pedestal bowl, she would whip the cream for the top.

By the time Skye was done, she had half an hour to change clothes and load the car. Wally was meeting her at her folks' since he had to work until six. Normally, he'd have been off at four, but the officer taking the afternoon shift had begged to come in a couple hours late because it was his daughter's birthday.

When Skye pulled into her parents' driveway, the outdoor display took her breath away. Despite the triple threat of the wedding, Loretta's pregnancy, and the holidays, May had still gone all out with decorations. Skye'd been avoiding her mother as much as possible—talking on the phone rather than visiting—so she hadn't been to the house since Thanksgiving. Now she stared in awe.

Her father had made a full-scale plywood sleigh and reindeers for the front lawn. In the driver's seat a life-size Santa held the reins. Mountains of brightly wrapped boxes filled the rear of the sled, and elves clambered over the piles. Wreaths and candles lit all the windows, and the garage doors were covered in green and red to look like giant packages.

Of course, May's concrete goose had gotten a new outfit. It wore a red dress, white apron, and fur cape with a red-and-white bonnet. Skye patted the bird's head as she walked past. One good thing about the holidays was that her mother's fowl wasn't wearing clothes that were a thinly veiled message to Skye.

The inside of the house was as festooned as the outside, with a tree in every room—sometimes more than one. As Skye entered the utility room, she saw that the washer and dryer tops were filled with coats and purses, and footwear littered the floor. With cream-color carpeting in the rest of the house, May didn't allow anyone past the dinette with his or her shoes on.

After slipping off her own ankle-high boots, Skye padded into the kitchen. Several of Skye's aunts and female cousins were busy preparing the meal, and she called quick greetings as she eased through the congestion to put her gifts under the huge fresh pine in the living room.

The men were gathered around the television watching *Lethal Weapon* or *Die Hard* or *Batman Returns*. Skye wasn't sure which, but it was one of those movies set during Christmastime where things were blown up and people were shot. Her uncle Dante, the town's mayor, was screaming at the hero, "Kill 'em all!" and Skye tapped him on the shoulder.

When Dante grunted his acknowledgment of her presence, Skye said, "If I were you, I wouldn't talk to the characters on the screen." She winked at him. "Tests have proven they can't hear you."

He rolled his eyes, snorted, and turned his attention back to the show. Skye sighed and returned to the kitchen to help with the food. She'd given up on ever achieving equality of the sexes at these gatherings. There was no use mentioning that the women were doing all the work while the men sat around and drank beer. As her dad would say, it was what it was.

More and more of the family arrived, and Skye began to watch the clock. Why wasn't Wally here? Had something happened to him? She chewed her lip. Should she call him? Resolving to give him a few more minutes, she went back to her assigned task—putting ice cubes in the plastic glasses next to the cans of soda lined up on the counter.

Finally, at six thirty, May pulled Skye partway down the hallway and whispered, "Where's Wally?"

Skye mentally squirmed under her mother's stare, but answered in a nonchalant voice, "Don't get your tinsel in a tangle, Mom. He probably went home to change clothes. He'll be here any minute."

"People are getting hungry." May gestured toward the living room.

"Go ahead and let them start eating. Wally won't mind."

"Well . . ." May trailed off as the phone rang. She took a step back toward the kitchen and snatched the receiver from the base. After she exchanged pleasantries, she listened for a few minutes, then hung up and said to Skye, "That was Sylvia at the PD." May worked as a dispatcher at the Scumble River Police Department, so she knew all the other women who manned the police, fire, and emergency desk. "There's been a fatal accident and Wally was called to the scene."

"Did she say who was killed?"

"No. They don't have an ID." May shook her head.

"How awful."

"Yes." May frowned. "I just hope it's not someone we

know." She shrugged, then added, "Wally told Sylvia to tell you he'll call when he has a chance. I guess that means he won't make it to the party. His first Christmas Eve with the family. I'm sorry, honey."

Skye nodded, then pasted a smile on her face. "That's okay. It's not his fault."

May put her arm around her daughter and they walked back to tell the others the news. Everyone was sympathetic, and Skye knew that Wally would be there if he were able, but she couldn't help wondering if this was what it would be like being the wife of a police officer. More to the point, was she prepared for all the missed holidays and lonely nights?

CHAPTER 4

Read Something into It

Because many of Skye's relatives wanted to go to Midnight Mass—which was strangely scheduled at eleven o'clock—the Christmas Eve party wound down early. After everyone left, May refused Skye's offer to help clean up and sent her away with a plate of food for Wally.

Fog started to roll in during Skye's short drive home, and she was relieved to pull into her garage. Juggling a box of gifts, the covered dish of leftovers, and her purse, she made her way carefully into the dark house.

It was almost as cold inside as outside. Her thermostat was programmed to set the furnace to sixty-five degrees at ten p.m.—her usual bedtime—and as soon as she deposited her load on the hall bench, she hurried to turn up the heat. While she poked the little button repeatedly, Bingo wound his way around her ankles, purring loudly.

Once the temperature was set to a toasty seventy and the leftovers were in the refrigerator, Skye grabbed the phone and called Wally's cell. When it went straight to voice mail, she left a message that she was home and for him to come over no matter the time. She wanted to spend a part of Christmas Eve with him, even if it meant a very late night.

Determined to stay up until Wally arrived, Skye changed into her flannel pajamas and settled on the white wicker love seat in the sunroom. Bingo was in his usual position on the matching chair's floral cushion. She shook her head at the black cat. He was an expert at the law of energy conservation. Apparently his knowledge of the first law of thermodynamics—energy can't be created or destroyed—led him to the conclusion that he should use as little of it as possible.

Skye patted Bingo's rump, then leaned back to watch *It's a Wonderful Life* for the eight hundredth time. Just as Clarence earned his wings, she heard the front door open. Clicking off the TV, Skye sprang to her feet and ran to greet Wally. He was shrugging off his duty jacket as she skidded into the foyer, and when he saw her, he tossed the coat on the bench and opened his arms.

Skye flew into his embrace and snuggled against his muscular chest. He smelled of hard work and Stetson aftershave. That, and the chiseled planes of his handsome face, indicating that he was a little on edge, made him even sexier than usual.

For a long minute, Wally held her close without speaking; then he turned up her chin and said, "I'm really sorry I missed your family's Christmas Eve party. Was your mom mad? Did she give you a hard time?"

His warm brown eyes held a look of concern. May had not been in favor of Skye marrying Wally. She had disapproved of his age, his religion, and his divorced status. Only after he had obtained an annulment and promised to consider converting to Catholicism had May relented and given them her blessing. As to her final objection, the age issue, she had finally admitted that a lot of men older than Wally fathered children.

"No, Mom was fine," Skye assured him. "In fact, she sent you supper if you're hungry."

"I'm starved." He released Skye. "I haven't had anything to eat since noon." He loosened his tie. "Not only did it take the tow truck operator forever to drag the car out of the river, but we had to wait for the coroner, too. Reid was in the city, and with traffic it took him a good ninety minutes to get back."

"I can imagine." Skye's ex-boyfriend Simon Reid was both the coroner and the owner of the local funeral home. He and Wally had settled into a polite professional relationship, but neither exactly liked the other.

"And after all that, we had trouble locating the next of kin. We finally called the number on a business card we found in the accident victim's wallet. And—"

"If the car was in the water," Skye interrupted him, "I'm surprised it was dry enough to read."

"It was one of those laminated ones with a magnetic backing."

"Ah." Skye nodded. "How did you decide that card had a personal connection to the woman?"

"The company it was advertising had the same last name as the victim," Wally explained, then continued his original thought. "The number on the card was answered by the victim's ex-husband's partner, and he gave us the ex's home phone number. The holidays complicate everything."

"Tell me about it." Skye's voice was tinged with sarcasm. "Remember? I'm the one trying to deal with our wedding details while everyone else only wants to think about Christmas." She nudged Wally toward the stairs. "Why don't you go take a hot shower and change into your sweats while I heat up dinner for you?"

"That would be great." Wally ran a hand over the stubble on his chin. "This was not how I planned to spend the evening, and I'm just plain tuckered out." He wrinkled his forehead. "Maybe I'm getting too old for police work."

"Hardly." Skye shook her head. Wally would be forty-four in February, and the slight gray at his temples only made him more attractive. "Anyone would be tired if they pulled a double shift and spent the last six or so hours out in the cold and wind on an empty stomach."

He shrugged, then trudged up the steps. Fifteen minutes later, they were seated at the kitchen table and Skye watched him inhale his dinner.

When Wally paused to take a swig of Sam Adams, she said, "Was the accident victim someone local?"

"Yes and no." Wally buttered one of the Parker House rolls that Skye had snagged and hidden away for him. May had used her mother-in-law's famous recipe, and the crusty brown buns had disappeared faster than a magician could palm a quarter.

"Which is it?" Skye frowned. "Yes or no?"

"Well, she's been living in Scumble River for the past six months, but she wasn't from here and she was moving away in a couple of weeks."

"Oh." Skye racked her brain for anyone she knew who fit that criteria, but when she came up empty, she asked, "So who was it?"

"Yvonne Osborn." Wally pushed back his empty plate and drained the last of his beer.

"Oh, my gosh!" Skye felt her chest tighten. "I was just talking to her yesterday."

"At the library?"

"Uh-huh. I was there working on my vows when that jerk who owns the new health club asked her out. And when Yvonne said no, he got really mad and grabbed her. I thought for a minute I'd have to run down to the PD and get one of your officers." Skye wrinkled her forehead. "If she hadn't Tasered him, I don't know what would have happened."

"Yvonne used a stun gun on someone Saturday morning?" Wally's expression was thoughtful.

"Uh-huh."

"Did the guy leave after that?"

"Grudgingly. He said something like 'You'll be sorry' and called her a bad name." Skye bit her lip. "He's a big guy, so it was sort of scary."

"Interesting." Wally narrowed his eyes.

"Why?"

"Well . . ." Wally shook his head. "I better not speculate."

"Come on." Skye punched him lightly on the arm. "It's not like I'm going to quote you to a reporter or take an ad out in the *Star*."

"Okay, but don't mention anything to Trixie," Wally cautioned.

"I promise." Skye's best friend and her matron of honor, Trixie Frayne, was writing a mystery, which meant that she considered any crime that took place in Scumble River fodder for her plot.

"The thing is that something about the accident scene seemed hinky to me."

"How so?"

"That's the problem." Wally got up and put his plate in the sink. "I can't put my finger on it, but something just doesn't seem right."

"Hmm." Skye could sympathize. As a school psych, there were times when her gut told her there was a problem that her psychological tests were not detecting. Unfortunately, like Wally, she needed proof in order to do anything about it.

Wally opened the refrigerator and peered inside.

"Are you still hungry?" Skye asked as he stared at the contents.

"Sort of." Wally snagged the Tupperware container that held the remaining zuppa Inglese and pried off the cover. "What's this?"

"It's a dessert." Skye joined him. "The Italian version of a trifle, only more fattening. Want to try it?"

"Sure." Wally got a spoon from the drawer and sat back down.

"I'm going to make some hot chocolate." Skye grabbed the milk carton from the fridge and turned the flame on under the teakettle. "Would you like some?"

"No, thanks."

While Skye measured unsweetened cocoa powder, sugar, and a pinch of salt into a saucepan, she considered what Wally had told her about the accident, then asked, "Where did the car go off the road?"

"That one-lane bridge, where Kinsman crosses over the river."

"The same spot I went off when that lunatic was trying to kill me?" Skye felt her stomach clench at the memory of the day she'd been forced to drive her car over the side of the bridge in order to save herself from a murderer.

"Almost exactly." Wally ate a spoonful of dessert. "I keep telling the mayor the city needs to widen that bridge or at least pave it."

The surface of the bridge consisted of narrow planks of wood that vehicles were supposed to position their tires on in order to cross safely.

"I agree, but Uncle Dante will never spend the money on it." Skye paused, recalling something that the librarian had mentioned in passing. "In fact, Yvonne said that Dante is going around saying the police department is useless."

"That's nothing new." Wally scooped the last crumbs of the zuppa Inglese onto his spoon. "He's been complaining about the police department budget breaking the city bank for as long as he's been mayor."

"So you don't think he's up to something?" Skye poured boiling water over the dry mixture and stirred.

"Who knows with Dante?" Wally got up and put the empty bowl next to the plate in the sink. "It sounds as if you and Yvonne had quite a conversation."

"We did." Skye added milk to the pan. "You sure you don't want a cup?"

"Nah. I'd rather have this." Wally opened the fridge, grabbed another bottle of Sam Adams, and opened it. "What else did you and Yvonne talk about?"

"That men judge women by how they look and teenagers need consequences." Skye poured the hot chocolate into a mug, then drizzled vanilla extract over the surface. "Oh, and that her ex-husband taught her how to take care of herself."

"I wonder why he felt the need to do that." Wally swigged his beer.

"I'm not sure." Skye sipped her cocoa. "At the time, I wondered whether he was the person who had instructed her on self-defense techniques, or the reason she needed to learn them."

Skye woke to rain pelting her bedroom windows. Wally slept peacefully beside her, and she debated whether to wake him up to give him an early-morning Christmas present. He'd been too exhausted last night to do more than snuggle for a few seconds before he fell asleep—which, considering her ghost problem, was probably for the best.

When Skye had inherited the house from Alma Griggs, she'd been both thrilled and dismayed. Thrilled that the elderly lady had thought so highly of her that she had entrusted Skye with her beloved home, but dismayed at the building's state of disrepair and the cost of renovating it.

Soon afterward, it became apparent that there was more wrong with the house than just a leaky roof and rusty pipes. The real drawback of the place was that the previous owner had never really left. And Mrs. Griggs's spirit clearly didn't like it when Skye entertained men in her home. Either that or she disliked Wally. Skye wasn't sure which, since he was the only guy she'd dated since moving into the haunted house.

As long as she and Wally only kissed and cuddled, everything was fine. But the minute they went any further, something in the place inevitably blew up, ignited, or malfunctioned. Having spent a small fortune on remodeling, and with the home-improvement loan to show for it, Skye was determined to live there once they were married. She had even tried to purge the house of the ghost.

Skye and Trixie had performed a ritual that Skye had found on the Internet, which involved salt and burning sage branches. However, instead of leaving, Mrs. Griggs had pushed the television off its stand, smashing it to smithereens. After that, Skye had been afraid to try another cleansing.

Since Father Burns had been skeptical and refused to do an exorcism, and Trixie had suggested that maybe Mrs. Griggs just didn't approve of premarital sex, Skye had been avoiding the situation. It was tricky, but somehow she had maneuvered things so that she and Wally made love only when they stayed overnight at his cottage. This had cut down considerably on her need to go to confession, but it hadn't been pleasant for either of their libidos.

With Mrs. Griggs's likely retribution in mind, instead of kissing Wally awake, Skye reluctantly got out of bed, slipped on her robe, and went downstairs to feed Bingo. Once the feline had his Fancy Feast, fresh water, and a clean litter box, she put on a pot of coffee. She'd planned a special breakfast, and while the French Roast was brewing, she set the dining room table with a white linen cloth, her Grandma Leofanti's Jadeite dishes, antique pink depression crystal goblets, and the sterling silver flatware that Wally's father had sent them as an engagement present.

Much to Skye's surprise, after May had forced her to compete in a culinary contest, she had found that she actually liked to cook. Not that she would ever admit it to her mother, but she found the planning and preparation satisfied her need for order, and Wally's appreciation of the results appealed to her nurturing instinct.

While Skye whisked together eggnog, eggs, and cinnamon for the French toast, she thought about Yvonne Osborn. The librarian had been a complex woman. From what Skye had heard and observed, she had a keen sense of right and wrong and was extremely impatient with those who didn't.

Cutting croissants in half lengthwise, Skye wondered if Yvonne's drop-dead-gorgeous exterior had led people to believe she would be laid-back, which made them resent her when she wasn't. Certainly, Chip Nicolet had been angered by Yvonne's refusal to go out with him.

When Skye heard Wally walking around upstairs, she put a pat of butter on the griddle to melt, then arranged slices of bacon on a rack and popped it into the microwave. While the French toast was frying and the bacon was being zapped, she split a red grapefruit, sprinkled brown sugar on top, and put the halves under the broiler.

A few seconds later, Wally walked into the kitchen dressed in sweatpants and a T-shirt. He kissed Skye. "Merry Christmas, darlin'."

Skye hugged him, wished him a merry Christmas, and directed, "Go sit down in the dining room. I have a surprise for you."

He sniffed appreciatively. "Is that what smells so good?"

"I sure hope so." Skye sent him off with a mug of coffee in one hand and a pitcher of spiced cranberry-apple juice in the other.

Once she had everything on the table, she sat down next to Wally and said, "Dig in before it gets cold." She waited impatiently while he ate the grapefruit, tasted the French toast, and took a bite of the bacon, then asked, "What do you think? Is it better than your usual Cap'n Crunch?"

"A thousand times better." He took her hand, brought it to his lips, and kissed her fingers. "Sugar, I've known you were the right woman for me since you were sixteen, but I had no idea how right you were. These past three years we've been together have been the happiest time in my life, and every day just gets better."

For a moment Skye couldn't speak. She had loved this man for more than two-thirds of her life, but until now, something had always kept them apart. Finally, she swallowed the lump in her throat and said, "Me too."

The remaining food forgotten, Wally stood, drew her to her feet, and claimed her lips. As their kiss deepened, he peeled off her robe and nightshirt. Then, once she was naked, he backed her against the wall. Skye was fumbling with the drawstring on Wally's sweatpants when the thunderous sound of dishes, crystal, and silverware crashing to the floor made her jerk her hand away.

She and Wally sprang apart, both gazing in disbelief at the sight of the overturned dining room table and the remains of their breakfast smeared across the Oriental rug. Skye clenched her fists, barely stopping herself from screaming at her resident ghost.

Before Skye could think of a reasonable explanation for the table's sudden ability to levitate—one that didn't involve a pain-in-the-butt poltergeist named Mrs. Griggs—the cell in Wally's pocket started to play "Hail to the Chief," the PD's emergency ringtone.

Cursing, Wally reached for the phone. He spoke briefly to the dispatcher, then clicked it off and turned to Skye. "Yvonne's death was no accident. Her car was forced off the road."

CHAPTER 5

Don't Be Shelfish

"Go." Skye pulled a winter white sweater dress over her head.

"There won't be anything I can do today." Wally zipped his pants.

Most of his clothes and personal belongings were already at Skye's house. He would bring over the rest of his things when they got back from their honeymoon. Then, once he was completely moved out of his bungalow, he'd list it with a real estate agent.

"But you'll feel better if you go into the PD and make sure." Skye smoothed on a pair of black tights. "You can drop me off at church."

"Well, I would like to take a look at the report that the lab sent over." Wally sat on the bed and put on his socks. "And maybe talk it over with one of the crime scene techs."

"Of course you would." Skye tugged on a pair of black knee-high boots.

"But I promised to go to Mass with you." Wally bent to tie his shoes.

"It's not a problem." Skye attached a red and green holly pin to the cowl of her dress. "I don't mind going to the service alone."

"Well . . ." Wally shrugged on his black-and-white her-ringbone blazer. "Okay, but I swear I'll only stay at the station until you get out of church."

"Great." Skye fluffed her chestnut curls and turned away from the mirror. "It's eight thirty. If I want a seat, we'd better get going."

It was drizzling as they walked out to his car, and he held an umbrella over her head. As she slid into the pas-senger seat, she smiled her thanks at him, assuring her-self that she was happy the call from the PD had come in when it had. The news that Yvonne had been forced off the road had distracted Wally, and he hadn't ques-tioned how the dining room table had tipped over on its own. The last thing Skye wanted was for him to begin to believe in Mrs. Griggs's ghost and change his mind about them living in her house after they were married.

She also understood—or told herself she did—why Wally needed to go into work even though it was Christ-mas Day. There had been a suspicious death, and he was the chief of police. It would be selfish of her to demand that he forget his job and stay with her. Wouldn't it?

The only sound during the ten-minute drive was the wipers sweeping back and forth. Out of the corner of her eye, Skye watched Wally navigate the slick roads. It was clear that his thoughts were already on the case, and she sighed. Would the rest of her life be like this? Always alone on special occasions?

When Wally pulled up in front of the church, he leaned over to kiss Skye before she got out of the car and said, "I'll be back at ten to pick you up."

"Perfect." She forced a happy note into her voice. "Then we can go home and open our presents." She put up the hood of her coat to protect her hair from the rain. "We don't have to be at Mom and Dad's until one."

As Wally drove off, Skye headed toward the white-steepled structure, ran up the steps, and entered the narthex. St. Francis had been built in the 1940s and reno-vated in the seventies, but in response to popular demand, the pastel walls and plain wooden altar had been restored to their previous gilded glory several years ago. Thank goodness the original stained-glass windows had been spared in the parish's earlier quest for modernization.

The interior looked festive with pine boughs, poinsettias, and a life-size Nativity. For a moment, Skye closed her eyes and imagined the same scene next Saturday. She had chosen a winter wonderland theme for her wedding, and while the pine boughs would be staying, the other decorations would be removed. The florist would string fairy lights against the back wall to resemble a starry night, loop white satin ribbons along the sidewalls to mimic snow, and place large hurricane vases filled with cranberries, oranges, and pears in front of the altar.

Focusing back on the present, Skye saw that the pews were already full, but she didn't see any of her relatives among the worshippers. May would have attended the six o'clock Mass and Skye figured Vince would go to the noon service, but she had hoped that some of her Leofanti cousins would be there.

Her father and his side of the family were Presbyterians—an irony that hadn't been lost on Skye when her mother had been so upset that Skye wanted to marry a non-Catholic. But then, May adhered to the Aldous Huxley quote, "Consistency is contrary to nature, contrary to life. The only completely consistent people are dead."

Skye dipped her fingers into the holy water and made the sign of the cross, then scanned the nave for an empty seat. Just as she was about to give up and climb the stairs to the choir loft, where folding chairs were set up for the holiday overflow, she saw an usher motioning to her. She hesitated. He was standing by a row near the altar. Parishioners were generally gracious and sweet unless someone tried to sit in what they considered "their" pew, and the front and back ones were usually the most highly prized and fiercely defended.

Still, most of the regulars were already seated, so Skye nodded to the usher and quickly walked toward him. While she genuflected, the rail-thin man sitting next to the aisle slid over and made room for her. She smiled her thanks, sat down, and shed her coat, then got to her knees and cleared her mind. She made herself forget about Yvonne's death, Wally's preoccupation with work, Mrs. Griggs's ghost, and her upcoming wedding.

When she finished her prayers, she eased back onto the pew and examined her neighbor. He looked familiar, but she couldn't remember where she'd seen him before. Was he a parent of one of the kids she had in counseling or one of the students she had evaluated? Or maybe he was just someone she'd seen around town.

Before she could figure it out, she heard music and the processional started down the aisle. As Father Burns began the Mass, Skye concentrated on the service. In a few moments, her worries drifted away, and it was a relief to allow the true meaning of Christmas to wash over her.

After communion, Father Burns made a few general announcements, concluding with, "Remember, it's smart to pick your friends—just not to pieces."

Rumor had it that some in the congregation didn't appreciate that the priest closed Mass with his words of wisdom, but Skye always found something to think about in his mild humor. She pondered today's message as they stood for the recessional. Friendships could be difficult enough, but for a person like Yvonne, who felt so strongly about right and wrong, relationships had to have been even tougher. Had one of her pals gotten fed up with her principles and killed her?

As "Joy to the World" was sung by the choir and Skye made her way down the aisle, she noticed a large cluster of parishioners having a heated discussion at the rear of the church. Nearing them, she heard Yvonne's name being mentioned, so she stepped out of the stream of worshippers heading toward the door and slipped behind the gossiping group.

They were so intent on getting their own opinions across, none of the folks seemed to notice when Skye eased in back of them. She stared at the bulletin board, hoping it looked as if she were studying an announcement that read:

CHOIR AUDITIONS WILL BE HELD TUESDAY, DECEMBER 26, AT 1 P.M. PLEASE COME AND TRY OUT. THEY NEED ALL THE HELP THEY CAN GET.

As Skye heard someone say, "If you ask me, that woman committed suicide," she used her peripheral vision to see who was speaking.

"Why would she do something like that?" A sweet-looking little old lady sighed. "Was she hooked on those awful drugs or something?"

Another woman touched her tight white poodlelike curls and said, "I overheard her having a big fight with her daughter in the parking lot of the library that afternoon right after the library closed at four."

"Why in heaven's name was the library open on Christmas Eve?" demanded a man dressed in a Western-style shirt, cowboy boots, and a bolo tie. "Let alone a Sunday afternoon?"

Another guy, this one wearing shiny polyester pants, asked, "Don't you remember the fuss last summer about the library being shut on too many holidays?"

"Oh, yeah. Right." The faux cowboy nodded. "The board decided it should be open every day except Thanksgiving, Christmas, Easter, and New Year's."

"I can't help thinking about the poor daughter." The sweet little old lady patted her chest. "I sure hope she doesn't feel guilty that her last words to her mama were mean ones."

"And don't forget Mrs. Osborn was divorced," the man in the boots added.

Poodle Hair poked him in the arm with her index finger. "If every divorced woman committed suicide, the men around here would have to start having sex with their sheep." She giggled. "Besides, most divorcées would kill their exes, not themselves."

"She's right," agreed a woman wearing a Christmas tree pin that was almost as big as the real thing. "Anyway, the news said it was an accident. What makes you think it wasn't?"

"I got a cousin over to the crime lab in Laurel," the counterfeit cowboy explained. "He said they got proof it wasn't no accident."

Voices rose as everyone in the crowd offered an opinion, and when they began to repeat themselves, Skye slunk away. She hurried down the front steps and out the double doors, intent on telling Wally that the county lab had a leak—not that that would be an enormous surprise to him. Keeping a secret in Scumble River or the surrounding area was like trying to carry water in a sieve—there were just too many holes to plug.

The rain had stopped, and a trio of fortysomething men had gathered in the middle of the sidewalk. Skye scanned the street, and when she didn't see Wally's car, she strolled slowly by the threesome. They were talking about Yvonne, too, and although Skye kept walking, as soon as she passed them, she ducked behind a large evergreen.

The men were discussing the librarian's tenure in Scumble River. Skye's pew mate seemed to be the leader of the triad. He leaned on a cane and rubbed his back. The other two men also appeared to be injured. One wore a cervical collar and the other had his arm in a sling. Had they been in some sort of accident together?

"Your neighbor was a real piece of work, King," Mr. Arm Sling griped.

King clutched his cane and sneered, "Tell me something I don't know, Artie."

"She about had a hissy fit when I tried to eat my lunch in the library." Artie shook his head. "All I had was a sandwich and chips. It wasn't as if I was going to spill a bowl of soup on her precious books."

"Yeah." Mr. Cervical Collar folded his arms. "Where else we gonna eat when it's cold out? It's not like there's a lunchroom for the city's maintenance crew."

Ah. So that was where Skye had seen King before. The maintenance workers were often in and out of city hall, which was right next to the PD and the library.

"Judy never minded us being there," King added.

"That's because she's a sweet kid, not a ball-busting witch," Artie grumbled.

"That was one good thing about getting hurt," Mr. Cervical Collar said. "At least we didn't have to deal with Miss I'm-Too-Good-for-You anymore."

"Maybe you guys didn't, but remember, Dutch, my property is right next to the place she was renting," King said. "All I heard from the minute she moved in there were complaints about my kids and animals. Somebody sure peed in that broad's cereal."

"So you told us, again and again," Artie whined. "What I don't understand is how she even heard any noise you made, let alone saw you doing anything. You live in the middle of a couple of acres and her house was in the center of a big piece of ground, too."

"'Cause she spied on me, you dope." King whacked his friend on his uninjured arm. "She was always out near my place with her binoculars."

"You've got to be shitting me! Was she some kind of pervert or something?" Dutch snorted back a laugh. "That's gotta be against the law. Did you ask her why in the hell she was looking at you?"

"Of course I did," King retorted. "What am I, a moron? I marched myself right up to her and asked what she thought she was doing and told her that in these parts we liked our privacy."

"What did she say?" Artie asked, adjusting his arm in the sling.

"She claimed she was bird-watching." King switched his cane to his other hand. "I said, in the middle of the freaking winter?"

"Yeah," his buddies echoed each other, egging him on. "She musta just been hot for you."

"I wish. She was really . . ."

When King trailed off, Skye stepped forward and peered through the evergreen's branches, thankful that there was no snow on the ground. At the same moment, the man in question swiveled his neck and saw her watching him and his friends.

King's mouth flattened into a mean line; he jerked his head in her direction and said to his buddies, "Let's go have some breakfast. My wife can whip us up something. Geez, she stayed home from church 'cause she claimed she had so much cooking to do. And we won't have to worry about some busybody sticking her nose in where it don't belong."

King's friends glared at Skye, then trailed after him as he limped toward a pickup parked in front of the building in a handicapped spot. Despite their injuries, all three men hopped into the cab without any perceptible difficulties, and the truck roared away.

Her face burning, Skye decided it was time to see if Wally had arrived. She checked the street in front of the church and the one on the side, but there was no sign of him. She decided he must be waiting in the parking lot. But when she walked around to the back of the church, he wasn't there either. *Great!* Her fiancé had forgotten about her on Christmas Day.

CHAPTER 6

By Book or by Crook

"I'm really sorry I was a few minutes late." Wally glanced at Skye as she got into the car. He'd finally arrived just as she was deciding whether to call him or hike over to the PD.

"Fifteen." Skye buckled her seat belt. "Fifteen is more than a few."

"It's just that it turned out the senior crime tech was available and willing to meet me at the bridge," Wally explained.

"He volunteered to come all the way from Laurel to Scumble River on Christmas Day?" Skye's voice held more than a hint of skepticism.

"That was the thing." Wally headed the T-bird toward Skye's house. "He lives in Clay Center, so he was close by, and his ex-wife wasn't dropping off his kids until ten thirty, so he had an hour free."

"I see." She kept her gaze on the windshield. "Why did you need to go back to the accident scene?"

"I wanted to have the tech show me how the vic's car was forced off the road." Wally glanced sideways at Skye, undoubtedly to check if she was still angry with him.

"Hmm." She adjusted the heat vent to blow on her cold

hands. She'd forgotten her gloves. "I can't quite picture how it happened, either."

"We can swing by now so I can show you," Wally offered, clearly still in appeasement mode. But after another quick look at Skye's expression, he said, "Or we could do it sometime tomorrow."

"Maybe tomorrow." She leaned her head against the side window.

"Right." Wally turned the car onto Brook Road; they were almost back at Skye's place. "I also wanted to have the guy see if there was any evidence that might have been missed the night before."

"Why?" Skye asked, curiosity winning over annoyance. Wally usually had a good reason for his actions. "Did you think the other techs had been careless?"

"Not exactly." Wally pulled into Skye's driveway. "But at the time we all thought it was an accident, so they might have overlooked something last night." He parked the T-bird in front of the house. "Now that we know she was forced off the road, I wanted a fresh pair of eyes to take a look and see if he could spot anything."

"That makes sense," Skye said as she and Wally got out of the car and walked up the steps.

Wally unlocked the front door and held it open for her. They took off their coats, hung them on the hall tree, and walked into the kitchen.

Skye filled the teakettle. "Did the tech recover any new evidence?"

"Yes." Wally got out a teapot, mugs, and spoons. "Quite a bit."

"What did he find?" Skye asked, adding several packets of sweetener to a tray.

"There were paint scrapings on the rail that matched the ones they found on the side of Yvonne's car." Wally opened a can of Earl Grey, spooned the leaves into an infuser, and placed the ball into the pot. "He also found fragments of glass that are probably from the perp's vehicle."

"Was it a hit-and-run?" Skye poured boiling water into the teapot. "Or do you think someone deliberately forced Yvonne into the river because they wanted her dead?"

"The tech said there's no way this could have been an accident. The pattern of the paint transfer on the side of the vic's car and the skid marks indicate that someone not only rammed into her, but they backed up and did it again." Wally lifted the tray from the counter and followed Skye into the sunroom. "Whoever ran her off that bridge meant to do it."

"How awful." Skye curled up on the love seat and Wally sat next to her. "In that case, I'd better tell you what I found out at church."

When she had finished recounting the various conversations she'd overheard, Wally slumped back and looked up at the ceiling. "It looks like we'll have our hands full of possible suspects."

"And I'm sorry to say, we may not even have uncovered the first page of the prologue yet." Skye leaned forward and poured tea into the mugs and handed Wally his. "I don't think I told you that I ran into Anthony on Saturday at the Gift Box in Clay Center."

"Not that I remember."

"He said people were really looking forward to Judy Martin's return because Yvonne had ticked off nearly every library patron she encountered." Skye added Sweet'N Low to her cup. "Not to mention whoever was complaining about her in the *Star*."

"Son of a buck!"

"Yeah." Skye stirred in the fake sugar. "The only thing worse than nobody having a motive is when everybody has one."

Wally nodded his agreement.

"Think about it." Skye sipped her tea. "Yvonne exposed people's shortcomings, which had to make them pretty darn uncomfortable. Not to mention that it looks like she annoyed them by insisting that they comply with every rule, no matter how trivial. If she didn't put up with even small infractions like eating a sandwich in the library, then what would she do if she caught someone doing something really bad?"

"Exactly."

"Folks may not understand Yvonne's kind of thinking, but communities need people like her," Skye mused. "If you let the small things go, it becomes too easy to turn a blind eye to the bigger things, until eventually there's anarchy."

"True." Wally frowned. "But being the one who stops the chaos from happening doesn't win you any popularity contests."

"Yvonne reminds me a lot of you." She poked Wally in the chest. "You'd never allow any hint of wrongdoing among your officers."

"Maybe." Wally shrugged, then changed the subject. "Anyway, I want to wait until the crime lab narrows down the color and make of the perp's vehicle before I talk to any of the possible suspects." He ran his fingers through his hair. "And at best, they won't have that information for me until tomorrow, and probably not until after lunch."

"Good." Skye put her mug down and snuggled next to him. "Can we forget about the case until then and focus on Christmas?"

"Definitely." Wally tilted her chin up for a kiss, then vowed, "I promise not to even think about the murder for the rest of the day."

"Yippee!" Skye bounced off the love seat and went over to the Christmas tree. She selected three presents and brought them to Wally. "Here. Open this first." She pointed to a box wrapped in silver. "It's the one you got in the Leofanti gift exchange."

May's extended family was too big for everyone to swap presents—only the kids got gifts from the whole group—so the adults picked names at Thanksgiving.

He looked at the tag attached to a big blue bow. "I see

my secret Santa was your cousin Ginger's husband, Flip." Wally tore off the paper and revealed a flat aluminum storage case. "Nice."

"What is it?" Skye stared at the label. CABELA'S was written in script on a forest green background.

Wally opened the lid and showed her the contents. "It's an all-in-one firearm-cleaning kit. How did Flip know I wanted this?"

"I'm guessing my mom told Ginger and Ginger told Flip. He must have been pretty darned happy because it gave him an excuse to go to Cabela's. He talks about that store the same way I talk about Von Maur." Skye paused, then added, "You do realize that now that you're going to be her son-in-law, May's taking notes on everything you say or do?"

"You're kidding!" Wally's eyebrows rose. "Why would she do that?"

"Come on. You've worked with her for more than eighteen years. You must have realized that she's elevated meddling to an Olympic sport. Why do you think she brings Vince his lunch every day? It's to keep an eye on him and nudge him into doing what she wants." Skye raised an eyebrow. "Have you noticed her talking to you more at work since we set the date?"

"Well, maybe." Wally shrugged. "It's hard to say. She was always pretty chatty."

"Okay." Skye bit her lip. "I should have warned you that Mom doesn't have any perception of personal boundaries where her kids are concerned. She drops in unexpectedly, requires daily phone contact, and has spies everywhere." She sighed. "In the future, be careful how much info you share with her. If she knows too much, she'll be able to plan a coup and take over our lives."

"I'll keep that in mind." Wally leaned back. "But I'm sure it won't be a problem for me like it is for you. You're her only daughter."

"Right." Skye stretched out the word. "I'm sure she's not interested at all in the potential father of her grandchildren." She stared at him, willing him to understand the seriousness of the situation. "It's taken a lot for me to stop her from interfering. I know people think I don't have a backbone where she's concerned, but I've drawn some tough lines, and it will be harder to enforce them with even the possibility of babies in the future."

Wally nodded, but Skye could tell he didn't fully understand, so she let the matter drop. She'd continue the discussion another time. Maybe after a few instances of May ambushing him, Wally would figure it out.

Gesturing to the gifts she'd arranged on the coffee table, Skye said, "Open the big one next. It's from me."

Wally loved the introductory selection from the Beer of the Month Club and immediately placed the six-pack in the fridge to chill. Next, he slid the paper off the Ford Thunderbird fiftieth-anniversary watch, and after admiring it, he put it on his wrist. Then he reached into his jacket pocket and pulled out a tiny box.

He gazed at it for several seconds before handing Skye the beautifully wrapped package and said, "I hope you'll wear these on our wedding day."

Skye carefully removed the paper and lifted the velvet lid. Inside was a pair of gold earrings: two swirling ribbons, one lined with shimmering baguette-cut diamonds and the other with glittering round diamonds, formed an X. She caught her breath. They were dazzling.

Wally looked into Skye's eyes and said, "Since X marks the spot on a treasure map and you are the treasure of my life, I had to get them for you."

Skye's throat closed and tears slid down her cheeks. No one had ever said anything like that to her before. A couple of men had told her that they loved her, but this was beyond being in love. Wally's words meant so much more. She swallowed, unable to speak.

"What's wrong?" Wally wrinkled his brow. "Don't you like them?"

"I love them and I love you!" Skye flung herself into

his arms and rained kisses all over his face. "You are everything I ever wanted in a man and had given up hope of finding. I never thought I could feel this way about anyone or that anyone would feel this way about me."

A few minutes later, as Skye and Wally were getting naked on the couch, Skye heard a low growl. She glanced to her right and gazed into a pair of yellow eyes. *Oh, my God!* How had a creature like that gotten into the house? Was Bingo okay?

Tapping Wally on the shoulder, Skye pointed silently at the gray caninelike animal standing in the sunroom's doorway.

He tensed, then put his lips to her ear and said softly, "Wolf."

Skye nodded and whispered, "Where's your gun?"

"In the safe in the bedroom," Wally answered, then said, "I'm going to get up slowly; then you do the same."

The wolf didn't move as Skye and Wally rose from the sofa, but once they were vertical, it turned and padded silently away. Wally quickly pulled on his pants, grabbed a wrought-iron lamp from an end table, and crept toward the door. Skye wrapped herself in the throw from the back of the love seat and followed him.

They both watched as the animal strolled into the kitchen and out the mysteriously open back door. Before it disappeared, the wolf turned its head and seemed to wink.

Wally rushed forward and slammed the back door. "What the hell just happened?"

Unwilling to share her belief that Mrs. Griggs had once again foiled their lovemaking, Skye said, "The door must not have fully latched after I put out the trash earlier and the wind must have blown it open."

"How about the wolf?"

"Maybe it smelled Bingo's food," Skye offered. She really, really didn't want Wally to be so spooked that he refused to live in her house after they were married.

Then her chest tightened and she gasped, "Bingo! We need to make sure the wolf didn't eat him."

Skye didn't take an easy breath until they located the cat. He was fast asleep on her bed, apparently unaware that his territory had been invaded by a wild animal.

Patting the snoozing feline, Skye glanced at the clock and screamed. It was a quarter to one. All thoughts of the wolf were erased from her mind, and she shot off the bed and ran into the bathroom. They had fifteen minutes to get dressed, load the car, and drive to her parents' house. Being late wasn't an option.

As she smoothed her hair, she yelled to Wally, "Throw on the rest of your clothes; then bring me my dress from the sunroom and put all the presents under the tree into the Bel Air." She knew they had too much stuff to fit into his Thunderbird.

By the time Skye tugged on her boots, she could hear Wally traipsing in and out of the house. When she ran down the stairs, he was holding her coat out for her. She shrugged into it, then sprinted into the kitchen, grabbed the side dish she'd been assigned—green bean casserole—and hurried out to the car.

Wally had the Chevy idling with the passenger door open, and as soon as she hopped in, he stomped on the gas pedal. He was as terrified of displeasing May as Skye was.

As Wally drove, Skye mentally ran through the list of what she was supposed to bring. She crossed her fingers that she hadn't forgotten anything. As with being allowed to make the zuppa Inglese for the party the night before, it had been a surprise that her mother had permitted her to cook. Except for extended family gatherings when everyone brought potluck, any meal at May's house was fully prepared by May.

While Skye hoped this new honor had been bestowed on her because her mom finally considered her a grown-up, more likely it was because May was overwhelmed with preparations for the wedding, the holiday, and Vince and Loretta's baby. Doubtlessly, Skye's mother was running herself ragged trying to control all three events.

Skye nodded to herself; yep, that had to be it. But a second later, she wrinkled her brow. She had a funny feeling that her mother had another iron in the fire. Something else had to be occupying some of May's attention, or Skye's recent maneuverings to avoid her mother wouldn't have been successful. Under normal circumstances, with the wedding so close, a single phone call a day wouldn't have satisfied May. If Skye wouldn't come to May, May would have camped out on Skye's doorstep. What was her mother doing instead?

Before Skye could find an answer, Wally asked, "Are you okay?"

"Uh-huh."

"You're awfully quiet."

"I was just thinking about Mom," Skye explained. "I realized that she hasn't been around as much as I would have expected."

"And that's a bad thing?"

"No." Skye bit her thumbnail. "I'm relieved, but something feels a little . . ."

"Hinky?"

"Yeah. That's the word." Skye nodded. "I'm afraid she's up to no good. At least *we* won't think it's good. Has she mentioned anything to you that you thought was odd, or done anything suspicious?"

"Not that I can remember." Wally scratched his head. "The only thing that comes to mind is that I was surprised she was taking next week off instead of this one. She's working her regular afternoon shift Tuesday through Thursday and traded with Thea for days on Friday."

"I guess she figured she'd need some time to recover," Skye mused. "Or maybe she thinks that Loretta will have the baby a week early."

"I'll bet that's it." Wally turned into Skye's parents'

driveway. "She did mention that she hopes her first grandchild isn't born while we're away on our honeymoon."

"Why would she care about that?"

"No idea." Wally shrugged. "But I wouldn't worry about it."

"Of course you wouldn't," Skye agreed, then muttered to herself as she exited that car, "But if you knew my mother like I do, you'd definitely be worried."

CHAPTER 7

Read Between the Lines

Tuesday morning, Skye jerked out of a deep sleep. She had been dreaming about her wedding day. They were at the part in the ceremony when Father Burns asked if there were any objections to the marriage, and suddenly people started popping up with protests as if the church were a giant toaster.

First, May jumped to her feet and yelled that the groom was too old. Next, Wally's ex-wife, Darlene, screamed that she still loved him, followed closely by Skye's ex-boyfriend Simon, who shouted that he still loved her. Then finally, just as Pope Benedict XVI came down the aisle to challenge Wally's annulment, the church exploded as if struck by a cruise missile.

Coming fully awake, Skye put her hand to her racing heart. What a nightmare. She turned to tell Wally about it, then remembered that he had said he was going into the police station early. She'd been tempted to beg off helping with the murder investigation. There were only four days until the wedding and she already had enough on her plate without adding the duties of police psych consultant. But in the end she knew her conscience would nag at her if she didn't do everything she could to find Yvonne's killer.

Skye checked the clock radio on the nightstand, then rocketed out of bed. *Shoot!* It was already past nine o'clock. Wally must have fed Bingo before he left, or the cat's stomach alarm would have gone off hours ago and he would have roused her, demanding his breakfast. She hoped Wally had also cleaned the litter box, because if he hadn't, the finicky feline might very well show his displeasure by leaving her a little gift—possibly right in the middle of the parlor on her new hand-knotted wool rug.

As Skye showered, she scrolled through her mental file of chores. It might be the twenty-sixth of December, but there were no after-Christmas sales in her future. Instead, she had to contact the photographer, florist, and DJ to go over the final arrangements, confirm the schedule of events, and make sure none of the vendors screwed up.

She was trying hard not to become the crazed bride her California cousin had been before her wedding, but after some of the mistakes that had already occurred, Skye had a newfound empathy for all the bridezillas she had sneered at in the past. It wasn't that she demanded perfection; she knew that would never happen. She just didn't want a disaster.

Since Wally had said he wouldn't need her at the PD until after lunch, Skye had almost three hours to work on the wedding. But first she had to figure out what to wear.

Because she had to dress up for her job as a school psychologist, she'd been looking forward to spending this week in sweats. Regrettably, there was no way she could take part in an interrogation looking like she'd just come from the gym, so instead of her comfy tracksuit, she put on a pair of camel wool slacks and a green cashmere sweater set that matched her eyes.

After checking that Bingo's litter box met his lofty standards, she fixed herself tea and an English muffin. Thus fortified, she started making phone calls to the

various vendors in her file. The DJ confirmed that he had
the two most important songs—the first dance, "At Last,"
sung by Etta James, and the father/daughter dance, "I
Loved Her First," sung by Heartland. The rest of the
playlist would be a combination of fifties, sixties, and seventies classics with some present-day country music
mixed in.

Next, Skye reiterated to the photographer that she
didn't want to take pictures of her and Wally together in
advance of the wedding. It might be a superstition, but
they'd had enough bad luck in their relationship, and she
wasn't taking a chance by allowing the groom to see her
in her bridal gown before the ceremony.

The call to the florist went quickly, and a few minutes
before noon, Skye closed her wedding organizer, grabbed
the lunch she had packed to share with Wally, and
headed to the PD. There were only a few cars in the lot
adjacent to the redbrick building shared by the police
station, city hall, and the library. As Skye passed the entrance to the stairs leading up to the library, she noticed
a black wreath hanging on the door. She paused, wondering how Yvonne's daughter was coping with her
death. Losing a parent was never easy, and now Christmas Eve would forever be associated with her mother's
passing. Skye pressed her lips together. No matter how
many murders she helped investigate, she would never
understand why someone would kill a fellow human being.

Sighing, Skye went into the station. She waved hello
to Thea, who was on the phone at the dispatcher's desk,
then used her key to let herself into the back. The cubi-
cles that the officers used to do paperwork were empty,
and the station was eerily quiet. But as she started to
climb the stairs to Wally's office, she heard voices coming
from the top of the steps.

Apparently Wally and Roy Quirk were standing in
the corridor that separated the police chief's office from
the mayor's, discussing staffing issues, because Skye heard

Wally say, "I know you don't like Zuchowski, but you've got to work with the tools you're given."

"Yeah, but it's unfortunate that Zuchowski is one of those tools." Skye reached the landing just in time to catch Quirk folding his arms across his chest and saying, "And he's going to be missing from the toolbox *again*. He called a few minutes ago to say he won't be coming in again today. The last shift he worked was days on Saturday."

"What in holy hell is the problem this time?" Wally's ears were red. "Don't tell me he has another family emergency."

"Nah." Sergeant Quirk was Wally's second in command and handled personnel scheduling. "He says he has the flu. Probably won't be able to take the duty again until next week."

"But you don't believe him?" Wally had his back to Skye.

"All I'm saying is it's mighty convenient timing." Quirk took a deep breath, the overdeveloped muscles of his chest threatening to pop the buttons on his uniform shirt. "Especially since he asked for this week off in order to go on vacation with his girlfriend."

Skye couldn't remember ever meeting Zuchowski. He'd been hired a little more than eighteen months ago, and it seemed as if he was never around the PD when Skye was there. Wally had mentioned him from time to time—mostly commenting on his absenteeism, tardiness, and poor performance. Now she wondered if she hadn't met him because he was never at work.

"Well," Wally drawled, "that is quite a coincidence."

"Maybe I'd better stop by his apartment." Quirk ran his hand over his shaved head. He was ex-military and didn't tolerate shirkers. "If he's sick, he might need some chicken soup."

"Good idea."

"And if he's not home?" Quirk's mouth tightened and a vein on the side of his neck pulsed. "Should I leave him a little get-well note?"

"Hmm." As Wally considered his options, he glanced around and finally noticed Skye. "Did you hear all this?" When she nodded he asked, "What do you think?"

"I think that if I ever want to actually meet the new guy, it better be soon."

Quirk snickered and gave her a thumbs-up. He and Skye had had some issues in the past, but things had gotten better recently—mostly due to a concerted effort on her part to make Quirk feel more comfortable. Still, it was clear that he found it confusing to work with her since he couldn't figure out her status. Was the psych consultant above or below the sergeant in rank? And did the fact that she was the chief's fiancée make a difference?

As Wally took Skye's hand, tugged her to his side, and gave her a hug, he said to Quirk, "If Zuchowski isn't there, don't let him know you stopped by. I'll deal with him when he finally *recovers* from his illness, and I think it's best if he doesn't have any warning."

"You got it, Chief." Quirk touched an imaginary hat brim. "I'll go over to Zuchowski's place right now." He turned and ran lightly down the stairs.

"So, besides an AWOL officer, anything else new around here?" Skye asked as she and Wally retreated to his office. "Any break on the murder?"

"The crime lab called a few minutes ago." Wally took a seat behind his desk. "According to the FBI's National Automotive Paint File and the PDQ, the paint chips at the scene come from a white 2006 Cadillac Escalade."

"PDQ?" Skye pulled the visitor's chair closer to the other side of the desk.

"The Royal Canadian Mounted Police's Paint Data Query system. Those databases cover vehicles marketed in North America after 1973." Wally picked up the sandwich Skye had put on a napkin in front of him. "The glass fragments confirm that the vehicle in question is that year and make."

"At least that's got to narrow it down. How many people drive a car that costs over fifty thousand dollars?"

"Not many," Wally agreed around a mouthful of ham, cheese, and whole wheat bread. Swallowing, he added, "However, there's a problem with locating vehicles involved in hit-and-runs. It's not as easy as those crime shows you watch on television make it seem."

"Oh?"

"I assigned one of the officers to start checking registrations, but the system's been down all morning. Even once it's up, after he looks into titleholders in the immediate area, it becomes exponentially more difficult to track ownership. If the killer lives more than forty or so miles away, we may never find him or her."

"Can't you inquire about suspicious damages at the repair shops?" Skye bit into her own sandwich.

"Yes. But there are hundreds of them." Wally started to peel an orange. "And again, the owner may use a place as far away as Chicago or Bloomington or even Springfield. The farther away, the less likely we'll locate it."

"How about putting out some kind of APB to all the shops in Illinois?" Skye took a swig of her Diet Coke.

"Unfortunately that's not possible." Wally opened the Ziploc bag of Christmas cookies and selected a frosted reindeer. "There are just too many and there's no organized list. I've got Martinez calling all the repair shops within a sixty-mile radius, but that will take her several days."

Zelda Martinez was Scumble River's only female officer, and also the newest hire, so she was often assigned the more routine tasks.

"Those guys I overheard at church mentioned being maintenance men." Skye popped an orange segment into her mouth and chewed thoughtfully. "I don't suppose they'd have the cash to own an Escalade?"

"Maybe not." Wally twitched his shoulders. "But you never know what kind of debt people are willing to go into for the car of their dreams." He grabbed a file from his in-box, flipped it open, and ran his finger down one of the pages. "The vic's husband is a land developer, so he'd definitely have the money for a luxury vehicle."

"So who do we talk to first?" Skye finished eating and tossed the debris in the trash can. "The maintenance men or the husband?"

"None of the above." Wally threw away his wrappers and slid a sheet of paper across the desktop. "I think we should start with the daughter."

"Why?" Skye scanned the page in front of her, noting that the girl's name was Phoebe and she had turned nineteen two weeks ago. "Because she argued with her mom right before the accident?"

"That's one of the reasons." Wally stood. "More important, we couldn't locate her that evening." He waited for Skye at the door. "When we finally contacted the vic's ex that night, he said their daughter was supposed to spend Christmas Eve with him, but she wasn't there."

"Did she show up at her dad's later?" Skye preceded Wally out of his office and down the stairs.

"Nope." Wally told Thea that he and Skye were heading out, then led the way into the garage. "The next day, the ex's new wife told Quirk that Phoebe never arrived at their house, and the girl didn't answer her cell until late the next morning. The current Mrs. Osborn said her husband was frantic because he was afraid Phoebe had been in the car with her mother."

"The poor man."

"Poor man, my butt," Wally snapped. "If the guy had contacted us, we could have told him there was no evidence of another passenger. The windows were all up, the seat belts were intact, and none of the doors had been opened once the vehicle was submerged."

"Interesting that he didn't call the police." Skye slid into the squad car. "I take it he gave you her cell number and you tried it that night?"

"Yep." Wally nodded as he joined Skye in the cruiser. "As soon as we confirmed Yvonne's identity, I had Quirk go to her house, and Phoebe wasn't there either."

"So our mission today is to see where Miss Phoebe

spent Christmas Eve?" She buckled her seat belt. "And find out if she drives an Escalade?"

"Exactly." Wally pulled the robin's-egg blue Caprice onto the street. "I also want you to see if you can tell what Phoebe's relationship with her mom was like."

"I'm on it." Skye could usually get a feeling for how kids got along with their parents by little things they said and their facial expressions. "I'm guessing Phoebe's out of high school. Does she go to college?"

"No. Her dad said there was some snafu with her application and she has to wait until next year to attend." Wally took a left onto Maryland Street. "Meanwhile, she's working part-time at your aunt's dance studio, which is where we're heading."

Olive Leofanti had opened the Scumble River School of Adult Dance a little more than a year ago. When her original partner had been unable to come up with her half of the money for the business, the future of the studio had seemed bleak. But in June, Olive had found another investor, changed the name of the school to Turning Pointe, and expanded to include lessons for children. Immediately, class size had begun to increase, and now the place seemed to be thriving.

Having two left feet, Skye hadn't been to the school since the grand opening, but her mother's daily family bulletins had kept her informed. Skye vaguely remembered May mentioning that Olive's new business partner was from out of state and that the woman had sent her daughter to represent her interests in the studio. But Skye didn't recall receiving a report about the new hire. May must be slipping—normally even a part-timer would have rated a mention.

As Wally made a right onto Basin Street, Skye commented, "You said we're going to the studio, but will Phoebe be at work today? After all, it's the day after Christmas and her mom died less than thirty-six hours ago. Surely, Aunt Olive wouldn't expect her to show up."

"According to Mr. Osborn, Turning Pointe is having a

recital tomorrow, and Phoebe insisted she couldn't let down her bosses and had to be there for the students."

"She sounds like a conscientious young woman." Skye rummaged in her purse, drew out a tube of lip gloss, and applied it.

"Yeah." Wally pulled into a parking spot in front of the school. "Except for the part about her disappearing the night her mom was killed."

"That is suspicious," Skye agreed.

As they walked through the double glass doors and into the lobby of the studio, Skye heard a cacophony of high-pitched, excited voices. She and Wally followed the sound to a large area that boasted polished wood floors and mirrored walls. Groups of females ranging in age from prepubescent to elderly were practicing everything from arabesques to hip-hop moves.

A beautiful woman in her late twenties or early thirties stood nearest the entrance. She was busy teaching a half dozen golden agers the steps to a jazz routine. When she noticed Wally, she told her group to take a break and approached him.

"Well, if it isn't Chief Boyd." The shapely blonde dressed in a skintight zebra-print leotard playfully tapped Wally's arm. "I haven't seen you in a while."

"Hi, Emmy." Wally smiled warmly at the stunning woman. "I've been too busy to get out to the club."

"That's a shame," Emmy purred. "We all missed you at the holiday shindig."

Skye had been standing a little behind Wally, taking in the exchange with growing unease. At the mention of a party, she decided it was time to interrupt. She cleared her throat and moved closer to Wally.

He glanced at her with a sheepish expression, then said to the lovely dancer, "I don't think you've met my fiancée, Skye Denison. Skye, this is Emerald Jones." As the two women shook hands, he explained, "Emmy and I are members of the Laurel Gun Club. We shoot together every Wednesday night. She's got the sweetest little Smith & Wesson Centennial 642CT and a Marlin 336XLR rifle."

"Really." Skye examined the tall, lithe woman who was beaming at Wally. "I've been thinking about learning to shoot. Wally's taught me a little, but I'd like to get more comfortable with guns. There's only so much protection pepper spray and a Taser can provide."

"True." Emmy tossed her ponytail. "And they aren't half as much fun."

"After the wedding, I'll have to come out to the club with Wally." Skye wasn't sure if she was making casual conversation or warning the gorgeous woman away from her man. "Maybe I'll see you there."

"As Wally said, I'm at the club every Wednesday night, and I also go most Sunday afternoons." Emmy arched a feathery brow and her sapphire blue eyes twinkled. "It would be nice to get to know you since I've heard so much about you."

"From Wally?" Skye asked, trying to figure out why it seemed as if she'd met Emmy before. There was something oddly familiar about the woman.

"Well, he does talk about you all the time." Emmy poked Wally's arm again. "But then, so does your aunt Olive and my mom's friend's son."

"Who's that?" Skye thought she remembered that Emmy's mother was from out of state. What was her connection with Scumble River?

"Simon Reid." Emmy wrinkled her cute little turned-up nose. "According to him, you're a paragon of virtue who can do no wrong and I'm as irresponsible as his mother." She widened her eyes. "Seriously, I only got into a tiny bit of trouble in Lost Wages. I didn't really *have* to leave town."

Uh-huh! Skye mentally slapped her forehead. That's who Emmy reminded her of—Simon's mother's friend Ruby. The statuesque blonde had hid out with Bunny Reid in Scumble River three or four years ago, when she was running from a shady casino owner. So Ruby was

Aunt Olive's partner. How in the heck had that happened? It had to be Bunny's doing.

"Believe me," Skye declared, "when Simon and I were dating, he never thought I was perfect."

Skye hid a smile. Simon was as straitlaced as they came. Depending on the kind of trouble Emmy had gotten into in Las Vegas, he would be having a fit that his mother was once again part of some harebrained scheme.

"That's not how he tells it." Emmy pouted.

"Although we broke up due to a misunderstanding, one of the reasons we never got back together was that he was always trying to change me," Skye reassured her. "And one of the reasons I love Wally so much is because he doesn't."

"Good to know." Emmy nodded to herself. "I can use that the next time Simon starts to give me a hard time about my past indiscretions."

Hmm! Interesting! Skye wondered how much time the vivacious blonde and the serious funeral director were spending together. Emmy seemed to be a younger version of Simon's mother, which would drive him crazy. Then again, Skye detected a certain spark in the dancer's eye when she talked about him. Was the attraction mutual?

"But we digress." Emmy turned to Wally. "I doubt you're here to take me up on the offer of a dance lesson for your wedding."

"You're right." Wally put his arm around Skye. "We won't be trying anything fancy. We're keeping things as simple as possible."

"At least as simple as my mother will allow," Skye clarified.

"May is a pistol, all right, but you're doing great." Wally winked, then turned serious. "We're here to talk to Phoebe Osborn."

"Oh, sure." Emmy grimaced. "Maybe I am as flighty as Simon keeps telling me I am. How could I forget that her mother was killed on Christmas Eve? Let me go find her for you."

"Is that her?" Skye pointed to a young woman who was the spitting image of what a teenage Yvonne might have looked like. "Over there by the rear wall?"

"Yes." Emmy nodded, then raised her voice to call, "Pheebs, over here."

The younger woman started to wave at Emmy; then her gaze went to Wally in his uniform. Her eyes widened and she tore across the length of the room, clearly heading for the door leading to the storage area at the opposite end.

At her first step, Wally shouted, "Halt, police!" Then he took off after her, yelling to Skye, "Cut her off in the alley!"

CHAPTER 8

Read Her the Riot Act

Skye rushed out of the dance school and raced around to the back of the building. At one end, a fence blocked any possible escape, so she ran toward the other side. She slid to a halt a nanosecond before the studio's rear door burst open and Phoebe flew out.

Clutching her purse in one hand and putting on her coat with the other, Phoebe glanced toward the chain-link barrier, then veered to her left. When she saw that Skye was blocking her getaway, Phoebe performed a graceful pirouette and darted around her.

Skye's arms closed on thin air and she stumbled forward, barely remaining upright. Making a hasty recovery, she swiveled and gave chase. Phoebe dug a set of keys from her jacket pocket and ran toward a bright green cube-shaped car.

Phoebe was looking over her shoulder at Skye when Wally stepped directly into her path. She attempted to stop, but she was going too fast and skidded into his chest. Even as she tried to twist away, he grabbed her arms, swung her around, and propelled her against the Scion's side.

He snapped on cuffs and said, "You have the right to remain silent."

Once Wally had finished reading the Miranda warning to Phoebe and secured her in the back of the squad car, Skye asked him, "How did you get out here so quickly?"

"When I saw Phoebe heading out the back exit, I turned around and ran for the front entrance." Wally opened the cruiser's front passenger door for Skye. "Since I knew you were on your way to block the alley, I figured I'd be ready to grab her in case she got past you."

"Good thinking." Skye slid into the Caprice; then, as Wally walked around to his side, she said to Phoebe, who was in tears, "Are you okay?"

The young woman shook her head; she was crying too hard to talk.

Before Skye could say anything more, Wally got into the Chevy and cautioned, "We need to wait to talk to her until we get to the station."

"Because she's under arrest for fleeing or attempting to elude a peace officer?" Skye guessed. Since being hired as the police psychological consultant, she had been studying the Illinois penal code.

Wally nodded, then looked at Phoebe in the rearview mirror and directed his next comment to her. "It's a Class A misdemeanor with a penalty of up to one year in jail and a fine of twenty-five hundred bucks." He stared at the young woman. "Of course, if you cooperate, I could decide not to file the charges."

After that, Wally was silent. Skye took the hint and kept her mouth shut, too. Once they reached the police station, Wally escorted a still weeping Phoebe into the interrogation room. The space was used more often for coffee breaks than for interviews, but it was set up with recording equipment that Wally immediately activated.

Stepping back into the hall, he said to Skye, "Good cop, bad cop?"

"Probably best." She nodded, not having to ask which role she was assigned.

"I'm going to act angry at you for being nice to her," Wally warned.

"And I'll make sure I seem scared of you," Skye confirmed.

"Ready?"

"Sure am."

When Wally and Skye returned to the interrogation room, he reminded Phoebe of her rights and asked if she wanted a lawyer. She sobbed her refusal and he introduced Skye as the police psych consultant.

Skye snagged a box of Kleenex from the counter, then took a seat next to Phoebe and handed her a tissue. "I know you're upset, but if you can stop crying and tell me what's wrong, I might be able to help you. Why did you run from us?"

"Because she forced her mother's car off the road," Wally said as he sat down across from the women and scowled. "Why else would she bolt?"

"I didn't kill her." Phoebe used both cuffed hands to push a hank of raven hair from her brow. She turned to Skye. "I don't know why I ran away. I guess I was just scared and panicked when I saw a cop. My dad and Uncle Hank say that all cops are corrupt and want to pin something on you."

Skye frowned. Phoebe seemed a lot younger than her nineteen years. And what kind of father told his daughter that the police were her enemy? Some parents had no common sense. Even if you felt that way, why instill in your child such fear and paranoia?

"Is your uncle Hank your father's brother?" Skye asked, recalling that Yvonne had been an only child.

"No. He's Dad's business partner. I just call him uncle because I've known him forever."

"Ah." Skye nodded. "I have an honorary Uncle Charlie who's like my mom's stand-in father."

"Yeah. Uncle Hank is sort of Dad's brother from another mother."

"If you two are finished bonding," Wally said, his tone

sarcastic, "maybe we can get back to why the prisoner was arrested."

"Sorry, Chief." Skye exchanged a frightened glanced with Phoebe. "What *were* you so scared of?"

"Everything." Phoebe's shoulders drooped. "Everyone has been hollering at me forever and I . . . I don't know where to turn anymore."

"Who's been yelling at you?" Skye asked, then added, "Start at the beginning."

"My mom and dad were mad about the whole college thing." Phoebe wiped her eyes, blew her nose, and tossed the used Kleenex on the table. "Mom was furious with me and Dad was pissed off at her for screwing things up." Phoebe sniffed. "It was a whacked-out mess."

"Why was your mom upset with you?" Skye plucked another tissue from the box and handed it to Phoebe. The situation seemed eerily similar to meetings at school when she tried to calm everyone down in order to get their stories straight and in perspective.

"I, uh, did something Mom didn't approve of." Phoebe studied her shackled hands as if they didn't belong to her. "So she wouldn't let me take the University of Chicago's offer to go there last fall."

"What did you do?" Skye asked, wondering why a mother would punish her daughter that way. Getting into the U of C was a major accomplishment, and there was no guarantee that upon reapplying the next year, a student would be accepted a second time.

"Mom was convinced I cheated on the SATs," Phoebe muttered.

"What made her think that?" Skye snuck a glance at Wally, who nodded his agreement at her line of questioning. When Phoebe didn't answer right away, Skye racked her brain for a possible reason and finally asked, "Did you score higher than she expected?"

"No." Phoebe shook her head. "She *expected* a perfect score."

"And did you get it?"

"Close." Phoebe sighed, then blurted out, "But then Mom found the check."

"The check?"

"See, I knew this girl who got a twenty-four hundred on the SATs, so Dad agreed to pay her to impersonate me. He got a fake ID with my name and her picture on it. Then we met in the parking lot before the test and I gave her my admission ticket."

"So after she took the exam for you, what happened?" Skye prodded.

"Dad had already paid her a thousand, and I was supposed to give her another thousand if she scored in the top one percent."

"Which she did?"

"Yes. With that score and my grades and extracurricular activities, I knew I could get into any college I wanted." Phoebe beamed, then added, "And I'm a good writer, so the admissions essays were a snap."

"But?"

"But ..." Phoebe tore off small pieces of tissue and constructed a mini ski slope in front of her. "Before I could make the second payment, Mom found the check. She made me tell her why Dad was giving this girl so much money. And when Mom heard what we'd done, she went ballistic."

"So she forced you to skip college this year, retake the SATs, and reapply with your own scores," Skye deduced, then asked Wally, "Is what they did illegal?"

"Yep." He ticked off the charges on his fingers. "Scheming to defraud, falsifying business records, and criminal impersonation." He pointed his remaining finger at Phoebe and asked, "Did your mother tell the authorities?"

"Uh-uh." Phoebe bit her lip. "But she told Dad that she would if she ever found out he tried anything dishonest again." Phoebe shook her head. "Mom really hated people who cheated or tried to scam the system. She always said that there was no such thing as a little white lie and no justification for anyone who took advantage of a loophole."

Skye nodded to herself. Phoebe's description of Yvonne fit the picture that everyone else had been painting. She seemed to be the kind of woman who set such high standards of behavior, it might be difficult to live with her.

As Skye thought about what Phoebe had revealed, Wally observed, "So your mom pretty much ruined your life. That gives you a really good motive to want to see her dead."

"I didn't kill her," Phoebe insisted. "I wasn't even mad at her anymore."

"Yeah. Right," Wally scoffed. "She screwed up your plans for college and made you get a job, and you expect me to believe you weren't upset with her?" He shook his head. "How dumb do you think I am?"

"You don't understand." Phoebe leaned forward, reaching out to Wally. "I retook the SATs in October and scored almost as high as that other girl did, and I heard a couple of weeks ago that I got into U of C again. In fact, Mom was so proud of me, she and I drove out to the housing development Dad's building to show him the acceptance letter."

"Congratulations," Wally sneered. "How about that year you wasted hanging out with your mom while all your friends went off to school?"

"I was bummed at first, but I had a chance to grow up." Phoebe's voice was firm. "I know I'll have a better college experience now because I understand that there are consequences for doing the wrong thing."

"How mature." Wally clapped mockingly. "So why were you fighting with your mom in the library parking lot on Christmas Eve?"

"It was stupid. I didn't want her to spend the night alone, so I told her I wasn't going over to my dad's house. His new wife is really nice, and I love my baby brother, but they have each other."

"You felt that they didn't need you as much as your mom did," Skye suggested.

"Uh-huh." Phoebe chewed her thumbnail. "But Mom said that she wasn't going to be alone and that a promise was a promise." Phoebe turned to Skye. "You understand how it is with mothers. Miss Olive says it's hard for you to make decisions that your mom doesn't agree with, too."

"It can be tough to draw the line." Skye shrugged noncommittally, but cringed inside. Did everyone think she was a pushover where May was concerned? She'd been really struggling to set limits with her mother, but maybe it was time to try harder.

"If you were arguing over spending the night at your father's place, where did you end up that evening?" Wally steered the questioning back on track. "You didn't go to your dad's and you didn't go home and you didn't answer your cell phone."

"Do I have to tell you?" Phoebe looked beseechingly at Skye.

"Yes." Skye patted her hand. "We need to know."

"The thing is, I really didn't want to go to my dad's." Phoebe rolled her eyes. "It's my half brother's first Christmas, and I knew Dad and my stepmother would be cooing and fussing over him. Heck, they probably recorded his every burp and bowel movement."

"Did you feel left out?" Skye asked. "Maybe it reminded you of a time when you and your dad and mom were all together for the holidays?"

"Yeah." Phoebe wiped a tear from her cheek. "It kind of hurts to see Dad starting over like that. Especially now that he has the son he always wanted."

"Like he doesn't love you anymore," Skye murmured sympathetically.

"How sad for you," Wally said, sticking to his role of bad cop. "Why didn't you just go home then?"

"Because I knew Mom would force me to go over to my father's."

"Then where did you go?" Wally demanded.

"I spent the night at the dance studio. There's a key to the back door hidden in a fake rock, and I used it to get in." Phoebe hung her head. "Please don't tell Miss Olive and Miss Emmy."

"Can you prove you were there?" Skye asked, then realized it didn't really matter since the medical examiner had said that due to the extremely cold temperature of the water, he couldn't give them a precise time of death. The anonymous 911 call reporting the accident had come in at five fifty-five, and Yvonne had been seen arguing with her daughter at four, so she could have been forced off the road anytime within that nearly two-hour stretch.

"No." Phoebe made a face. "There's a little break room in the back with a sofa and a fridge. I had the tray of veggies and dip that Mom had made for me to bring to Dad's, so I just hung out and surfed the net on my laptop." She grinned. "Miss Emmy insisted that the studio had to have Wi-Fi, so I was all set."

"Why didn't you answer your cell?" Wally made a note on the pad of paper in front of him.

"The battery ran out and I didn't have my charger with me." Phoebe twitched her shoulders. "Besides, there was no one I wanted to talk to."

"If your mother wasn't going to be alone, did she say who she was spending the evening with?" Skye asked.

"I was mad at her for lecturing me about doing the right thing, so I didn't ask, but my guess is it was this guy she'd been going out with for the past couple of months. His name's Tom Riley. He owns the bakery in Laurel."

After a few more questions, Wally asked Skye to step into the hallway and said, "What's your impression? Do you believe her?"

"I think so. If her story checks out about the new SAT score and being reaccepted to U of C, she really doesn't have much of a motive."

"Yeah." Wally ran his fingers through his hair. "If she

were going to kill her mom, it probably would have been in the summer when Yvonne put the kibosh on her scheme to cheat her way into college."

"Can you have the crime lab see if she was using her laptop from the dance studio that night?" Skye asked. "I know it doesn't provide an alibi since the ME is still trying to figure out the TOD, but it would confirm that part of what she told us."

"I was thinking the same thing myself," Wally agreed, then grimaced. "And that weird car she was heading to when I nabbed her sure isn't an Escalade. What in the hell was that thing? It looked like a shoe box."

"It's a Scion," Skye explained. "It's made by Toyota to appeal to teens and young twenties. I've seen them on commercials, but not around Scumble River. They might be a little too trendy for parents in our neck of the woods to buy their kids."

"Probably. Around here they get an old pickup or hand-me-down car from mom and dad." Wally glanced through the window at Phoebe, who was sitting slumped over with her head in her hands. "I'll ask her to turn over her laptop to me, then make a few calls to see if her story checks out."

"Good." Skye looked at her watch. "It's still early. Who do you want to interview next?"

"The vic's husband." Wally looked back at Phoebe. "I want to get to him before he and his daughter have a chance to compare notes. I'll have Martinez babysit Phoebe while we talk to her dad."

"Where does he live?"

"He's built one of those mini mansions near Laurel. It's right by the I-80 exit, so an easy commute to the city."

"Okay." Skye mentally ran through her to-do list. "How about if I meet you back here around four?"

"You have time to go with me?" Wally asked with a cautious note in his voice. "I thought maybe you had wedding stuff to do."

"*We* do have wedding tasks to accomplish." Skye

stared at him until he squirmed. "But I figure if I help you with the case, you'll have time to help me with the wedding details." She arched a brow. "Besides, since it will take us nearly an hour to drive to the other side of Laurel, you'll have plenty of time to tell me all about Emmy Jones."

"Well . . ." Wally stammered.

Skye cut him off and added, "I especially want to hear about how you know her so well."

CHAPTER 9

Due as I Say

Skye decided to use the short time she had to drive out to talk to her sister-in-law. She wanted to check on how Loretta was feeling and see if she could still fit into her bridesmaid's dress. Loretta's baby was due in exactly two weeks and her middle seemed to be expanding at an alarmingly fast rate.

Vince and Loretta had opted to build a house after being unable to find exactly what they wanted in the area. Skye hadn't been surprised by their decision. She'd known that her friend wouldn't be satisfied with anything less than perfection. She'd also known that Vince would move heaven and earth to fulfill his new wife's every wish. For a man who had dated nearly every pretty girl in three counties, he was an astonishingly devoted husband.

Loretta and Skye were both alums of Alpha Sigma Alpha sorority, and since Loretta was a hotshot defense attorney in Chicago, Skye had originally reached out to her several years ago to defend Vince on a murder charge. Then, despite Loretta's often-declared aversion to small towns and their citizens, she had fallen in love with Skye's brother, married him, and agreed to live in Scumble River.

It helped that Loretta was able to do so much of her job from home and had to go into the city only for meetings and trials, but it had still been a tremendous sacrifice on Loretta's part to consent to live in her husband's hometown rather than remain in Chicago. It was a sacrifice that Vince was well aware of and was determined to reward.

Skye and Vince's father, Jed, had deeded a good-size parcel of land to his son and new daughter-in-law from forty acres that Jed had purchased several years ago. It was located a couple of miles down the road from May and Jed's place on the Stanley side of County Line Road. Skye was heading there now.

Vince and Loretta had begun construction nine months ago—shortly before Loretta got pregnant—and they had moved in only a week ago. Although Skye had seen the place during various stages of development, this would be her first visit since it was finished.

As she turned down the long lane leading to the house, she tried to visualize the oaks, pecans, and hickories interspersed with redbuds, hawthorns, pawpaws, yellowwoods, and crab apples that her sister-in-law intended to have planted in the spring. The tree allée would make an elegant entrance to the spectacular home that Loretta had designed, with only a tiny bit of input from an architect, Vince, and both their mothers.

Skye parked along the circular driveway—praying her car didn't leave an oil stain or any other kind of mark on the pristine concrete pavers. She strolled up the cobblestone walkway leading to the double mahogany doors, rang the bell, and smiled when she heard the percussion solo from Iron Butterfly's "In-a-Gadda-Da-Vida." Vince must have won the argument for the programmable doorbell's musical selection.

Vince might have stopped performing with his band, the Plastic Santas, in order to be home on weekends, but he would always be a drummer at heart—even though he owned a beauty salon and cut hair for a living.

Several seconds went by, and Skye was considering ringing the bell again when Loretta finally appeared. She put her hands on her hips and said, "Hey, girl. I didn't think you'd have time to visit your preggo sister this week."

Skye hugged her, then said, "I only have forty-five minutes—but I wanted to see how you are." She stepped back. "You're radiant."

It was a trite phrase, but it described her friend to a tee. Loretta's dark brown skin glowed with health, and from the back, with her six-foot-tall, lean-muscled body and impeccably coiffed coal black braids, she appeared ready to walk a fashion runway. Only when she turned and her stomach was visible did it look like she had swallowed twin baby elephants.

"Yeah. I'm gorgeous, all right. The fact that I can't sleep, can barely get up from a chair without help, and have to pee constantly is immaterial," Loretta said with a sneer.

"Uh." Skye couldn't argue with her friend's statement. At thirty-six and a half weeks pregnant, Loretta had to be extremely uncomfortable.

"Why did you have to choose red for your bridesmaids dresses?" Loretta took Skye's hand and pulled her inside, then tugged her through the foyer and the family room and into the kitchen, complaining as they walked, "I'm going to look like an overripe tomato."

"I'm sure you'll be beautiful." Skye would never admit that she shared her friend's fear, which was why she wanted to get a peek at Loretta in the gown. "Besides, you agreed on the color." Skye gazed around the mammoth space, counting three sinks and two dishwashers before she said, "I'm still amazed at the size of this kitchen. You could feed an entire baseball lineup, or at least a basketball team."

"Yeah." Loretta eased onto a stool. "It did get a little out of hand," she admitted. "Still, I'm shocked at how much of the space we do use."

"Hey." Skye took a seat next to her. "You only build your dream house once. You might as well have what you want."

"True." Loretta rested her hands on her belly. "Anyway, besides the obvious reason that you're getting married in four days, why are you on such a tight schedule?"

"Did you hear that the car crash on Christmas Eve, the one that kept Wally from the family party, wasn't an accident?"

"No. I've been so busy with the house and finishing up my last case before I went on maternity leave. I haven't been listening to the news or reading the paper." Loretta selected a cookie from the tray on the counter in front of her and slid the treats over to Skye. "What's the scoop?"

"Wally was skeptical from the beginning," Skye said, then explained what the crime lab had discovered, finishing with, "So we're interviewing the people Yvonne had a disagreement with, hoping to come up with someone with a motive and the opportunity to commit the crime."

"I can't believe you're working an investigation this close to your big day." Loretta popped the last bite of cookie into her mouth, chewed, and swallowed. "Don't you have a million last-minute things to do?"

"Sort of." Skye shrugged. "But I think I have it all under control for now, at least as much as it can be." She pushed the cookie tray back toward Loretta. She was already afraid that with all the holiday treats she'd been eating, her bridal gown wouldn't fit.

"Is May driving you crazy?" Loretta selected another cookie. "She nearly drove me insane when we were building the house. Then, when she found out about the baby, I thought I would have to get an unlisted number and a guard dog to have any privacy." Loretta crunched off Frosty's head. "And she was laid-back compared to my mother."

"Mom's been fairly reasonable," Skye confessed. "Our last big disagreement was about the wedding presents. She wanted them all sent to her place so she could display them properly." Skye made air quotation marks with her fingers. "I wasn't thrilled about her conducting guided tours of our gifts, but in the end, I didn't care enough to fight about it. If you want to see the kind of loot you missed getting by eloping, drop by Mom and Dad's and take a peek in Vince's old bedroom." Skye winked. "Just keep behind the velvet ropes and don't try to touch the crystal or she'll call the security guard to take you away."

"Thanks, but I'll take a pass." Loretta snickered. "We'll rake in the gifts for presenting both sets of parents with their first grandchild, so I'm not too worried about missing the wedding booty."

"Not to mention the swag you'll get at the house-warming," Skye reminded her. "You're still planning to have it after the baby's born, right?"

Loretta nodded, then said, "Speaking of the house, want the grand tour?"

"Definitely." Skye helped her sister-in-law to her feet and said, "Lead on."

Loretta started in the family room. "This is where we'll spend most of our time." She swept her arm around the enormous room featuring a wet bar at one end and a fireplace at the other.

"Nice."

"You saw the dining and living rooms when we walked from the front door to the kitchen, so let me show you the master suite."

They made their way to the opposite end of the house, where the master suite took up the whole west side. In addition to a gorgeous bedroom with French doors leading to a patio and an in-ground pool, there was a huge bathroom and a double walk-in closet that shared a dressing area. When the place was under construction, Skye hadn't been aware of the magnificence of the suite, but now she was stunned by the lavishness.

Granted, Loretta was a partner in a prestigious law firm, but Skye wondered just how much money attorneys made. For sure, her brother couldn't afford anything half as luxurious as this. Even with free land and tapping into all the family connections for cheap labor, it had to have cost them close to a million. They probably had an enormous mortgage, but Vince would have never been able to qualify for such a big loan, even if his income was double what Skye figured it was from the hair salon.

Once Loretta had shown Skye the three upstairs bedrooms and the massive garage, they ended up back near the master bedroom, admiring the nursery. Skye spent an appropriate amount of time *ooh*ing and *aah*ing over the delicate mushroom-and-ecru color scheme, the soft fawn carpet, the draperies tied back with heavy tassels to give the curtains a scalloped look, and the elegant iron scroll-worked crib.

Then, after complimenting the cherub chandelier and chatting about the baby's arrival, Skye asked Loretta, "Would you mind trying on your bridesmaids dress for me?"

"Seriously?" Loretta screwed up her face. "You want me to take off my clothes, shimmy into that gown, and model it for you?"

"Yep." Skye nodded. "That about covers it." Tilting her head, she said, "Pretty please with chocolate syrup and peanut butter on top?" Vince had confided that Hershey's and Peter Pan were Loretta's latest cravings. "I made Frannie do the same thing the minute she got home from college last week, and poor Trixie has had hers on at least a half dozen times in the past month."

Frannie Ryan had been the coeditor of the student newspaper that Skye and Trixie sponsored at Scumble River High. Her mother had passed away many years ago, and she and Skye had become extremely close during the girl's school years. They'd continued to grow their relationship while Frannie attended the local junior college as a freshman and sophomore before transferring to the University of Illinois last fall.

"If I must," Loretta grumbled, then shuffled into the

master bedroom. "I live to make you happy." She slipped into the walk-in closet, adding, "But just remember, Frannie and Trixie aren't eight and a half months pregnant."

"Which is why I appreciate you trying on the dress for me so much." Skye waited in the bedroom, wanting to see it in a grand reveal once Loretta had the gown on rather than as she got into it.

Skye heard rustling and a few choice words; then Loretta shouted, "Did Wally ever bring up the subject of a prenup?"

"No." Skye had asked Loretta to look over an agreement if Wally asked her to sign one. She'd assumed that because of his family's wealth, he would want her to consent to a prenuptial before they were married. "And when I mentioned it, he said we didn't need one. We weren't getting divorced, and if anything happened to him, he wanted me to have everything he owned."

"That's a surprise." Loretta's voice was awed. "Nowadays, a prenup is the norm for people who get married in their thirties or forties and have any significant assets."

"That's what I thought," Skye agreed. "Which was why I was sure he'd want one." If Loretta only knew that Wally's father was a Texas oil millionaire, she'd really be shocked. "It certainly can't be because he thinks I have any money. He knows I just paid off my credit cards last year and that I have a home-improvement loan."

"*C'est la vie.*" Loretta's tone indicated that she had lost interest in the conversation. "I'll be out in a second."

Several agonizing minutes later, Loretta emerged from the closet and Skye held her breath. Her attendants were of wildly varying sizes—Trixie was five-foot-two and wore a size 4; Frannie was six inches taller and six sizes larger; and then there was Loretta, who towered over both women and now had a stomach roughly the dimension of an extralarge exercise ball.

Exhaling, Skye slumped in relief. The poinsettia red silky taffeta gown looked gorgeous on her friend. The maternity version had an empire waist, but the rest was identical to the other bridesmaids' dresses. The straps were sewn at an asymmetrical vee, and there was a diamanté snowflake-shaped embellishment where they merged at the sweetheart neckline.

"You look incredible," Skye said, thrilled she could tell the truth.

"Yes, I do." Loretta spun around and peered at herself in the full-length mirror. "What do you think of my shoes?" She lifted the hem.

Skye glanced down at Loretta's feet and saw fabulous black satin peep-toe pumps with a sparkling brooch and an hourglass heel. "Stunning." She loved them. She had told her attendants they could wear any shoes they wanted as long as they were black, but now she wished she'd asked them all to buy the ones Loretta had on.

"The dress fits perfectly." Loretta looked over her shoulder and down at her derriere. "Does it make my ass look big?"

"Not at all." Skye kept her face expressionless, sure that her sister-in-law would not be amused if she mentioned that compared to her front, Loretta's rear end was minuscule. "You look great."

"That reminds me, did I mention that a few hours before her car went off the bridge, I talked to that librarian who was killed?" Loretta kicked off her pumps and retreated to the walk-in closet.

"What reminds you?" Skye followed Loretta and helped her out of the gown.

"The subject of big butts." Loretta wiggled into her maternity jeans.

"Okay." Skye hung up the bridesmaids dress. "I surrender. How do big butts jog your memory about your encounter with a dead librarian?"

"You know how I've been trying to wind up my part of that case I've been working on? So I can turn it over to the attorney who's covering for me while I'm on maternity leave?"

"Yes."

"Well, I finally finished about three o'clock Christmas Eve, and just as I was about to e-mail everything to my paralegal, the power went out." Loretta slid her T-shirt over her head and slipped on her loafers. "The trial starts today, and I needed to get the info to the firm ASAP in order for my replacement to have time to go over it before he walked into court."

"So you went to the library to use their Internet," Skye guessed.

"Exactly." Loretta eased onto the vanity bench and smoothed her hair. "It was the only place I could think of that was open and had Wi-Fi."

"Okay, now I know why you were at the library." Skye wrinkled her brow. "So tell me the connection between large rear ends and Yvonne."

"We were chatting about the negatives of being pregnant," Loretta explained, "and she said that when she was expecting, both her boobs and her butt got so big that she felt like Dita Von Teese."

"Who?"

"The Queen of Burlesque." Loretta shrugged. "She has this really knockout hourglass figure."

"I get it. Yvonne had an amazing shape, too," Skye commented, then added, "An attribute I'm not sure she was entirely comfortable with."

"She mentioned that men hit on her all the time, even when she was preggers," Loretta confirmed. "She said she was sick and tired of guys seeing her only as a body and not being interested in her brain."

"I suppose if you look like a *Cosmo* model, you have to expect that."

"Yeah." Loretta nodded. "But it wasn't as if she dressed to show off her assets."

"True."

"She said she was going to a party with this man she'd been seeing for the past couple of months who seemed different, and she had to leave straight from the library because she was meeting him in Laurel at five. She was wearing this really chic bronze Armani suit, but it wasn't very sexy." Loretta made a face. "I told her she should go home and change into something slinkier."

"Why?" Skye asked. "Yvonne clearly didn't want that kind of image."

"I don't think it was that she didn't want to look sexy," Loretta corrected. "I think she just didn't want that to be *all* that people thought she was. So I told her that clearly, if she'd been dating this guy for a while, he'd already passed her test and deserved a treat."

"What did Yvonne say?"

"She agreed."

CHAPTER 10

Beyond the Tale

"So tell me about Emmy Jones." Skye made herself comfortable in the squad car's passenger seat, prepared to interrogate Wally during the entire drive to Laurel if necessary.

"There's nothing to tell." Wally slid a quick glance at Skye.

"Come on. Really?" She raised a brow. "A hot dancer who is an expert markswoman, a woman you see frequently yet have never mentioned to me." She shook her head. "I bet there's lots to tell."

"I'm not sure what you want to hear." Wally took another hasty peek at Skye, then returned his attention to the two-lane blacktop. "We shoot together. That's all."

"How long have you known her?" Skye asked, realizing she would have to dig the information out of Wally—not unlike her counseling sessions with most adolescent boys.

"Six months or so," Wally answered, clearly reluctant to continue the conversation. "I think she started coming to the club in June, and it was at least four or five weeks after that when we first competed against each other."

He shrugged. "Since it wasn't that important, I didn't keep track."

"Hmm." Skye remembered that July had been the height of her wedding planning frenzy. "Why didn't you ever mention her to me?"

"I already told you—it didn't seem that important." Wally tugged on his tie. "She was just one of the guys at the club." He looked at her sharply. "Think about it. Have I talked about any of them?"

"No," Skye admitted. "But I'm assuming the rest of the *guys* aren't babes."

"There are other women who belong to the gun club," Wally insisted. "Tomi Jackson, Luella Calhoun, and Kathryn Steele all shoot."

"Let's see." Skye kept track on her fingers. "Tomi is in her sixties or seventies, Luella prefers girls, and you're usually at odds with Kathryn because her newspaper reporters frequently interfere with your investigations."

"That's not the point," Wally argued. "The point I'm making is that I've never told you they were members of the gun club either."

"Okay." Skye crossed her arms. "Let's set aside the issue of your not telling me about Emmy. Did you know that she was Ruby's daughter?"

"No." Wally braked for a stop sign. "I knew she was living with Bunny, but not why. I just figured that Bunny was renting out her extra room to make money for more Botox or plastic surgery. Like the time she accepted counterfeit money in exchange for closing down the bowling alley for that bachelor party or that cat show/ speed dating thing she tried to pull off eight months ago."

"Did you know Emmy had gotten into trouble in Las Vegas?" Skye asked.

"No." He took his turn at the four-way, then said, "Emmy and I don't talk that much, and when we do, we usually discuss weapons."

"She seemed to know a lot more about you than just what guns you like to shoot." Skye tapped her fingers on the dashboard. "She asked if we were there for dance lessons for the wedding."

"Because when I first met her she indicated she was available." Wally's expression was wary. "But before you jump to conclusions, I made sure she knew that I was getting married in a few months. I guess I should have told you, but you were so busy during the summer. I didn't want to waste the little bit of time we had together on something trivial."

"Oh." A faint flush rose in Skye's cheeks. Between her job as a lifeguard at the recreation club—which Wally had suggested she not take this year—and her mother insisting that she do multiple cake and food tastings for the reception, Skye had barely seen Wally. That might have been a serious error on her part.

Wally abruptly pulled the car over to the side of the road, turned to Skye, and took both her hands in his. "Why are you suddenly so jealous? That's not like you at all." He studied her face. "I know you don't truly think I would ever cheat on you with Emmy or anyone else, so what's really going on?"

"I guess I have bridal jitters." Skye caressed Wally's palm with her thumb and gazed into his dark chocolate eyes. "A part of me is convinced that I'm not the kind of woman who gets a happily ever after, so I keep thinking the wicked queen will show up at the last minute, wave her magic wand, and make you disappear."

"Darlin'." Wally leaned over the console, cupped her cheek, and between kisses on her upturned face, he said, "That'll never happen. I would shoot the wand to pieces before she could say 'abracadabra.' You're stuck with me until death do us part."

"I know I'm being silly and I'm sorry." Skye pressed her lips to his, determined to show him that she was re-morseful for having doubted him. When they came up for air, she said, "Four more days and I promise to return to the land of the sane." She tilted her head. "Or at least my usual brand of insanity."

"I'm looking forward to that." Wally kissed her temple, then eased the Caprice back onto the asphalt. "Now can we discuss the case?"

"If we must." Skye pretended reluctance, then asked, "I take it since we're driving all the way over to Laurel, you're certain Yvonne's husband will be home. Did you call him and make an appointment?"

"No. I like to surprise possible suspects. When they're off balance, they don't always think before they speak and sometimes they blurt out something incriminating." Wally slowed as a trio of deer ran onto the road, stared at the oncoming squad car, then scampered away. "What I did was phone his company to see if he was there. His secretary said that he was taking the day off to care for his son because his wife was sick with the flu."

"We're going into a house with flu germs?" Skye's voice rose an octave.

"We have to talk to him." Wally gripped the wheel so tightly, his knuckles turned white. "So we really don't have much choice."

"But what if we catch the flu and are sick for the wedding?"

Wally's jaw clenched, but he repeated patiently, "I have no choice." The muscle under his left eye twitched. "If you want, you can wait in the car."

"No," Skye conceded. "You're right." She started to bite her thumbnail, then stopped and sat on her hands. She had an appointment for a manicure on the twenty-eighth and wanted her nails to be in good shape. "Maybe we could wear masks and gloves."

"Seriously?" Wally's nostrils flared. "You want to conduct an interview wearing a mask? Are you sure you don't want the whole hazmat suit?" he teased.

"I guess not," Skye conceded, rolling her eyes at her own foolishness. "I suppose it would be a little tough to establish any kind of rapport dressed as if we thought he had the plague."

"You think?"

"But I don't want to sneeze my way down the aisle either." Skye wrinkled her nose. "Or spend our honeymoon in bed—at least not in bed sick."

"Definitely not." Wally winked at her. "I have big plans for how we spend our time in bed."

"Me too." Skye's heart did a tap dance, thinking of the sexy lingerie she'd received from her friends at last month's personal shower.

"If we make sure not to touch our faces and wash our hands with sanitizer as soon as we get back in the car, we'll be okay," he soothed. "Besides, we both had our flu shots."

"Sure." Skye nodded, not really convinced but seeing no use in pursuing the subject. Instead, she said, "Does Yvonne's husband drive an Escalade?"

Wally shook his head.

"Did you find out anything new about the case while I was gone this afternoon?"

"Not much." Wally braked at a stoplight. They had entered Laurel's city limits and were driving through town toward the highway. "Quirk escorted Phoebe home and she produced the SAT scores and the U of C acceptance letter. She also gave him her laptop and consented to have it examined by the crime lab. We'll drop it off after we talk to her dad."

"So you'll authorize her release once we've talked to her dad?" When Wally nodded, Skye said, "That's good. It sounds as if it's pretty unlikely she killed her mother."

"Right." The light turned green and Wally drove forward. "The only other interesting thing is that as we suspected, Zuchowski wasn't home."

"Oh, oh." Skye flipped down the visor. "Are you going to fire him?"

"I haven't decided yet." Wally frowned. "I hate to leave the department shorthanded while I'm away on our honeymoon, so I might put him on probation instead."

"That's a good compromise." Skye took a brush from

her purse and fixed her hair. "Back to the case, I might have some information. I went to see Loretta during that hour I had free."

"Checking to see if her bridesmaids dress fits," Wally guessed. "Did she try it on for you?"

"Yes, and it looks great." Skye applied apricot lip gloss, then wiped her fingers on a tissue. "While Loretta was modeling the gown, she mentioned that she saw Yvonne the afternoon before she died."

"What time?"

"Loretta chatted with her while Yvonne was closing up the library," Skye answered. "So it must have been four o'clock."

"What did they talk about?" Wally asked, getting into the left-turn lane.

"Big butts." She paused to enjoy Wally's startled reaction, then described Loretta and the librarian's conversation. When Skye was finished, she asked, "You saw Yvonne when they pulled her out of the water, right?" At Wally's nod, she added, "Do you remember what she was wearing?"

"She had on this tight red dress with pleats across here." Wally gestured to his upper chest. "And what do you call those thin straps?"

"Spaghetti."

"Yeah, those." Wally nodded. "And she had this fancy coat that looked like it was supposed to go with the dress. It was red satin, too, but it had big black flowers all over it."

"So she did go home and change," Skye murmured almost to herself.

"She must have. She definitely wasn't wearing the brown suit Loretta saw her in." He rubbed his chin. "Until Phoebe told us about that Tom Riley guy, we wondered why she was heading away from her house. She must have been on her way to Laurel to meet him."

"So we know she left the library parking lot after quarreling with Phoebe, drove home, and changed clothes." Skye listed Yvonne's last-known activities aloud so Wally could follow her line of reasoning. "That means we can narrow down the TOD."

"Right." Wally pulled up to the entrance of the Pheasant Creek subdivision and flashed his badge at the guard. Once the yellow and black gate was raised and Wally had driven through, he said, "How long do you think it would take her to put on different clothes?"

"Well . . ." Skye reflected on what she knew about Yvonne. She was fairly sure the librarian hadn't been the type to fuss much with her hair and makeup. "Considering the situation, she would have been in a hurry, so I'd say maybe ten or fifteen minutes, tops."

"Which means if we allow fifteen minutes for the argument with her daughter and ten minutes to drive home, we can now assume she was forced off the road between four forty-five and five fifty-five," Wally calculated.

"Not exactly a precise TOD, but better than the two-hour window we had before." Skye examined the widely spaced houses as Wally steered the cruiser down a street lined with tiny trees and huge homes.

"Slightly." Wally pulled into a long driveway. "Here's Neil Osborn's place."

"Fancy." Skye studied the imposing faux Tudor castle. "I hadn't realized that there was this kind of affluence in Laurel."

"It's less than an hour from Chicago and handy to I-80, so people are taking advantage of the cheap land." Wally parked behind a nondescript Honda. "In this area they can build a fifty-five-hundred-square-foot house for the same amount a duplex would cost in the city."

"True." Skye nodded, then asked, "Have you contacted Tom Riley yet?"

"No." Wally got out, walked around the Chevy to Skye's side, and opened her door. "The bakery closes at two, and Phoebe doesn't know where he lives and doesn't have his personal telephone number. I've got Martinez running down his address."

"If he was the one Yvonne was meeting, I wonder what he did when she failed to show up for their date," Skye remarked as they walked toward the house.

"That's a good question." Wally rang the bell. "He should have either been upset at being stood up or concerned for her welfare."

"Unless he killed her," Skye said, staring thoughtfully into space.

Before Wally could respond, the huge oak door banged open and a short, fiftysomething man wearing an expensive suit charged past him, flung himself inside the Civic, and drove away, his tires squealing.

Another fiftysomething man, this one taller and dressed in jeans and a sweatshirt, appeared in the doorway, scowled at the departing Honda, then turned to Wally and Skye and said, "Can I help you?"

"Neil Osborn?" The man nodded, and Wally said, "I'm Chief Boyd from the Scumble River Police, and this is Skye Denison, our department's psych consultant. We're here to talk to you about your ex-wife's death."

"Sure." Stepping aside, Neil said, "Come on in, but I have to warn you my wife has the flu and I think my son might be getting it, too."

"Then we won't shake hands." Wally crossed the threshold. "Where's the best place for us to sit? Where we won't disturb your family?"

"Let's go to my den." Neil led them across a large foyer and down a short hallway. "I've got the baby monitor so I can hear Neil Junior if he cries."

Neil showed Wally and Skye into a large room decorated with sports memorabilia and neon beer signs. The two choices for seating were barstools or a row of black leather theater chairs lined up facing a massive flat-screen television.

Wally nodded imperceptibly toward the stools, and Skye quickly said to Neil, "What a lovely bar. Do you mind if we sit here?"

"Thanks. Sure. Have a seat." Neil grinned. "I designed

it myself. I salvaged this black mesquite from a church they were leveling." He ran a hand over the bar's surface. "You can't buy wood like this anymore."

"Gorgeous." Skye beamed. "I've been remodeling a house and have been trying to keep as much of the original structure as possible."

"Yvonne loved old houses." He wrinkled his forehead. "She hated to see any building torn down. Which was kind of hard to avoid in my business."

"How long had you and your ex-wife been divorced?" Wally asked.

"It'll be three years this summer." Neil stood behind the bar and leaned on the polished surface.

"We talked to your daughter today about where she was Christmas Eve," Wally said, watching the older man closely. "Did you know she and your ex had had a disagreement right before Yvonne was killed?"

"Mothers and daughters argue a lot." Neil thrust his fingers through his short salt-and-pepper hair. "It's no big deal."

"Phoebe claims that she didn't want to spend Christmas Eve with you, and her mom said she had to because she had given you her word." Wally sat back. "Does that sound like something they'd fight about?"

"Yeah." Neil sighed. "The divorce was hard on Phoebe. And even though she and my wife get along pretty well, she's still not comfortable spending much time with us. We try to include her, but with the new baby, it's hard to give her the attention she wants."

Wally and Skye exchanged glances. Neil had confirmed what Phoebe had told them. She raised a questioning brow and he nodded.

Skye took a breath and said, "Phoebe also told us about the SAT scheme that Yvonne foiled." She tilted her head. "That had to upset you. All that money down the drain."

"I won't lie to you. I was mad when it happened, but I came to realize she was right." Neil's expression was shamefaced. "It was a moron move. I don't want to teach my little girl to be a cheater."

Skye murmured wordless encouragement for him to keep talking.

"But Yvonne and I had an amicable divorce." Neil exhaled loudly. "We didn't have any hard feelings between us, and we made a point to stay friends so Phoebe wouldn't be caught in the middle."

"It seems as if your ex-wife had a pretty strong sense of right and wrong," Wally interjected. "Was that a problem between you two?"

"One of many." Neil shrugged. "There were no shades of gray on Yvonne's color wheel." He shook his head. "It was hard being married to someone who always insisted that you do the right thing."

"I can imagine," Skye said. "It must have been rough having to look into that kind of mirror every day. Probably not easy having someone like her as a mom either. Did Phoebe resent Yvonne?"

"No more than any other teenager resents their parents' rules." Neil stared over Skye's head. "But Yvonne was never one to look the other way, and I wouldn't be surprised if that's what got her killed."

CHAPTER 11

Babble like a Book

It took only a few minutes to establish that Neil didn't have a good alibi. He claimed that he had been with his wife and son during the time his ex was killed, but neither of them could be considered reliable witnesses. Wally then asked him a few more questions, but Neil maintained that he and Yvonne had had an amiable divorce. It was clear that the guy was either innocent of the murder or too smooth to incriminate himself.

When the baby started to cry and Neil edged toward the door to the hallway, Skye quickly asked, "Who was the man rushing away when we arrived?"

"My business partner, Hank Gaskin."

"Phoebe mentioned that you two are more like brothers than partners." Skye smiled. "In fact, she called him Uncle Hank. What was he so upset about?"

"Nothing." Neil's expression was bland. "He was just in a hurry."

Wally and Skye exchanged skeptical looks, but silently agreed that Neil wouldn't tell them any more. They said goodbye and left Yvonne's ex to tend to his ailing family.

As soon as they got into the squad car, Skye grabbed

the bottle of Purell she'd set at the ready on the dashboard. She motioned for Wally to hold out his palms, then squeezed a large dollop of the clear gel onto his fingers. After he rubbed in the liquid, he took his cell from his pocket, called the PD, and authorized Phoebe's release.

While Wally was on the phone, Skye disinfected her own hands, then used a tissue saturated with the sanitizer to swab her purse and the door handles. When she finished wiping down the cruiser's interior, Wally started up the Caprice, put it in gear, and pulled out of the drive.

As they headed toward town, he said, "If we don't get a break in the case soon, we'll have to come back and talk to the new Mrs. Osborn. I would have liked to question her today, but I draw the line at interrogating a sick woman."

"Good thing." Skye shuddered. "The air around her would be full of germs."

"Remind me again, how many more days until you're sane again?" Wally laughed without humor.

"Sorry." Skye managed a smile. "That did sound a little cold."

"Just a tad." Wally patted her knee. "Let's drop off Phoebe's computer, then get some dinner. Where do you want to eat?"

"It's hard to pick." Skye thought for a moment. There were lots of restaurant choices in Laurel versus the two or three places in Scumble River. "Kinkade's is nice and we haven't been to Harry's in long time." Skye slid a questioning glance at Wally. "Unless that's where your dad is holding our rehearsal dinner?"

"I have no idea where he's taking us." Wally parked the Chevy behind the crime lab and grabbed the plastic evidence bag containing Phoebe's laptop from the rear seat. "Just remember, if you're unhappy with his choice, I was the one who said we shouldn't let him surprise us."

As Wally walked toward the building, Skye nervously jiggled her foot. She hoped Wally's strained relationship with his father wouldn't become a problem this coming weekend. Understandably, the oil millionaire wanted his son to take over the family empire. But Wally had no interest in running CB International, which made for considerable tension between the two of them.

It didn't help matters that Carson constantly tried to persuade Wally to change his mind. Carson had tried guilt, claiming to be sick; bribery, showering his son with presents; and even an elaborate scheme to buy a factory near Scumble River in order to involve Wally in the company. When none of that had worked, he'd turned his attention to Skye. Currently, his plan appeared to be to lure her to his side with extravagant gifts, and once she was there, persuade her to convince Wally that running CB International was his destiny.

Ten minutes later, Skye was still worrying about Wally and his father when Wally returned to the squad car and said, "How do you feel about Italian for dinner? The crime tech said Little Mario's just moved into a new building on Branch and the food is great."

"Yum." Skye's stomach growled. "In my opinion, nothing's as good as my mom's Italian cooking, but I'm always willing to try to prove that notion wrong." She put away the to-do list she'd been holding. "Do you want to drive by Riley's Bakery on our way? It might be interesting to see the place."

"Sure." Wally steered the Caprice out of the lot. "It's on the main drag, so we can go past, then take a side street over to Branch."

As they expected, the bakery's display window was dark, but Skye could see that the shop was a nice size and had a good location. Tom Riley was almost certainly making a good living with his business.

Wally slowed as they cruised by. "The bakery's hours are six to two. I'm guessing morning is the busiest, so my plan is to come over here to talk to him around one thirty."

"Do you want me to go with you?" Skye asked, trying

to remember her schedule for the next day and hoping she could fit in the visit.

"If you have time." Wally's expression was sober. "Riley might not know about Yvonne's death yet, since Phoebe claimed not to have talked to him. She said he and her mother had been dating for a couple of months, so he might take the news that Yvonne's dead pretty hard. It would be good to have you there, in the event he has a meltdown."

"Okay." Skye grabbed her appointment book from her purse and flipped to December. She ran her finger down the page until she reached the twenty-seventh. "I'm picking up my wedding gown at nine, and it's a good hour to Barrington, so I might not be home until eleven. Then I have to go to the bank to get cash for the DJ and limousine driver and a money order for the photographer, since only the florist and cake maker will accept a personal check."

"I could take care of that for you," Wally offered. "Just give me a list of the balances and I'll put them all in separate envelopes."

"Great!" Skye was happy that she and Wally had decided to open a joint checking account so that either of them could take care of the bills. "That would be a real time saver for me."

"When do we need to hand over the final payments?" Wally asked.

"The day of the wedding. I was going to pay the full amount up front, but then someone told me it wasn't a good idea." Skye massaged her temple. "Knowing that they won't get the rest of their fee until they show up gives them an incentive to do a better job."

"That's a smart move." Wally nodded approvingly.

"You know, even though I think Mom and Dad were relieved that we insisted on paying for our own wedding, I'm sure they feel a little uncomfortable that they aren't footing the bill." Skye pursed her lips. "What if we give Dad the envelopes and put him in charge of settling up with the vendors?" She thought a moment and added, "He doesn't have much to do besides escort me down the aisle and the father/daughter dance at the reception, so it might make him feel more a part of the whole she-bang."

"Good idea." Wally eased the Chevy into a spot near Little Mario's entrance, then went around to open Skye's door. "Still, I'm glad we're taking care of the cost. Even keeping things simple like we've tried to do, I would guess that shelling out nearly twenty-five thousand would be a strain for your parents."

"Definitely. Coming up with twenty-five grand would be tough for nearly anyone except a guy with a trust fund," Skye teased Wally. Up until now, he'd lived on his police salary and had seldom touched the money his mother had left him, but he'd said his mom would have wanted him to use the cash for their wedding expenses.

As soon as they entered the restaurant, Skye was impressed with its new look. Little Mario's previous incarnation had been a congested space with less than a dozen tables crowded under bright neon lights. This building had two large rooms and a bar all lit softly to enhance the dining experience.

Since it was nearly seven, which in a small town was late for dinner on a Tuesday night, Wally's request for a booth in a back corner was easily fulfilled and they were seated right away.

Their server appeared immediately and placed a basket of warm bread in the center of the table. She poured olive oil into a saucer, added grated parmesan cheese and freshly ground pepper, and then asked for their drink orders. Because Wally was in uniform and driving a squad car, he asked for iced tea instead of his typical Sam Adams, and Skye stuck to her usual Diet Coke with a slice of lime.

As Skye and Wally looked over the menus, she said, "I'm torn. I'm starving, but I'm also a little worried that my wedding gown won't fit. The holidays have really thrown my eating habits out of whack, and I'm afraid the dress will be too tight."

"I'm sure it will be okay." Wally covered her hand with his. "Any extra calories you've eaten will have been burned off by nervous energy. Besides, you're beautiful the way you are."

"Thank you." Skye smiled. "But I always dreamed that when I got married, I'd look like my Barbie did in her wedding gown."

"Hey." Wally tore off a piece of bread, dragged it through the oil mixture, and fed it to her. "If Barbie's so great, why do you have to buy her friends?"

Skye snickered.

"And if your dress is tight, you can always put on one of those Spanx thingies, right?"

She nodded, her mouth full. She was so lucky. A lot of men would have told her that missing a meal would improve her curvy figure, but Wally seemed to love her whether she was fat, thin, or anywhere in between.

After they ordered—tortellini paesano for her and pasta casareccia for him—Wally leaned back and sighed. "I sure hope we can wrap up this case before we leave on our honeymoon. Don't get me wrong. Quirk is a good police officer, but he hasn't had much practice investigating a murder on his own, and this is such an unusual situation."

"We'll figure it out before we go." Skye paused to allow the waitress to serve their salads. Then, as she forked up a bite of the mixed greens, she added firmly, "And if we don't, Quirk will do fine."

Wally nodded, clearly unconvinced. "It's just that the longer it takes to solve a case, the less likely that it will be solved."

Skye made a sympathetic sound, thinking that Wally reminded her how crucial time was every time they worked together. Before she could come up with a response other than "so you've said," a rowdy crowd of late teen and early twentysomethings burst through the entrance. When the group was seated in the booth next to Wally and Skye, his lips tightened at the interruption of their quiet dinner.

Skye opened her mouth to soothe his obvious displeasure, but shut it when she heard one of the guys say, "Janet, did you hear that librarian bi-atch who gave you a hard time a couple of weeks ago at the Christmas concert in Scumble River was killed over the weekend?"

Wally started to speak, but Skye held her index finger to her lips, cupped her ear, and jerked her head toward the rear of their booth. She was thankful that the kids behind them were evidently too self-involved to notice that there was a police officer present, even though Wally was dressed in his uniform. "Yeah, Cody," Janet answered. "Della blogged about it yesterday."

"I'm surprised she actually wrote about something interesting." Cody guffawed. "The last time I read her blog, it was all about her dog taking a dump in her neighbor's yard, how mean the guy was about the whole thing, and what kind of bag she used to clean up after the hound."

"Yeah. That's what she writes about, all right. And her baby niece's diapers." Janet giggled. "That girl is obsessed with poop. Believe me, I only read her blog in order to make fun of her."

"Did she mention how she found out about the murder?" Cody asked. "The *Laurel Daily Herald* didn't have anything about it on their Web site, and it wasn't on the radio until this morning. The 'rents always listen to the local station while we eat breakfast, and the announcer called the story breaking news."

"Della's brother's wife has a part-time job at the county building," Janet explained. "And she overheard some of the lab geeks talking about how it looked like an accident at first but was really a murder."

Wally ground his teeth, and Skye shot him a sympathetic look. She understood his frustration, but there were no secrets in a small town. Besides, the PD had released the news to the local media, so it wasn't as if the crime techs had let the cat out of the bag.

"I bet you're happy the wicked witch is dead," Cody said, egging her on.

"Of course not." Janet sounded offended. "Did you drink a second can of dumb today? I'd never be glad someone died." The young woman's tone turned thoughtful. "But she didn't have to get so bent out of shape. It was none of her business that I was powdering my nose."

As the bunch at the adjacent table cracked up, Skye and Wally exchanged a puzzled look. Why did Yvonne care if the girl was putting on makeup?

"She did almost get you busted," a second male voice piped up. "You were just lucky that the cop on duty at the concert was crushing on you."

Wally stiffened and Skye patted his hand. They'd said the concert was in Scumble River, which meant that the officer who'd let the young woman off was one of Wally's employees. Who had worked the event?

"I am irresistible," Janet drawled. "And Larry knew if he arrested me for doing a little blow, I'd have to let his boss know about his own dirty little habits. Who do you think's my snowman?"

That explained it. Janet hadn't been putting on makeup; she'd been snorting cocaine, Skye realized, then murmured almost to herself, "But who is Larry?"

"Zuchowski," Wally mouthed, then muttered, "Lawrence Zuchowski."

"That explains his absenteeism," Skye whispered. "What are you going to do?"

"Fire his ass, then arrest him for dealing," Wally hissed. "But first I'll check our evidence closet to see if Zuchowski is getting his supply from the PD."

"Shit!" Skye swore. "If he is, Uncle Dante will have a field day. You know he's on a kick about how useless the police department is."

"In this case, the mayor just might be right."

CHAPTER 12

Chilled to the Tome

After hearing about Zuchowski's criminal activities, Wally barely ate his dinner and answered all of Skye's attempts at conversation in monosyllables. Midway through the meal, she gave up trying to lighten his mood and concentrated on finishing her tortellini. They both refused dessert, and she was relieved to be back in the squad car heading home.

Thoughts of Zuchowski's betrayal occupied Skye's mind for most of the trip, and they were crossing into the Scumble River city limits when a horrible notion hit her and she gasped.

"What's wrong?" Wally glanced at her.

"I just had an awful idea."

"Worse than an officer I hired dealing drugs that he might have stolen from my evidence closet?" Wally's expression was grim.

"Unfortunately." Skye twisted her hands. She hated to make Wally feel even worse than he already did, but she had to say it. "What if Zuchowski murdered Yvonne to keep her quiet? She had to be upset that he didn't arrest that girl she'd caught snorting cocaine."

"Son of a B!" Wally roared. "You're right; that's a lot worse."

"Sorry."

He stared out the windshield for so long that Skye worried he'd become catatonic, but finally he said, "You're right. We have to consider the possibility that Zuchowski is the killer." He hit the steering wheel. "First thing tomorrow, we find out for sure if he's in town or not. Now I hope he did leave on vacation with his girl-friend on Saturday like Quirk suspects."

"Why don't we swing by his place now and check?" Skye suggested, hoping to alleviate Wally's concerns.

"Because Zuchowski not being home right this min-ute wouldn't prove anything," Wally snapped, then added in an apologetic tone, "We have to make him admit he's out of state and has been since before the murder was committed."

"You're right." Skye shrugged. "I didn't think it through."

Wally was silent until he pulled into the police station garage. Once they were out of the squad car, he said, "You go ahead home."

"Aren't you coming?" Skye asked. Since they'd be-come engaged, either she'd stayed over at Wally's house or he'd slept at her place nearly every night.

"No." Wally gestured to the door leading into the PD. "I want to check the evidence closet. This is a good time to do it because the mayor's not as likely to pop in at ten at night as he is during the day."

"That's true." Skye stroked his sleeve. "Uncle Dante is a real early-to-bed, early-to-rise kind of guy." She paused, then asked, "But isn't Mom dispatching to-night?"

"Yes." Wally's lips tightened. "Are you thinking she might tell Dante?"

"Not to get you in trouble." Skye frowned. "But she's not good at lying, so if he ever asked her, she'd probably blurt out the truth. And even if she didn't, her body language would give it away."

"Good to know." Wally hugged Skye. "I'll ask Martinez to stay after her shift ends to act as my witness. Then, when May leaves at eleven, we'll take inventory."

"That's definitely the safest way to do it." Skye put her hands on his chest. "You can come over after you finish. I might even wait up for you."

"It'll be late," Wally warned. "We won't get started until eleven thirty, and the accounting will take at least a couple of hours."

"I can use the time to pack for our honeymoon. You did say we're going somewhere warm, right? Is it Hawaii or the Bahamas?"

"Why? Is that where you want to go?" Wally arched an eyebrow.

Skye pretended to pout.

"It's a surprise, remember?" Wally trailed a finger down her cheek. "A surprise means not knowing ahead of time."

"Fine." She thumped his shoulder. "So are you coming over later?"

"I better not." Wally blew out a long breath. "I wouldn't be very good company and I'll be up early. It's better if I let you get your rest."

"Okay." Skye kissed him. "Then I'll meet you at the station at twelve thirty tomorrow. And I'll go to the bank. It looks as if you'll have your hands full."

"So it seems." Wally gave her one final hug, then released her. As he walked her to the Bel Air, he said, "Thanks for understanding, sweetheart. I really had hoped to be able to help you more these last few days." Wally held the Chevy's door open for her, and after she slid in, he said, "Let me know if there's something you can't do or something you absolutely need me to do."

"Believe me, I will." Skye put her key in the ignition.

"And since I've done almost everything else for the wedding, you can write all the thank-you notes when we get back from our honeymoon."

At his sudden stricken expression, Skye snickered to herself, waved, and drove away.

Waking the next morning, Skye realized that Wally had been right. She would have been exhausted if she had waited up for him the night before. As it was, when she'd arrived home, she'd barely had the energy to feed Bingo, clean his litter box, and drag herself up the stairs to bed before collapsing into a dreamless sleep.

Now, as she stepped into the shower, everything they'd learned yesterday whirled through her mind. A picture of Yvonne was beginning to form. She'd been a gorgeous woman who loved her daughter, but stood firm when Phoebe crossed the line. It couldn't have been easy to refuse to allow the girl to go to college on schedule or to stand up to her ex-husband about the situation.

Skye poured shampoo into her palm, then lathered her hair while she thought about the conversation she and Wally had overheard at Little Mario's restaurant. It would have been a lot simpler for Yvonne to pretend not to have seen Janet snorting cocaine than for her to report the girl's drug use to the police.

Had the librarian stuck around to witness the arrest? Skye didn't think so. From what she knew about Yvonne, the woman would have been satisfied that she had done the honorable thing and expected the officer to do his duty. But would Yvonne have checked to see if Janet had been charged? Skye doubted it.

On the other hand, the *Star*'s Police Beat column listed the arrests made each previous week, so it would have been easy to notice that charges hadn't been filed against the young woman. Even if Yvonne hadn't known Janet's name, if there was no female in her early twenties arrested for cocaine usage in the paper, the librarian could have put two and two together and realized the officer to whom she'd reported the crime hadn't followed through.

Skye turned off the water and grabbed a towel. The real question was, would Yvonne have sought out Zuchowski to question why Janet hadn't been prosecuted, or would she have taken her concern to his boss— either Wally or Quirk? Skye was fairly certain the librarian would have gone up the chain of command, and clearly she hadn't spoken to Wally. Had she talked to the sergeant?

Again, Skye was reasonably sure that Quirk would have brought the matter to Wally's attention. Especially since it was clear that the sergeant was fed up with Zuchowski's behavior. If nothing else, Quirk would have put a note in the rookie's file.

After drying and flatironing her hair, Skye applied her makeup and put on a pair of black flannel slacks and a red turtleneck sweater. She packed the lingerie she planned to wear underneath her bridal gown in a duffel bag, then grabbed her wedding shoes.

Before adding the box to her carryall, she lifted the lid and admired the elegant peep-toe sling-backs. She fingered the Swarovski crystal on the side of the instep and the tiny white fur poof on the strap. They were perfect. It had been difficult finding a pair with a reasonable heel, but even though Wally was a good five inches taller than she was and she could have worn stilettos, she hadn't wanted to spend the entire day with sore feet.

Checking her watch, Skye hurried downstairs. Where had the time gone? She fed Bingo, gulped down a bowl of Special K, and headed to Barrington. It would have been nice to have some company on the long drive, but Loretta was increasingly uncomfortable riding in a car, Trixie wasn't arriving home from her husband's family holiday party until late afternoon, and Frannie was spending every minute she could with her boyfriend, Justin Boward.

Justin was a year younger than Frannie and still at-

tending Joliet Junior College. He and Frannie hoped
he'd be accepted to the University of Illinois for his final
two years so that they could be together. Skye had her
fingers crossed that he'd get in too. She was afraid that
since his girlfriend had made the cut, if he didn't, his confidence would be shattered. Which might end the young
couple's relationship.

If Justin wasn't accepted, Skye wasn't sure how he'd
react. If need be, she was prepared to step in and pick up
the pieces. He'd been in counseling with her from eighth
grade until partway through high school, and she wasn't
willing to let all her hard work go down the drain. He
was her friend, and that was as important a relationship
as when he'd been her student.

With that happy thought, Skye arrived at the bridal
salon. As she walked through the doorway, the dial on
the shop's French tabernacle clock showed precisely
nine a.m. Although her dress fit perfectly, the appointment still took nearly ninety minutes. Part of the time
was spent settling the bill, which involved a phone call to
her cousin in California, who was picking up the tab for
the gown as per a longstanding agreement she had with
Skye. The dress was payment to Skye for having stepped
in as the bridal coordinator at her cousin's wedding when
the original planner was murdered.

An hour later, Skye was back in Scumble River. She
went directly to her parents' house to drop off her wedding dress. She and her bridesmaids would be getting
ready at her folks' place, so it seemed easier to store the
gown there. This plan would also prevent Wally from
accidentally—or on purpose—seeing the dress before
the ceremony.

When Skye arrived at her parents', her father's old
blue pickup was parked in the driveway. Because it was
winter, Jed, who was a farmer, wasn't in the fields; instead
he spent a lot of time in his heated garage, tinkering with
machinery and other projects. Before going into the
house, Skye opened the pedestrian door to say hello.

Jed's dog, a brown Labrador named Chocolate, shot to his feet and raced toward Skye. Thankful that she had left her gown in the car, she braced herself, then squatted down and hugged the excited animal.

"You staying for lunch?" asked Jed, who was never one to waste words.

"I'm meeting Wally at twelve thirty to go interview someone over in Laurel concerning the librarian's murder." Skye was well aware that her folks ate at noon on the dot. "So if I do, I'll have to eat and run."

"No importance." Jed turned back to the motor he had in pieces on his workbench.

"Mom might not see it that way." Skye knew her father wasn't saying the woman's murder wasn't important, but instead that it wasn't a problem if Skye had to leave immediately after the meal.

"Don't tell Ma. Just go." Jed took off his International Harvester cap and scratched his head. "Life's easier if you plow around the stump."

"You're so right, Dad." Skye patted Chocolate goodbye, then retrieved the garment bag containing her wedding gown from the backseat of her Bel Air and went inside. She was anxious to see if May had kept her promise to remove all the interior Christmas decorations so the photos taken as the bridal party dressed wouldn't highlight the holiday. Being born in December, Skye had spent years having Christmas overshadow her birthday, and she wasn't going to allow it to happen to her wedding, too.

As Skye entered the utility room, she saw that it was still decked out in pine boughs festooned with big red satin bows and sprigs of holly. Stepping into the kitchen, she noted the countertop held a Santa cookie jar, reindeer salt and pepper shakers, and a napkin holder in the shape of a snowman. The sight of the three-foot-tall white tree adorned with shiny green ornaments, which stood in the corner of the dinette, added to her displeasure.

Skye took a deep, cleansing breath, counted to ten, then bit her tongue. Her mother had until Saturday, so there was no use starting an argument now. If worse came to worst, Skye would sic Trixie and Frannie on the decorations before the photographer got started. And she'd haul the multiple Christmas trees out of the house and onto the trash heap herself.

May had been intent on adding ingredients to a pot simmering on the stovetop and hadn't noticed her daughter's arrival, but as she turned and saw Skye, she snapped, "What happened between you and Wally last night?"

"Hello to you, too, Mom." Skye kept her tone neutral. An upset May was a dangerous May. "And to answer your question, nothing happened. We interviewed Yvonne's husband, went to dinner, and came home." She deliberately omitted the conversation she and Wally had overheard at the restaurant. "Why do you ask?"

"Because instead of spending the night with his fiancée, like he should have four days before his wedding, he was at the police station until all hours of the morning." May waved a wooden spoon at Skye. "And he wasn't alone. Zelda Martinez was with him. Her shift was over and he asked her to stick around. You need to put a stop to that immediately. She's a beautiful, much *younger* woman."

"Whoa." Skye's head was spinning. She could hardly believe that her mother had just admitted that Skye and Wally usually slept together. It was an issue that May had been in denial about since Wally and Skye had started seeing each other three years ago.

The additional fact that her mother seemed concerned that Skye and Wally might be fighting was mindboggling. Up until last March, May would have been thrilled to see her daughter angry with Wally. She would have been urging Skye to break up with him and take Simon back. Now May was worried that Wally was cheating on her daughter. Would wonders never cease?

Either May had done a complete one-eighty and become a fan of Wally, or she was so invested in the wedding, she couldn't bear to let anything stop it. Both scenarios worked for Skye, and she hurried to assure her mother that everything was fine between her and her groom.

"If you two are so darn hunky dory, why was Wally at the PD so late last night?" May went back to her cooking, but she didn't let the matter rest. "And why did he have Zelda there until the wee hours? Dante's going to blow his stack at Wally paying her overtime."

"Wally has a lot of work to do with Yvonne's murder and all, so he probably needed Zelda to do research, or background checks, or something like that," Skye prevaricated. For good measure, she added, "He wants the case solved before we go on our honeymoon."

"Speaking of that, you're going to love what Wally has planned."

"You know where we're going?" Skye asked, incredulous at the idea that her mother knew and she didn't. "How did you find out? Who told you? Did Wally tell you? Where are we going?"

"Of course I know, and I can't tell you where. I promised Wally I would keep it a secret, and I never break my promises. He checked with me to see if I thought you would like his idea, which I did. I even gave him a money-saving tip," she bragged.

"You've got to be kidding me." Skye was stunned at the whole concept of Wally and her mother maneuvering behind her back. What had Wally been thinking, consulting May? Skye took another cleansing breath. Then, before she blurted out something she'd regret, she said, "Let me hang up my dress and you can tell me all about it."

As Skye passed her mother heading toward the hall, May grabbed her arm. "Hang it in your room. Don't go into my bedroom."

"Okay," Skye agreed. "Why?"

"There's a surprise for you in there that I don't want you to see until later."

A surprise? May's surprises were rarely good ones. Skye shuddered and took yet another cleansing breath. At this rate, she'd hyperventilate and need a brown paper bag to keep from passing out before the wedding.

CHAPTER 13

Cock-and-Bull Story

Skye was beginning to feel as if she spent her whole life in a car and ninety-five percent of that time on the road to Laurel. She'd been a little late meeting Wally at the PD, so when she arrived, he thrust a folder at her, told her to read its contents on the way, and nearly shoved her into the police cruiser.

As ordered, she'd devoted the past half hour to studying the file. Several of Wally's officers had spent all of yesterday confirming information from the witness and suspect statements that had been taken the previous day.

They'd verified that the library had indeed been open on Christmas Eve until four in the afternoon. Loretta's description of Yvonne's attire had been corroborated by another patron. And the parishioner who had overheard Yvonne and her daughter arguing had been located, and she had substantiated that the quarrel she'd observed appeared to be about where the young woman would spend the night.

On the forensic side, the crime lab had confirmed that Phoebe's laptop had indeed been used at the dance studio during the time she claimed to have been there.

Skye closed the folder with a sigh. Apparently everyone they'd talked to so far had been telling the truth, which meant they were back to square one. No wonder Wally seemed so grumpy. Either that or his bad mood had to do with the Zuchowski situation. She wasn't sure which scenario was worse.

Deciding she had to deal with his crankiness eventually and it was better to get it over with right away, Skye asked, "So how did the evidence closet inventory go?"

"Everything was accounted for." Wally scowled. "But I'm having the drugs that were stored there reevaluated to make sure they are what they're labeled and Zuchowski didn't substitute something and steal the real thing. We're dropping the samples off before we talk to Tom Riley."

"How long will the tests take?" Skye was glad that nothing had been missing, but clearly, Wally wasn't satisfied. "Any chance we'll know today?" She hoped they'd have the results quickly so Wally could stop worrying that he'd been lax in his duty.

"Yeah." Wally combed his fingers through his hair. "The process is relatively simple. They'll call as soon as they get through."

"Was Zuchowski in Scumble River the night of Yvonne's murder?"

"Thank God, no." Wally's expression brightened slightly. "I never thought I'd be happy to learn one of my officers had lied in order to get time off, but I guess I'd rather he was a liar than a murderer."

"Good choice." Skye could feel Wally's stress radiating outward like sonar waves.

"Quirk finally got him on the phone this morning, and after some not so gentle persuasion, Zuchowski caved like a cardboard box and admitted he was on vacation and had been since Saturday night." Wally winced and massaged his temple. "He's flying home this evening and has been ordered to report to the station before midnight. And to bring his airline ticket receipts and his girlfriend with him."

"And once you have proof of his alibi, I'm sure you'll feel better."

"Right," Wally grunted. "Then all I have to deal with is that he's a druggie who has been selling to his friends and looking the other way while they party."

"At least you'll know he's not the killer."

"Too bad we don't know who is." Wally's face was set in hard, tight lines.

"We'll figure it out," Skye assured him; then, trying to cheer him up, she teased, "Mom was in quite a tizzy about you working late and being alone with the young and oh so beautiful Zelda Martinez."

"You're kidding me." Wally's brows shot into his hairline.

"Nope." Skye grinned. "She thought we'd had a fight and you were cheating on me. Isn't it great that she's changed her mind about you, and not only wants us to be together, but is determined that nothing will stand in the way of our marriage?"

"I suppose that's one way of looking at it." Wally shot Skye a sharp look. "You didn't tell her what was really going on, did you?"

"Of course not. I was the one who warned you not to let her know," Skye huffed. "I just said that you were extremely busy with the murder investigation and that you wanted to solve the case before we left on our honeymoon." She paused, then glared at him. "And by the way, why in the world would you tell Mom where we're going when you won't even tell me?"

"I didn't," Wally protested. "I mean, not intentionally. She saw some brochures on my desk, and she sort of guessed, so I figured I might as well ask her if she thought you'd like what I was considering. And it turned out she was pretty darn helpful."

"Really?" Skye was happy that her mom and Wally were getting along better, so why did she have such a bad feeling about the whole thing? She mentally shrugged. She was probably just paranoid where her mother was concerned.

"Uh-huh."

When Wally didn't continue, Skye asked, "How was she helpful?" It was always good to check May's version of events against reality.

"She tipped me off to a good deal," Wally answered, then quickly added, "Not that I was concerned about the cost, but this way I could get us even nicer accommodations."

"Hey, I love a bargain, and I know you're not cheap," Skye assured him.

"I just want to make sure you know that I'd pay any amount of money to make you happy."

"Being with you makes me happy." Skye leaned over the console and laid her head on his shoulder. "As long as we can have time alone without any distractions, I'll be thrilled with any honeymoon spot you pick."

"Me too." Wally cupped her cheek. "Just you, me, and a sunny day."

Skye stayed resting against him until a pothole bounced them apart. When she settled back into her seat, she said, "Having lunch with my parents today put me off schedule and I didn't have enough time to stop at the bank to get the checks and cash we need for the wedding vendors. Do you think we'll finish here while it's still open?"

The Scumble River First National Bank had extremely limited hours of operation and was closed for more holidays than the schools. Most people found it a challenge to get to the bank to do business during the narrow window of opportunity, but complaints did little good. It was a privately held company, and the owner ran it like a fiefdom.

"Probably. It's going on one thirty now, so say an hour with the vic's boyfriend and an hour to get home, we should be in town by four and I think the bank is open until five today." Wally shrugged. "But it's hard to say how long an interview will take or what will come up. If you can't go tomorrow, maybe I can."

"Let me think." Skye tried to remember what she had

scheduled for Thursday, then gave up and grabbed the big blue wedding organizer from her tote bag. The binder was heavy, but she'd decided several weeks ago that carrying the extra weight was worth the effort in order to keep track of everything. "Frannie and Trixie are coming over at ten to help me make the favors. Then we're taking them, the seating plan, the place cards, and the guest book to the Country Mansion's reception coordinator. So if I'm at the bank when it opens at nine, I should be in good shape."

"Okay." Wally pulled to a stop in front of the crime lab. "But let me know in the morning if you want me to get the cash and checks." He got out of the Caprice, retrieved the carton of evidence bags from the trunk, and as he closed the driver's door said, "I'll be back in a couple of minutes."

While Skye waited for him, she ran a fingertip down her list. So far, she was on schedule. She had prepared the ceremony and reception boxes with the items that were needed for each event—programs, unity candle, emergency kits, etc.—and they were stashed in the foyer ready to be picked up by her aunt Minnie, who had volunteered to be in charge of their safe arrival at the church and restaurant.

When Skye got home today, she would place her hose, jewelry, makeup, and the backup list with the vendors' phone numbers into the duffel that already contained her lingerie and shoes, then put that carryall in the front hall as well. She'd already given the wedding-day schedule to her attendants, the groomsmen, the ushers, her parents, and Wally's father.

As Skye was sliding the organizer back into her tote bag, Wally got into the squad car and said, "They're going to rush the tests and will call my cell in a couple of hours with the results."

"Good." Skye smiled; then, as Wally pulled the Chevy away from the curb, she asked, "Have your guys picked up their tuxes yet?"

"I guess so." Wally would be wearing his dress uniform, but most of the other male members of the wedding party were renting tuxes. "I told them to get them by the twenty-sixth."

"Call them tomorrow and make sure none of them forgot," Skye commanded. "I'm not worried about my dad or Uncle Charlie—Mom will have made sure they have theirs—and your father and cousin are wearing their own, so that just leaves Vince and Justin and the two ushers. Come to think about it, I'm sure Mom has Vince's tux under control, so you just need to check on the ushers and Justin."

"Got it." Wally nodded. "I'll take care of the calls tonight. I might be too busy in the morning." He glanced at her. "Anything else?"

"When's Quentin arriving?" Skye asked. "The last time you talked to him, you told me he wasn't sure because of some big deal he was working on. You said he might be out of the country this week."

Quentin Boyd was Wally's first cousin on his father's side and second in command at CB International—a position Wally's dad wanted him to take. Even though Quentin's father had died when he was a teenager and he'd lived with Wally and his parents, the two men had never been close. Skye had been surprised when Wally had asked him to be his best man.

"He'll be here sometime tomorrow." Wally parked the cruiser in front of Riley's Bakery. "I don't have the exact time."

"So he finished the deal and is back in the United States?" Skye asked, getting out of the car and stepping over the curb.

"I guess."

"Is your dad coming in on the same flight?" Skye asked as Wally joined her on the sidewalk. "Are he and Quentin staying with you?"

"They're both flying in on the company plane. And they're staying in the presidential suite at the Drake in

Chicago." He smiled ruefully. "Dad's philosophy is that cash is like compost. It's just a pile of crap unless it's spread around."

"Oh." Skye found it difficult to imagine just how different Wally's father and cousin's lives were from her own.

"Besides, my house doesn't quite live up to their standards. There's only one guest room and one bathroom, and neither my dad nor my cousin has ever learned to share. Not to mention no maids or room service." As Wally held open the shop's door for Skye, he added, "Remember, I gave Dorothy two weeks off. She'll start back working for us at your house the Monday we get home from our honeymoon."

Dorothy Snyder was Wally's housekeeper. Skye wasn't sure how she felt about having her clean and cook for them, especially since Dorothy was one of May's best friends. But Wally had convinced Skye that Dorothy needed the work, so she'd agreed to the woman's continued employment. She only hoped that Dorothy wouldn't report their every move to May.

"Before I forget," Skye said, putting aside the housekeeper issue, "you need to make sure to give Quentin the ring and the marriage license."

"Got it on my preceremony list," Wally assured her.

Having ticked those items off, Skye cleared the wedding from her mind and prepared to focus on the case. As they stepped inside the bakery, she looked around. The shop gave off an aura of welcome and hospitality with sunlight streaming through the plate-glass window and the air smelling of sugar, cinnamon, and fresh bread.

Half a dozen small tables and chairs were grouped on one side of the space along with a buffet holding two coffee carafes, a selection of sugar packets, stirrers, and a thermos of cream. Glass display cases lined the opposite wall. The store was empty, which wasn't surprising since it was less than ten minutes before closing time.

A bell had rung when Skye and Wally entered, and now a compact man hurried from the kitchen, wiping his hands on a towel. "Can I help you folks?" he asked, tucking the towel into the string tie of his apron. "I'm afraid we're out of most items."

"Are you Tom Riley?" Wally asked.

"Sure am."

Wally introduced himself and Skye, then said, "We're here to speak to you about Yvonne Osborn. I understand you two were dating?"

"Yes." Tom ran his hands through his ginger-colored hair, and his warm smile turned sad. "We'd been seeing each other since Halloween."

"And you're aware that she died suddenly on Sunday evening?" Wally asked.

"Yes." Tom nodded. "I heard about it on the radio yesterday morning."

"You didn't know until Tuesday?" Wally skewered the baker with a disbelieving stare. "Didn't you call her to find out what happened to her when she failed to show up for your date on Sunday?"

Skye flicked a glance at Wally. Had they established for sure that Tom Riley had been the man Yvonne was meeting Christmas Eve, or was this an interrogation technique? She'd noticed that during suspect interviews, Wally often stated something as if it were true whether he was sure of the information or not.

"I left a message on her cell, her home phone, and the library, and when she didn't call me back, I wasn't sure what to think," Tom explained. "I knew the police wouldn't be able to do anything since I wasn't a relative, and I had no idea who else to call. I didn't have her daughter's number and it wasn't listed anywhere."

Yvonne's cell phone had been retrieved from her purse, but the river water had made it impossible to access. The crime techs were trying to dry it out, but held out little hope that they'd ever recover any data from it. And the library had been closed until today. But why hadn't Phoebe returned Tom's call when she heard him on the family's answering machine?

"So you did nothing." Wally was clearly taking the bad-cop role again.

"Can you tell us what you were thinking and why you made that decision?" Skye asked, employing a counseling method she often used at school.

"I considered checking with Yvonne's ex-husband, but they didn't get along very well, so I decided not to." Tom collapsed against a counter, his shoulders sagging and tears running down his cheeks. "I wish I had done something."

"Let's sit down." Skye glanced at Wally, who nodded his approval. She took the baker's arm and settled him at the nearest table. "Is it okay if we turn off the 'open' sign and lock up?"

"Sure." Tom wiped his face with his apron. "Sorry. I've been trying not to think about Yvonne. We'd only been together briefly, but we really connected."

"Take your time." Skye pulled her chair close to Tom's while Wally handled the door. She waited until he returned and took a seat, then asked the baker, "You said that Yvonne didn't get along with her ex-husband. Was it the normal stuff or something more?"

"A lot more." Tom fingered an empty cup that hadn't been cleared away. "She said he had the morals of a politician and the ethics of a television evangelist. She despised everything he stood for—conspicuous consumption, greed, and success at any cost."

"So it wasn't an amicable divorce." Skye wanted to make sure she was clear about what Tom was saying since it contradicted Neil Osborn's claims. "There definitely were hard feelings between Yvonne and her ex, and they hadn't stayed friends?"

"The only contact they had concerned their daughter and Osborn's attempt to corrupt Phoebe," Tom stated firmly. "Yvonne didn't share the specifics with me, but my take on it was that Osborn had tried to somehow buy the girl's acceptance into college."

"Yes." Skye nodded. "We heard about that incident,

but it was my understanding that they had sorted it out, and everyone, including Mr. Osborn, regretted their actions in the matter."

"Hardly." Tom snorted. "He was royally ticked that Yvonne had interfered in his scheme and livid that she had prevented their daughter from going to the University of Chicago last fall." Tom shrugged. "Apparently, Phoebe had come to see her mother's point of view, but Osborn sure hadn't."

"Did Yvonne ever say why she had married Mr. Osborn in the first place?" Skye couldn't imagine a couple that was more ill-suited.

"She claimed he used to be different." Tom shook his head. "She said his original plan was to build ecofriendly housing for middle-income families and rehab buildings using green technology. But then he was corrupted by the money people were throwing at the whole conservation movement, and being environmentally responsible turned into a scam."

Wally nudged Skye's knee with his own, indicating that he wanted to take over the interview; then he said to Tom, "How did you and Yvonne meet?"

"At the Stanley County Motorcycle Association." Tom smiled. "She was at the fall rally, and we got to talking and hit it off."

"A couple of police officers I know are members of that group, and I think I remember them saying that the rally is held at the end of September. Correct?" When Tom nodded, Wally asked, "Did you and Yvonne start dating right after you met at the club get-together?"

"No. We ran into each other a few more times—at the amateur-theater-group tryouts, a poker party given by mutual friends, and the Lions Club fish fry. Then I finally got up the nerve to ask her out."

"You had a lot in common," Skye said, still trying to picture Yvonne riding a Harley. "I imagine finding a woman with such diverse interests is rare."

"It is." Tom's tone revealed the depth of his sadness at

losing such a unique girlfriend. "I'd never met a woman like her before. She was so much fun and would try anything once, as long as it was legal and didn't harm anyone else." He shook his head. "People who didn't really know Yvonne thought she was rigid and sanctimonious, but really all she wanted was to do the right thing."

Skye murmured, "And that might have been what got her killed."

CHAPTER 14

In a Binding

Wally asked Tom Riley a few more questions about his relationship with Yvonne, then inquired as to his whereabouts during Sunday night when she was being forced off the bridge. The baker claimed to have been making local deliveries from three to five thirty that day. He had arrived at the last place—a children's birthday party—at five fifteen, which meant there was no way he could have been at the crime scene between four forty-five and five fifty-five. It was at least three-quarters of an hour's drive between Laurel and Scumble River.

Tom provided the numbers of his customers that afternoon, and Wally moved a few steps away to phone them to verify the baker's alibi. As Skye listened to those one-sided conversations, her cell rang. She checked the caller ID and grimaced. Why was Isla Nugent, the woman making her wedding cake, calling?

"I am so sorry," Isla apologized as soon as Skye said hello.

When Skye had hired Isla, the cake maker had been thrilled. Everyone in Scumble River agreed that Maggie Broacher, one of May's best friends, was the premier special occasion cake maker in town, and she normally would have been the one to make Skye's cake. But Maggie, her husband, Jonah, their kids, and grandchildren were spending Christmas week at a resort in the Bahamas. The family wouldn't be arriving home until Friday night, and since that wouldn't allow enough time to bake and decorate a wedding cake, Maggie had recommended Isla.

"What are you sorry about?" Skye asked Isla, her grip tightening on the tiny cell phone. "Please tell me it has nothing to do with my cake."

"When I turned my oven on this morning, it exploded and the kitchen went up in flames before the fire department could put it out." Isla's voice rose.

"Are you okay?" Skye forced herself to ask, not wanting to sound completely heartless. She added for good measure, "Was anyone hurt?"

"I'm fine." Isla exhaled. "We're all fine. No one else was home, and I ran out the back door."

"Are you insured?" Skye asked, willing herself to show concern before she grilled the poor woman about the fate of her cake.

"Yes. I'll be able to replace everything—eventually . . ." Isla trailed off. "But I can't even order stuff until I get the insurance check."

"Will you be able to make my cake?" Skye finally allowed herself to ask, feeling that under the circumstances she'd been as understanding as could be expected.

"No," Isla admitted. "There's no way I can do it. All my equipment is ruined, and I don't have anywhere to bake or decorate."

"Oh, my God!" Skye moaned, then silently beseeched the Almighty. *Really? Really?* She was trying to be laid-back. She wasn't being a bridezilla. What had she done? Why was this happening to her?

Wally held his phone to his chest and asked, "What's wrong?"

"No wedding cake." Skye briefly explained, then realized that Isla was still on the line and begged, "You don't have spare cakes in the freezer? You could decorate them at my house. Or you could even bake the cakes there. I have a big kitchen and I could help."

"I'm so sorry, but it takes special pans and tools, and I just don't have any extras." Isla paused, then said, "But I do have your topper. It was in the dining room, so it wasn't damaged."

"That's something, I guess." Skye's tone was flat. While she was thrilled that her one-of-a-kind, special-order topper, with the groom in a police uniform and the bride with chestnut hair and green eyes, was safe, she had no idea what she would put it on. Maybe she could create a Twinkie, Ding Dong, and Sno Ball structure like the one the Dooziers had made for Elvis's wedding. Skye's lips twitched. Wouldn't that send May over the edge?

Focusing, Skye arranged with Isla to drop off the topper at the police station—she'd let Isla explain to May about the absent wedding cake—then said goodbye. As Wally wrapped up his call with Tom Riley's last delivery customer, Skye slumped in her chair. What would she do?

Skye was so sunk in despair, it took her a few minutes to recognize that the baker was speaking to her. She tuned in just in time to hear him say, "So I could do it."

"What?" Skye blinked away the tears she'd been holding back and concentrated on the man standing over her. "Could you repeat that please?"

"I said I couldn't help overhearing that your baker won't be able to make your cake." Tom twisted his apron, a faint flush on his freckled cheeks. "So I offered to do it."

"The wedding is Saturday," Skye warned, not wanting to get her hopes up.

"Well, if you don't mind keeping it simple, I could make a cake by then." Tom gazed over her head, apparently visualizing a calendar because he said, "Today's the twenty-seventh, so if I bake the layers after you leave this afternoon, I can ice it in the morning and stack it after the shop closes tomorrow, which gives me Friday afternoon to decorate it." He paused, then cautioned, "But you have to be satisfied with the ingredients I have on hand."

"I don't have a problem with that." Skye looked over at Wally. How did he feel about hiring someone involved in an ongoing investigation? When he stared back at her without responding, she prodded, "Is it okay with you if Tom makes our wedding cake?"

Wally twitched, seeming to surface from some sort of reverie, thought for a second, and shrugged. "His alibi checked out, so he's no longer a suspect. And since I'm certain there are others who can testify that Yvonne and her ex didn't get along, he's not a vital witness to anything, so sure. Why not?"

"Then you're hired." Skye jumped from her chair and hugged the startled baker. "Thank you so, so, so much. You really saved the day."

"You're, uh, welcome." Tom patted her awkwardly on the back, then stepped away. "Do you have time to fill out the order form now?"

"Definitely." Skye glanced at Wally, and at his nod, she turned to Tom and said, "When do I need to get the topper to you?"

"Friday before two thirty," Tom answered as he rummaged behind the counter for an order pad and pencil. "Have a seat and let's get started. How many guests are you expecting?"

"Three hundred and ninety at last count." Skye took Wally's hand and murmured, "Mom added a few since the last time I told you."

"What a surprise," Wally teased. "She's determined to outdo your California cousin's wedding, and since you won't let her go over-the-top with decor or entertainment, she's doing it with sheer volume."

"For that number of servings, you'll need four tiers." Tom made a note on his form. "You can have all the same flavor or different ones for each layer."

"We were going to have two chocolate, a yellow, and a white." Skye chewed her lip. "We were thinking those flavors would cover all the bases so that there should be something everyone likes. Are you able to do that?"

"Sure." Tom chewed on the end of his pencil. "I could also do red velvet for one of the chocolate tiers, since it's my specialty."

"That would be amazing." Skye beamed. "I adore red velvet. It's a shame we can't have Wally's favorite. He loves carrot cake."

"I can do carrot cake in place of the white, which can be a little bland."

"Great!" Skye leaned over to hug the baker again, but when he flinched, she contented herself with patting his arm. "You're amazing."

"Nah." Tom flushed, then got back to business. "With red velvet and carrot, I'd go with a cream cheese icing for the filling," he suggested. "Do you want fondant or buttercream frosting?"

"Buttercream," Skye decided, then added, "Our theme is winter wonderland and my bridesmaids are wearing red." She tilted her head. "Can you do anything with that for the decoration?"

"I have just the thing." Tom's hazel eyes glowed and he got up, trotted into the back, and returned carrying a box. "We could use these." He scooped up a handful of delicate crystal and silver snowflakes. "I ordered these for a cake I'm making in February, so I have plenty of time to reorder if you want them."

"They're perfect," Skye crooned, touching one with her fingertip.

"And how about a fondant red ribbon and bow with the ribbons trailing down the tiers?"

"Brilliant."

Tom scribbled furiously on his form, then asked, "Do you have any ideas for decorating the cake table?"

"My gown is trimmed in white faux fur, so maybe red-and-white marabou boas," Skye suggested. "The florist said they'd have extra evergreen boughs, so we could twist the boas around those."

"Wonderful. I have to drive to the grocery store tomorrow night. I'll go to the Meijer on Boughton Road in Bolingbrook so I can get the boas at the Hobby Lobby down the street. I can call my friend Jan who works there and make sure what we need is in stock." Tom whipped a calculator from his pocket, punched several buttons, frowned, entered in a few more numbers, then announced, "I can do what you want for six hundred dollars. Is that okay?"

Before Skye could answer, Wally declared, "Sold." He took out his wallet, handed the baker his Platinum American Express, and said, "Charge it."

"Thanks. I owe you one for the rush job." Wally spoke into his cell phone as he and Skye sat in the parked squad car. "If you can keep this whole thing quiet, I'd appreciate it."

"The drugs in the evidence closet were what they should have been," Skye deduced, putting together his side of the conversation with his relieved expression. "Which means whatever Zuchowski was selling, it wasn't police property and you weren't negligent."

"Thank goodness for small favors." Wally eased the Caprice onto the street and headed out of Laurel. "But I still have a bad apple on my force, and the mayor will have a field day with that."

"You can handle Uncle Dante," Skye reassured him. "And if he gives you a hard time, we'll sic my mother on him. In a few days you'll be her son-in-law, and no one messes with May's kids, not even her brother."

"That would be an interesting battle to observe." Wally's lips twitched. "But I screwed up and I have to fix this mess myself."

"Which you will." Skye realized that they were driving in the direction of Scumble River rather than I-80. "Aren't we going to go reinterview Neil Osborn? I thought you wanted to confront him about his lies regarding his relationship with Yvonne."

"I think this time we should talk to the vic's ex when he's at work rather than comfortable in his own home," Wally explained. "Besides, I want to verify what Tom told us regarding Yvonne's feelings about Osborn before I question him again."

"That makes sense." Skye checked her watch. It was almost five o'clock. So much for getting to the bank while it was still open.

"Phoebe gave me a list of Yvonne's friends and her previous colleagues, so I'll call them and see what their impressions were of her feelings for her ex. Then I'd like to go talk to Chip Nicolet. His health club closes at nine, so I want to get there about eight forty-five." Wally glanced at Skye. "I'll understand if you don't have time to come with me."

"Thanks, but I'm fine." Skye crossed her fingers that she was telling the truth. "I think I have everything under control."

"Excellent." Wally grinned at her. "Since you witnessed the altercation between him and Yvonne, it'll be helpful to have you at the interview."

"Let's see. It'll be close to six when we get to town, so that gives you two and a half hours to make your calls." Skye thought about what tasks she could accomplish while Wally was busy. "How about I meet you back at the station at eight thirty?"

"Sounds good." He paused, a guilty look on his face. "Unless you want to stop and get some supper before we start working."

"What if we swing through Mickey D's drive-up?" Skye suggested. "That way you can eat at your desk and I'll take mine home."

"You're the best." Wally squeezed Skye's knee. "Thanks for understanding."

Once they reached Scumble River, picked up their dinner from McDonald's, and Skye was in her Bel Air, she realized that she should have gone into the PD to tell her mother that she had arranged for another wedding cake. She wasn't sure when Isla was dropping off the topper, but May needed to know that the matter had been handled before she went monster-of-the-bride on the poor woman.

As soon as Skye got inside her house, she phoned her mother to explain the cake situation. Predictably, May didn't take the news well, but after being reassured that a replacement had already been ordered, she calmed down enough to agree that a fire was not Isla's fault. After a torrent of other wedding-related questions, comments, suggestions, and concerns, Skye was finally able to say goodbye to her mother and feed Bingo.

The impatient black cat had been rubbing against Skye's ankles, purring loudly and meowing the whole time she talked to her mother. Now he watched intently as Skye opened the cupboard door, selected a can of Fancy Feast, and popped off the top. She scooped half into his bowl, then snapped on a plastic lid and put the remainder in the fridge.

Skye placed his dish on the floor and Bingo rushed toward it, but before he reached the food, he skidded to a stop. Scrambling backward, he rose on his hind legs and did what Skye could only describe as a kitty conga; then with his fur bristling, he ran from the room.

What in the heck had happened? Skye hadn't heard anything and she was alone in the kitchen. Wait. She sniffed. What was that smell? It was citrusy, but with a hint of jasmine and patchouli. Skye had noticed the same scent before and done some research. It was a perfume called Tabu that had been popular in the 1930s, and it had been Mrs. Griggs's favorite cologne.

Was the ghost here? Was the former owner's spirit what had scared Bingo? But why would the pesky poltergeist be around now? Wally wasn't even in the house, let alone getting frisky. Great! Was Mrs. Griggs going to start haunting her all the time?

Skye shrugged. At least nothing had caught on fire or been broken, and it wouldn't hurt Bingo to lose a few pounds.

After gulping down her Caesar salad, Skye headed upstairs. It was past time to pack for her honeymoon. Last August, she'd hit the end of summer sales at Coldwater Creek and Macy's at the Bolingbrook Promenade and at Von Maur in Lombard, and she now hoped she had everything she needed. Finding shorts, capris, or lightweight dresses in the dead of winter in Illinois wasn't something she wanted to attempt.

Sixty minutes later, while she was trying to decide if she really needed both white and black sandals, her doorbell rang. Skye frowned. She wasn't expecting anyone and her house's location on a seldom-used rural road meant she rarely had drop-in visitors.

With a sense of dread, Skye ran down the steps and peered out the window next to the door. Clutching her chest, she moaned. What was Earl Doozier doing on her front porch, and why was he holding a dog dressed in a pink tutu?

CHAPTER 15

Truth Is Stranger
Than Fiction

Skye backed slowly away from the door, afraid the stress of the wedding had finally made her lose her mind and she was hallucinating. The dog in Earl's arms looked a lot like a furry ballerina. Along with a tulle skirt, it was wearing a tiny rose-colored tee with a heart-shaped chiffon appliqué and itsy-bitsy pink ballet slippers on each of its four paws.

The bell rang again, followed by a series of urgent knocks, and Skye reluctantly approached the window to take another peek. She pushed the curtain aside and nearly had a heart attack. Earl's face was pressed against the glass, distorting his already decidedly odd features into a grotesque parody of himself.

Earl spotted Skye at the same time she saw him, which pretty much removed the option of pretending that she was out. Even as she recognized that she shouldn't, she unlocked the dead bolt. It was probably a bad decision, but she couldn't hurt the peculiar little man's feelings by snubbing him. Not being completely crazy, she left the chain on and opened the door only a crack.

"Miz Skye, I's so glad you're to home." Earl's usual

mossy grin was lacking. "Youse gotta tell me what to do with it."

"It being the dog?" Skye guessed, then added, "It is a dog, right?" Knowing the Dooziers' proclivity for in-breeding, she was half afraid the tiny creature Earl held in his arms might be his niece. His brother Elvis's wife *had* given birth rather recently.

"A course it's a pooch. Her name's Sugar Plum." Earl shoved his camo trucker hat farther back on his head and scratched the bald spot he revealed. "Whatcha think it was, one of my kids?" He hooted at his own wit, mak-ing a sound that was a cross between an owl in heat and a whooping police siren.

"No." Skye laughed weakly. "Certainly not." She added quickly, "I've just never seen an animal like it before. What breed is she?"

"Hell if I know." Earl held the small canine up and examined it. "Looks like some kinda mix of a bunch a those itty-bitty dogs that those rich women on TV carry around in their pocketbooks."

"True." Skye nodded. The pup did resemble a spoiled rich girl's purse dog.

"Alls I can say is accordin' to that biddy over to the south a me, this here dog belongs to her daughter and costs a lot of moolah and she's gonna have a shit fit if she finds out I have it." He twitched his bony shoulders. "Glenda said we could get rid of it by havin' it stuffed and givin' it to you for a weddin' present. Sort of a con-versation starter."

"No!" Skye squealed at the thought of the cute little puppy being mummified. "A wedding gift should never be something prepared by a taxidermist."

"Then what should I do with it?"

"Give Sugar Plum back to her owner," Skye advised, glancing at her watch. She had to leave for the police station in fifteen minutes.

"I tried," he griped, hitching up his neon orange sweat-pants. "But no one's to home, and when I leave the mutt on the step, she jus' runs on back to my place like one a those boomerangs."

"Hmm." Skye considered the problem. "I guess you really can't teach an old dog—"

Earl interrupted her, "New math."

"Right." Skye rolled her eyes. When would she learn not to use adages around Earl?

"Anyway, it's strange that she keeps returning to your house." Skye leaned on the jamb. "Are you feeding her?"

"Nope. She's in love with Blue." Earl grinned. "Don't you remember? I told you t'other day on the phone that he's a lot like his daddy—a real good f—"

"Stop," Skye ordered, raising her hand like a traffic cop. "So Juliet here can't get enough of your hound dog Romeo." Skye thought fast. "Here's what I suggest you do. Call your neighbor and leave her a message that you have her daughter's pet and will return Sugar Plum as soon as you hear from her. Keep the little hussy away from Blue until her owner picks her up. Under no circumstances allow them to get romantic." She stared at Earl. "Is that clear?"

"By romantic you mean humpin', right?" Earl patted his crotch. "Like me an' Glenda, but without the beer and fried pork rinds?"

"Right." Skye closed her eyes and wondered what kind of mental scrub brush she'd need to get that image out of her mind. "No conjugal visits whatsoever."

"Okay." Earl nodded slowly, then repeated Skye's instructions. "Call Miz Osborn, leave a message, keep the dogs apart."

"Exactly. Call, leave a *polite* message, and keep Sugar Plum in the house and Blue in his pen." In Earl's case, as with many of the students she worked with, Skye found it a good idea to repeat the directions several times and be ultraclear. "I'm sorry to rush you, but—" She started to close the door and stopped, interrupting herself. "Did you say Osborn?" When Earl nodded, Skye spelled out, "Yvonne Osborn, the librarian, was your neighbor?"

"Yeah." Earl made a face. "For the last six months of hell."

"Why didn't I realize she lived by you?" Skye muttered. "I'm an idiot."

"Uh-uh, Miz Skye." Earl patted her arm. "Youse the smartest woman I know."

"Thank you, Earl." She felt like smacking herself upside the head. She and Wally had figured out that Yvonne was on her way to Laurel from her house when her car went off the bridge, and Skye knew that the bridge marked the entrance to Doozier territory. After all, Cattail Path was the next intersection. "That's sweet of you to say, but in this case, I think my brain might have blown a circuit."

"Why, Miz Skye?" Earl asked, his high, domed forehead wrinkling in concern. "I don't see nothin' oozin' out your ears."

"Because last Sunday Yvonne Osborn was killed when her car was forced into the river, and I didn't realize she was the neighbor you were talking about," Skye explained.

"She's dead?" Earl squealed. "I didn't have nothin' to do with it, Miz Skye." He backed away, a wild look in his muddy brown eyes.

"That's not what I meant, Earl," Skye assured him, then paused.

Could he have been behind the wheel of the Escalade that shoved Yvonne's car into the river? The Dooziers didn't own that kind of vehicle, but he might have "borrowed" it, and the librarian had been giving him a hard time about his hound. No. Skye mentally shook her head. If Earl had killed Yvonne, he was too wily to complain to Skye and admit he had possession of the murdered woman's dog. He might be one fruitcake short of Christmas, but he wasn't the candied cherry that got baked into the dessert. His survival instinct was too sharp to leap into that oven.

"Youse know me." Earl continued backing away, then

darted forward and shoved the dog through the door's narrow opening and into Skye's arms. "Iffen I offed her, I'd a shot her, and you can check my guns. They ain't been fired in weeks."

"Wait," Skye called as Earl hurried down the porch steps. "Don't you dare leave this animal with me. Take her back right now."

"No!" Earl shrieked, hopping onto a riding lawn mower with red sled-shaped plywood pieces duct taped to both sides. "I can't have no dead woman's dog. Youse knows the law won't understand."

"Who is Yvonne's other neighbor?" Skye unhooked the chain and ran outside. "Who's the guy that you said was upset with her?"

"King Housley," Earl yelled, clapping a Santa hat over his trucker cap and gathering the reins of his pseudosleigh.

He'd taken half a dozen stuffed deer heads and mounted them on poles, then attached the poles to the front of the mower. The whole shebang was supposed to resemble a team of reindeer, but it looked more like a *Nightmare Before Christmas* than the *Night Before Christmas*.

Before Skye could react, Earl stomped on the wannabe sled's accelerator and sped down her driveway, the lawn mower's souped-up engine backfiring until Santa, aka Earl, was clear out of sight.

King was the name of the guy she'd overheard with his buddies in front of church on Christmas morning. Had Wally spoken to the three maintenance men? She had to remember to ask him about that.

Shivering, Skye headed toward her car. The weather this winter had been unseasonably mild for Illinois — forties during the day and high twenties at night — but it was still chilly. They'd been fortunate to avoid frigid temps and huge snowstorms so far, and Skye could only hope that her luck would hold out. She prayed there wouldn't be a blizzard during her wedding. She certainly didn't want any of her guests skidding off the road. She also needed the day after to be clear. Whatever their honeymoon destination turned out to be, she knew they'd have to fly to get anywhere balmy.

Skye instinctively cuddled the small animal to her chest, and Sugar Plum licked her face and whimpered. The pup's sweet expression seemed to be begging Skye to find out who had killed her mistress's mother. Or maybe the pooch just wanted a doggy treat. Sadly, she didn't have any tidbits, and it wasn't looking too good for solving the crime either.

After depositing Sugar Plum in the Bel Air and promising her she'd be out in a minute, Skye ran back inside the house to shut off the lights, get her purse, and lock up. She'd learned her lesson a while back when she'd rescued another victim's pet. Bingo did not play well with others, and the last thing she needed was a ticked-off feline alone with vital wedding bits and pieces lying everywhere, just ready to be torn apart.

On the previous occasion, she'd lost her favorite pair of Cole Haan black pumps to Bingo's teeth and claws. She had no idea what he'd target this time, but she wasn't taking any chances with her beautiful peep-toe slingback wedding shoes.

Once Skye reached the police station, she tried to hurry past her mother, who was working the dispatcher's desk, but May rushed to the counter and yelled, "What on God's green earth is that?"

"Yvonne Osborn's daughter's dog," Skye called over her shoulder as she used her key to open the inner door. "I'm late. I'll explain later."

It took a while to tell Wally about her Doozier encounter, because as she described the visit, his fits of laughter kept interrupting her.

He finally sobered up enough to ask, "So you're sure Earl had nothing to do with the murder? He was mad at Yvonne and he wouldn't be above stealing a car to run her off the bridge."

"I'm not a hundred percent," she said, idly scratching

the little dog's ears, "but he'd be on the bottom of my suspect list."

"Yeah, on a scale of one to ten, annoying him about a dog is probably a one or two." Wally reached into his drawer and came out with a package of beef jerky. He peeled the cellophane wrapper off and offered the stick to Sugar Plum. "And if he were going to kill her, he'd shoot her and bury her where we'd never find the body."

"On the other hand, those maintenance men I overheard at church had a grudge against Yvonne and they could steal a car just as easily as Earl could." Skye fetched a coffee cup, filled it with water from the carafe on Wally's desk, and put it down for the tiny pooch. When she resumed her seat, she asked, "Did you talk to any of them?"

"Quirk interviewed the trio right after you told me about their conversation." Wally pulled a folder from a pile and flipped through the pages inside. "It's interesting that all three men are collecting disability from the Scumble River Public Works Department."

"What happened?" Skye asked, watching Sugar Plum as she walked around the room's perimeter sniffing the corners. Skye hoped female dogs didn't mark their territory.

"Let's see." Wally paused to read the report, then said, "According to Quirk, they were hurt when a dump truck that Kenneth—aka King—Housley was driving went off the road. The other two men were standing on the shoulder and he sideswiped them."

"Isn't that an odd coincidence?" Skye murmured almost to herself, then looked up and asked, "Are we going to reinterview them?"

"Yep." Wally nodded. "Tonight we'll talk to Chip Nicolet; tomorrow we'll requestion Neil Osborn and the three injured amigos."

"Remember, I won't be free until the afternoon," Skye reminded him. "And our bachelor/bachelorette party starts at seven p.m. sharp." Because several of their attendants and friends were coming into Scumble River from out of town, the parties were being held closer to the wedding date than Skye would have preferred.

"Right." Wally ran a hand through his hair. "How about if I speak to Artie and Dutch and save the neighbor and the ex for you?"

"That sounds like a good division of labor," Skye agreed. "King's definitely the most likely suspect. Yvonne was allegedly spying on him, and he sounded mad enough about it to strangle her."

"If you can meet me here at two tomorrow afternoon, we should be able to get it all in." Wally made a note on his calendar.

"That should be doable." Skye pointed at the cute canine sleeping at her feet. "Now, what do we do about Sugar Plum?"

"Turn her over to her owner." Wally pulled the phone toward him and dialed. A few beats later, he said, "Phoebe? Chief Boyd here. Someone has turned in your pet. Can you pick her up?" He listened for a second, then said, "Good. She'll be with the dispatcher. I have to warn you, May's not an animal lover, so I'd get here sooner rather than later if I were you."

Skye stifled a giggle at the look on her mother's face when Wally handed her Sugar Plum and ordered her to look after the pooch until Phoebe Osborn showed up. May held the dog at arm's length before setting the animal on a chair and commanding the dog to stay put.

May glared at Wally before silently returning to her computer. Skye was convinced her mother was plotting her revenge as she banged away on the keyboard.

As Skye and Wally drove the five miles to Chip's fitness center, she said to him, "Earlier, you mentioned wanting to catch Neil Osborn on the job when we speak to him tomorrow. Is his office in Laurel?"

"No. Naperville." Wally pulled the squad car into the Guns and Poses parking lot. "But the development he's working on is in Lawnton."

"And that's where we'll find him?" Skye asked, pushing open the heavy glass door to the gym. "At the work site, not in his headquarters?"

"That's what his secretary told me when I talked to her this afternoon." Wally followed Skye into the health club's empty reception area. "Turns out that, like me, Osborn's secretary is originally from Texas, so we kind of hit it off."

"Oh, really?" Skye arched a brow before smiling to indicate she was okay with him using his down-home charm on the woman to gather information.

"Anyway," Wally went on, "she's not real fond of her boss. In fact, she's looking for another job because she says Osborn can't keep his hands to himself and has quite a temper when someone stands up to him or prevents him from getting what he wants."

"Hmm." Skye examined the vacant lobby and uninhabited front desk. "That sure is a different image than the one he presented to us."

"Yes, it is." Wally walked toward a hallway leading into the rest of the facility. "From the other calls I made, it seems Osborn put on quite an act for us. All of the vic's friends say that Yvonne and her ex not only didn't get along, they actually disagreed on everything from politics to religion to child rearing."

"Wow!" Skye trailed Wally down the passageway. "He certainly sold us a bill of goods." She shook her head. "That I believed him really makes me question my instincts as a psychologist."

"The term sociopath was used by a couple of Yvonne's previous colleagues, the ones who worked with her when she was going through the divorce. Of course, they only knew him from Yvonne's perspective, so their opinions are biased." Wally stepped into the main workout room and scanned the area. "Looks like everyone's gone for the night."

"Well, it is five minutes before the place closes," Skye commented.

"True." Wally sighed. "I was hoping to get here earlier, but . . ."

He trailed off, and Skye bit her lip. She knew he was too nice to say that it was her fault their plan had gotten off schedule because she'd been late and saddled with Yvonne's dog.

Touching his hand, she apologized. "I should never have answered the door, especially after I saw Earl standing there."

"No big deal," he assured her. "Stuff happens." He took her elbow and guided her back into the hallway, where they continued their search.

When they didn't find anyone in the half dozen smaller activity rooms or the swimming pool, Skye said, "Maybe Chip's in his office, which is probably in the rear of the building."

"I bet you're right. Let's go see."

As they started to walk away from the pool area, Skye stopped abruptly. "Wait." A sound was coming from the dressing rooms. She tilted her head and asked, "Did you hear that?"

"Yeah. It was a sort of moaning, I think."

"Maybe the gym is haunted by exercise-crazed spirits," Skye snickered. "Or poor souls who died trying to lose that last pound."

"You know I don't believe in ghosts." Wally was undoubtedly referring to Skye's pet poltergeist, Mrs. Griggs. "Which means that sound was real." He edged past Skye, then strode toward the noise. As he eased open the door to the men's locker room, he ordered, "Stay behind me."

Skye let Wally get a few feet inside before poking her head around the door. Initially, his broad shoulders blocked her view, but when he started to retreat, she saw Emmy Jones in the arms of Simon Reid. Both of them were too preoccupied with each other to notice Wally's entrance.

Emmy and Simon weren't quite naked, but it was clear they wished they were, and Skye had to stifle a gasp. It wasn't that she still loved Simon—all she felt for him now was friendship—but it was a shock to see him kissing another woman. Especially in a public place.

When Skye and Simon had dated, he'd been adamant that any display of affection needed to be in private. Apparently, Emmy brought out the uninhibited side of his personality. The side Skye had never been able to bring to the surface.

CHAPTER 16

Draw the Line

Skye snatched Wally's arm and pulled him out of the locker room, grabbing the door a split second before it slammed shut. As she eased it closed, she thanked the stars above that neither Simon nor Emmy had seen them. It would have been too darned humiliating to be caught watching her ex-boyfriend make out with his new sweetheart.

Wally's shoulders were shaking with muted laughter as Skye dragged him past the pool and into the hallway. When they were finally in the clear, he cracked up, leaning against the wall and howling.

After a minute or so, Skye smacked him on the arm. "I don't see what's so funny."

"The look on your face. You were horrified." Wally took a breath, then chuckled again. "I don't think you could have been any more appalled if you had walked in on your parents having sex."

"Thanks." Skye whacked him again. "Another image I need to get out of my mind."

"I have to admit." Wally's tone was admiring. "I didn't think Reid had it in him." He shook his head. "Of course, with them both wearing only bathing suits—geez! Emmy in a bikini would probably melt most men's . . ." Apparently noticing Skye's displeased expression, Wally trailed off and quickly added, "Not that I . . . I mean she's not my type, but other guys . . ."

Skye turned and walked stiffly away. She was upset on so many levels she couldn't sort them out, and Wally's words weren't helping. She might not love Simon, but observing your ex in the arms of a younger, thinner, more beautiful woman would be hard for anyone to stomach. Then there was Wally's attitude, not to mention his remark about the swimsuit-clad Emmy. It was just too much to take this close to her wedding.

Noticing the restroom to her right, Skye stomped inside, slammed the door shut, and turned the lock. She slumped against the sink, stared into the mirror, and wiped away a tear. Why was Wally being such a jerk? She felt sorry for herself for a few more seconds, then sniffed and realized that maybe the fault was hers, not his. It could be that she was being too sensitive. It had been sort of funny, seeing Simon so out of control. Even so, the remark about how hot Emmy was had been uncalled for.

Straightening her shoulders, Skye emerged from the ladies' room to find Wally staring uneasily at the doorway. She met his worried gaze with a cool look.

He stepped toward her, cleared his throat, and said, "I apologize. I don't know what got into me. I shouldn't have laughed."

"No. You shouldn't have." Although Skye usually hated to see anyone feeling uncomfortable, she was determined to let him squirm.

"I realize now how embarrassing the situation was for you." Wally edged closer.

"Exactly." She allowed him to take her in his arms and rested her head on his shoulder. "Awkward would be putting it mildly."

"And what I said about Emmy in a bikini was stupid." Wally smoothed Skye's hair. "You know I think you're the most beautiful woman in the world, right?" When she didn't answer, he cupped her chin and tilted her face up. "You believe me, don't you?"

"It's fine." Skye didn't meet his eyes. "I know you love me. And I know you find me attractive. But I also know that I'm not beautiful. And I'm all right with that—at least most of the time."

Wally started to protest, but Skye shook her head and instead he asked, "We're okay, though?" He kissed her temple. "I am sorry."

"We're good." Skye stepped away and said, "I'm just being silly and overemotional. It must be bridal hormones or something."

Before Wally could respond, Chip Nicolet rounded a corner of the hallway holding a sheaf of papers and talking into his cell. When he caught sight of Skye and Wally, he stared at them for a moment, zeroing in on Wally's uniform, then muttered something into his phone and clicked it off.

Pasting a smile on his face, Chip walked toward Wally and said, "Chief Boyd. What can I do for you? Are you here to join up?"

"We'd like to speak to you about an incident that occurred a few days ago at the Scumble River Library." Wally's stance was relaxed, but his gaze never left the health club owner's. "I was told that you had an altercation with Yvonne Osborn."

"It was just a misunderstanding." Chip shoved his phone and the papers he was holding into the back pocket of his jeans and crossed his beefy arms. "I asked her out; she declined. I thought she was playing hard to get, so I asked again. But that was it. No harm, no foul."

"She used a stun gun on you," Wally said, his voice conveying a subtle challenge. "That sounds like a problem to me."

"Like I said, she misinterpreted my intentions and overreacted." He shrugged his massive shoulders. "It was no biggie."

Seeing that the men had apparently reached a stalemate, Skye introduced herself and said, "I'm the police department psych consultant, and I actually witnessed your run-in with Ms. Osborn."

"That's mighty convenient," Chip huffed. "I don't remember seeing you."

"Nonetheless, I was there. I'm sure you wouldn't notice a woman like me unless I was either in your way or you wanted something from me." Skye waited for him to dispute her allegation, and when he didn't, she continued. "And after you grabbed her and she Tasered you, you said, 'You'll be sorry for that, bitch.'"

Chip made a sound that was halfway between denial and exasperation.

Skye ignored his displeasure and asked, "Did you indeed make her sorry?" When he didn't answer right away, she prodded, "Perhaps by lying in wait, then following her and running her car off the road."

"Shit!" Chip narrowed his eyes. "So that's what this is about. She had an accident and is blaming me. She sure holds a grudge."

"She doesn't anymore," Wally said, rejoining the conversation. "Yvonne Osborn died last Sunday."

"She *what*?" Chip jumped as if he'd been Tasered again. "How?"

"Her car was forced into the river." Wally's tone was impassive. "I'm surprised no one mentioned it to you or that you didn't hear about it on the radio or read about it in the Laurel paper."

"I don't listen to the news or get the paper. It's too boring. If it isn't an AOL headline, I don't want to know about it," Chip muttered. Then, finally seeming to realize why Wally and Skye were questioning him, he protested, "I'm no killer."

"Hardly anyone says that they are," Skye murmured. "Maybe you didn't mean for her to die. Maybe you just wanted to wreck her car." Skye tilted her head. "After all, Yvonne spurned your advances, demeaned you, and then zapped you in the crotch. Together they make a pretty good motive for revenge."

Ignoring Skye's accusations, Chip turned to Wally and asked, "When did it happen?"

"Between four forty-five and five fifty-five p.m.," Wally answered.

"And she was in town when she was forced off the road?" Chip demanded.

"Yes." Wally studied the agitated man. "The bridge by Cattail Path."

"Then I have about twenty witnesses who can tell you that I was nowhere near Scumble River Sunday night." Chip let out a breath, clearly relieved. "I was in Joliet at my family's Christmas Eve party from five until close to midnight." He smiled triumphantly. "In fact, there's a video of me lifting up a couch with five of my little cousins sitting on it while singing 'Rudolph the Red-Nosed Reindeer.' It's on YouTube."

"We'll need the names and phone numbers of everyone there and the URL for that YouTube video." Wally took out his notepad and flipped it open.

"I have it all in my office." Chip seemed happy to cooperate and led them toward the rear of the fitness center. "I've got the video on my computer. I'm going to use it in an ad for the club."

Once Chip showed them the clip and provided the party's guest list, Wally said to him, "I'll ask that you stay here with Ms. Denison while I call and confirm your alibis."

"But I got places to go, people to see," Chip complained.

"This shouldn't take too long." Wally folded his arms. "Just take it easy."

"But I'm not too good with being patient," Chip grumbled.

"Challenge yourself." Wally waited until the health club owner grudgingly took a seat behind his desk, then left.

Chip muttered something under his breath, then

pulled out the papers he'd put in his pocket, leaned back in his chair, and leered at Skye. "I hope you're into watching. This could be really exciting. I might even use a calculator and a spreadsheet."

An hour later, when Wally finally returned and told Chip that he was in the clear, Skye jumped from her chair and barely stopped herself from running out the door. To make room for her wedding organizer, she'd taken out the book she usually carried in her purse, which meant she'd had nothing to do for the past sixty minutes except observe Chip chew on his pencil and swear at the computer. Boredom had set in after the first few unimaginative curse words, and by the time Wally appeared, Skye was almost comatose.

Driving back to the police station, Wally announced with a disgusted expression, "Another suspect bites the dust. I sure hope something comes of our reinterviews with the husband or the neighbor."

"Me too," Skye agreed. At the rate they were going, the murder wouldn't be solved before they left on their honeymoon. She knew Wally wouldn't have a good time with an open case hanging over his head, and if he wasn't happy, she doubted she would be either.

When Skye's alarm went off at seven the next morning, she wasn't surprised to see Wally's side of the bed empty. He'd had a restless night, and she vaguely remembered hearing him get up before dawn. When she'd checked the clock and discovered that it wasn't even five a.m., she'd gone back to sleep.

Yawning, she stumbled downstairs, fed Bingo, and made herself a strong cup of coffee using her new favorite toy, the Keurig coffeemaker she'd received as a shower gift from her coworkers. When she and Wally ate breakfast together, it was easier to use her good old Mr. Coffee to brew a whole pot. But when she was alone, she loved all the different flavors the Keurig setup offered.

Carrying her mug back to her bedroom, she took contented sips of the French Roast Extra Bold as she made the bed, applied her makeup, and set her hair in hot rollers. Finally, she stared into her closet, waiting for inspiration to strike. She wasn't sure how to dress for the day's widely varying activities. Making the reception favors might be messy, but she didn't know if she'd have enough time to change clothes afterward•before meeting Wally at the station.

After a few minutes, when nothing jumped off the hanger and screamed "wear me," she settled for a pair of dark jeans and a long-sleeved red T-shirt. Before leaving for the interviews, she would add a jacket to look more professional.

Once Skye was ready, she arranged the materials they would require to assemble the favors on the kitchen table, made a list of the cash and checks she would need to pay off her vendors, and was at the bank when it opened at nine.

It took nearly an hour to complete her transactions, mostly because the teller on duty was her cousin Ginger Leofanti, and Ginger wanted to discuss what she was wearing to Skye's bachelorette party that night. Ginger explained that she was leaning toward a red minidress with red high heels, but she didn't want to outshine Skye's choice.

After reassuring her cousin that her outfit was fine, Skye arrived home just in time to greet her bridesmaid and matron of honor. Frannie was first through the door, with Trixie close behind her. Both women hugged Skye, then tried to speak at the same time.

Frannie won. "Justin got into U of I!"

"That's awesome!" Skye was relieved. "Is he requesting the Illinois Street residence hall?" She knew Frannie's father had insisted she stay in Wardall on a girls-only floor. If Justin lived in Townsend, the guys' dorm, the couple could be together in the ISR common areas.

"He hasn't decided yet." Frannie didn't quite meet Skye's eyes. "He just found out yesterday, so everything is still up in the air."

Skye was fairly sure Frannie and Justin had endlessly discussed their options. What were the two young people plotting? Mentally shrugging, she decided it wasn't her problem. She was no longer their school psychologist; now she was just their friend, especially since she had finally persuaded both of them to call her by her first name instead of Ms. D.

Trixie interrupted Skye's thoughts by poking her in the shoulder and said, "Owen's family drove me freaking crazy this year. I'm not big on Christmas anyway—I mean, basically it's sitting in front of a dead tree eating candy out of your socks."

Frannie snickered.

"You owe me big-time for making Owen and me postpone our trip until after your big day," Trixie informed Skye. "I could have been in the Caribbean for the holidays instead of in the middle of an Indiana cornfield with people who think underwear and towels are fun gifts."

Trixie's husband, Owen, had surprised her with a Christmas-week cruise, but he'd agreed to rebook it for the week after so Trixie wouldn't miss Skye's wedding. At the time, Trixie had been happy to delay her vacation. Apparently, after spending several days with her in-laws, she'd had second thoughts.

"Sorry you had such a bad holiday," Skye said. "But it wasn't much fun around here either." She explained about the murder and the investigation, concluding with, "Wally missed Christmas Eve and has been preoccupied with the case ever since." Realizing how bad that sounded, she added, "Not that I don't understand that a murder preempts everything, but it has been a little hard doing all the stuff for the wedding by myself."

"You poor thing." Trixie hugged Skye again and whispered into her ear, "You're always so independent, it never occurred to me, but this is really an emotional roller coaster for you, isn't it, sweetie?"

"More than I ever expected." Skye sniffed. "Getting married changes so much."

"I'm sorry." Frannie put her arm around Skye's shoulder. "I should have been helping you since I got home from school instead of being so selfish and spending the time with Justin."

"That's okay." Skye shook her head. "It's not so bad getting all the little details and arrangements done; it's just dealing with the mood swings that I hate."

"Well, we're here now." Trixie stepped back and took Skye's hand. "You can tell us all about it while we get to work on those favors."

"Right this way." Skye beamed at her friends. She felt better already.

The three of them dove into making the 390 hot cocoa giveaways. As Skye filled disposable, cone-shaped cake decorating bags with instant hot chocolate mix, she poured out her heart to her friends. She rarely talked about her feelings. Most of the time hers was the shoulder everyone cried on, and it felt good to let go and talk about what had been running through her mind for the past week. She told them about all her doubts and fears.

Trixie and Frannie listened and made sympathetic noises, but didn't comment on anything until Skye said, "It's just that I suddenly realized that with Wally being the chief of police, I'll never be able to count on him for the holidays or any of the special occasions in our lives. His job will always have to come first."

"Right." Trixie tied a red ribbon around one of the sheer plastic bags where the chocolate mix ended, leaving room to add the next ingredient. "But a lot of the time you'll be working with him on the investigations."

"True." Skye's teeth caught her lower lip and worried it for a moment before she said, "And one of the things that I love about him is what he stands for, that he always tries to do the right thing." She frowned, then added, "At least almost always."

"Almost?" Frannie asked as she began scooping a quarter cup of miniature marshmallows into each bag and securing the second bow. "Is there something you haven't told us?"

"Well." Skye debated, admitting her jealousy. "Maybe one little thing."

"Oh?" Frannie and Trixie said in unison, both raising their brows. "What's that?"

"It's not a what." Skye passed the last of the bags with the hot chocolate mix to Trixie, then began fastening the completed bags with the third red ribbon, this one with a heart-shaped tag attached that read: OUR WARMEST THANKS, SKYE & WALLY. "It's a who."

"That sounds bad." There was a worried look in Frannie's brown eyes.

"Yes, it does." Trixie thrust out her pixielike chin and demanded, "Spill."

"Her name is Emerald, aka Emmy Jones, and she's an instructor at my aunt Olive's dance studio." Skye wrinkled her nose. "She's also the daughter of a friend of Bunny's and is living with her above the bowling alley."

"Uh-oh." Frannie shook her head. "What has Miss Bunny done now?"

"Not Bunny; it's Wally and Simon."

"Oh?" Trixie's voice held more than a hint of curiosity.

Skye started to explain about Wally knowing the dancer from his gun club, but Frannie interrupted, "I didn't know Wally liked to shoot."

"Duh." Trixie sniggered. "Of course he likes to shoot. He's the chief of police and he was born and raised in Texas. What do you think his hobby would be? Collecting stamps?"

"Anyway," Skye said, steering the conversation back to what she'd been saying. When she was finished, she summed it all up with, "So apparently Emmy and Wally have developed quite a friendship."

Trixie said, "And you're jealous?"

"Not really," Skye protested, then admitted, "Maybe

a little, but I trust Wally. I know he'd never cheat. I'm just hurt that he didn't tell me about her. Why would he keep that a secret?"

"He didn't. Guys just don't always think to share stuff like that." Trixie tossed her head. "Get used to it."

"Yeah." The furrows in Skye's forehead smoothed out. "You're right. Any other time, I don't think it would have upset me. My hormones seem all out of whack."

"Maybe you have bridal PMS." Frannie giggled.

"Maybe." Skye's shoulder's drooped. "But something else feels wrong." She told them about the kiss she'd witnessed between Emmy and Simon at the fitness center.

"But that's a good thing, isn't it?" Trixie tilted her head questioningly. "Aren't you happy that Simon's found someone?"

"I am."

"And if Emmy's involved with Simon, you don't have to worry about her and Wally," Frannie pointed out.

"I'm not." Skye looked at the ceiling. "I can't explain."

"It's the green-eyed monster. It has you by the heart." Trixie gave Skye a long look. "You don't want Simon, but it bothers you that he's moved on."

"I hope I'm not that petty." Skye made a face. "But from what I've told you about Emmy and what you both know about Simon, don't they strike you as an odd match?"

"He's just proving the old saying that you marry your mother." Trixie snickered.

"Oh, my God!" Skye fought a grin and lost. "That's it. Emmy reminds me of what Bunny must have been like as a young woman." Her smile faded. "And look how well that turned out for Simon's father. Bunny ended up leaving him with a small child to bring up on his own. I sure don't want anything like that to happen to Simon."

Frannie and Trixie exchanged anxious glances, but didn't comment. Clearly, they too were beginning to worry about Simon's new relationship.

CHAPTER 17

Read Him like a Book

Skye felt a lot better after sharing her feelings with Trixie and Frannie—even if she still had a niggling concern that Simon's choice of girlfriend would cause him trouble. Over fried chicken at the Feed Bag—Scumble River's only sit-down restaurant—she and her pals had a good time catching up on one another's lives. Being around her friends lifted her spirits as nothing else had. It was almost as if they were her guardian angels and they used their own wings to help her remember how to keep aloft.

After lunch everyone went their separate ways. Skye delivered the favors, seating plan, place cards, and guest book to the Country Mansion's reception coordinator, then hurried back to the police station.

As they headed out to question King Housley, Skye asked Wally, "Did Phoebe pick up Sugar Plum last night?"

"Yes." Wally chuckled. "But not soon enough for your mother."

"Uh-oh." Skye rolled her eyes. "Did Sugar Plum pee or poop inside the station?" May didn't tolerate messes and would have had a hissy fit if she had to clean up after an animal.

"Not that I know of, but May left me a formal note of

complaint, indicating that dog sitting was not in her job description." He shrugged. "I guess it's a good thing the dispatchers aren't unionized or I'd be in trouble."

"Mom doesn't need a union." Skye adjusted the seat belt, which was cutting into her neck. "If she's upset with you, you're already in hot water. You'd better watch your back."

"Right." Wally snorted, plainly unconcerned. "The dog weighed less than six pounds. How much bother could she have been?"

Skye recognized a rhetorical question when she heard one and instead of answering, said, "So did Zuchowski show up?"

"With his bleached blond alibi in tow." Wally's expression hardened. "He's in the clear for the murder—both the woman he was with and the airline ticket receipts prove he was out of town the night Yvonne was killed— and he didn't steal from the evidence closet. I just wish I had proof he sold drugs and could arrest him. But none of his customers will come forward and testify, so I had to settle for firing him."

"Being let go without a letter of reference means that in all probability he'll never work as a police officer again." Skye gazed off into the distance. "And either he'll continue selling drugs and eventually get caught or this whole affair will be the wake-up call he needs. One way or the other, you got a bad cop off the streets."

"Hopefully." Wally's face was a twisted knot of frustration.

Skye waited a few seconds, then changed the subject. "Did your dad and cousin arrive safely?" She rubbed her hand across her eyes. "I've been worried a snowstorm somewhere would ground them. We've been really lucky with a mild winter so far."

"Quentin texted me about one a.m." Wally steered the Caprice over the notoriously narrow bridge leading to Cattail Path. "He and my father didn't get in until after midnight and went straight to their suite."

"Good thing they have today to rest." Skye was relieved that all the out-of-town folks in her bridal party were now present and accounted for. "Trixie's back in town, I picked up the cash and checks, the favors are done, and everything has been dropped off at the Country Mansion."

"You got a lot accomplished." Wally shook his head and muttered, "More than I did—that's for sure."

As they drove slowly past the Doozier property, Skye noticed that, as usual, the yard was littered with car parts, dead appliances, and broken-down furniture. A new addition to the mix was a desiccated Christmas tree lying by the driveway and twinkle lights spelling out MARY KRISMAS adorning the wire fence.

Skye barely blinked at Earl's slaughter of the English language. "Sorry you didn't have a more productive morning. Were you at least able to talk to Dutch and Artie?" When Wally nodded, she questioned, "How did that go?"

"It went." Wally's lips tightened. "Neither had much to add to what they originally told Quirk. Yvonne was a pain in the butt, but they hadn't had to deal with her since their accident. And they figured since Judy was due back soon, Yvonne wouldn't be working at the library anymore by the time they recovered and went back to work."

"Which leaves us with King Housley and Neil Osborn as our remaining suspects."

"That about sums it up." Wally was silent, then shook his head and forced a smile. "Do you have anything else you need to do today?"

After visualizing her schedule, Skye answered, "Just finish packing for our honeymoon. I had a mani/pedi at five, but I postponed that until tomorrow."

"Good." Wally nodded, then pointed and said, "That's the vic's place."

Skye examined the librarian's rental. It was a nondescript ranch-style house with gray siding and white trim.

Its decorations were limited to a tasteful evergreen wreath on the door and white candles in the windows. How sad that Yvonne would never spend another holiday with her daughter.

A minute later, Wally pulled the squad car into a short driveway that led to an iron gate blocking the entrance to an oak-lined lane. He turned off the Chevy and gestured to the padlocked entrance. "Looks as if Housley doesn't want any unexpected visitors driving up to his place."

"I'm surprised he doesn't have a fence." Skye examined the heavily wooded area in front of her. Each of the houses on Cattail Path was situated on several acres of property and surrounded by trees.

"Me too. Maybe he figures that most salesmen and Jehovah's Witnesses are too lazy to hike in." Wally got out of the cruiser and opened the passenger door for Skye. "We'll have to walk from here."

Trudging up the long dirt track, Skye was glad she'd worn flats. Wally held her elbow, making sure she didn't trip on the rutted surface, but it was rough going. Thank goodness the lane wasn't covered with snow and ice, or they'd really have had a difficult time. They were both silent, as if they'd agreed it was best to approach the house without announcing their presence.

Just before they rounded a slight bend in the lane, Wally stopped suddenly, pulled Skye closer, and asked quietly, "Do you hear that?"

Skye nodded and kept her voice low as she replied, "It's sort of a *ch-thunk! Cer-rack.*" She tilted her head. "Do you know what it is?"

"I can't put my finger on it, but it sounds familiar," Wally whispered before taking the lead. He moved noiselessly toward the sound. Abruptly, he pulled Skye behind a huge Douglas fir. She peered between the branches and saw a guy chopping wood. He was facing away from them, but a second later, he turned to pick up another log, and she recognized King Housley. He no longer appeared to need his cane.

She turned to Wally and mouthed, "That's him." Putting her lips to Wally's ear, she asked, "But what happened to his injury?"

"Good question," Wally murmured almost inaudibly. He got out his phone, thumbed the video button, and aimed it at King as the miraculously healed man swung his ax, splitting the huge piece of wood in half with ease.

Once Wally had recorded King bending, chopping, and carrying a heavy load of kindling toward the house, he and Skye returned to the driveway and approached the residence from the front.

There was no doorbell, but after three or four loud knocks, Housley yanked open the door and snarled, "Yeah, what do you want?"

"I'm Chief Boyd and this is Ms. Denison, the police department psychological consultant." Wally's voice was unruffled and his posture was relaxed, but his hand rested on his nightstick. "We'd like to speak to you about your neighbor Yvonne Osborn."

"The other cop already talked to me." King leaned heavily on his cane.

"We have a few more questions to ask you." Wally took a step forward, but Housley didn't budge. "I understand that you two were having problems because you felt that she was spying on you."

"So?" Housley's tone was surly. "No one cared when I called the station and complained that she was a freaking Peeping Tammy."

"I apologize, and I'll look into why your complaint was ignored." Wally moved closer to the threshold. "Our questions will only take a few minutes."

"Go ahead." King grimaced. "But make it quick. I'm having a bad day with the pain and all, and it's almost time for my pill."

"Why don't we go inside, where you can be more comfortable?" Skye pasted a concerned expression on her face.

"You got a warrant?" King blocked their entrance.

"In fact, I changed my mind. I'm through talking to you people."

"I don't think so." Wally stuck his foot in the doorway, whipped out his phone, and said, "Take a look at this, Mr. Housley."

As King focused in on the little screen, his face reddened. Suddenly, he raised his cane and swung it toward Wally, who ducked, grabbed the walking stick in midswipe, and hauled the man out onto the front porch. When Housley attempted to run, Wally grabbed him by the shirt collar, spun him around, and handcuffed him.

King ranted about his rights until Wally said, "I guess now we'll do this at the station." Turning to Skye, he directed, "See if Housley's wife is around and if she has the key to the gate."

"Don't you give it to them, Hazel!" Housley screamed. "You hear me?"

Skye found Housley's wife in the kitchen. The tiny woman was seated at a table, gripping a dish towel in her gnarled fingers. Although the appliances and furniture had seen better days, everything was spotless. This lady's cleaning habits would give May a run for her money.

Hazel didn't look up when Skye approached her, but she sobbed, "King didn't kill that librarian." Apparently, Mrs. Housley had been eavesdropping on the drama that had taken place on her front porch. "The radio said she died sometime between four and six. Me and King were in Clay Center the afternoon of Christmas Eve from three thirty to past seven."

"Can anyone else verify that?" Skye asked. She instinctively knew that the woman would lie for her husband, but whether it would be out of love, loyalty, or fear, she wasn't sure. Maybe a combination of all three. "Preferably someone not related to your husband."

"Yeah." Hazel smoothed the towel and folded it in a precise square. "We were at our church over to Clay Center. The little kids put on a Nativity play, and then there was a potluck. We sat with the minister and his family."

"That's good, then." Skye patted the woman's shoulder. "But there's still the matter of the attempted assault on a police officer."

"Could the chief forget about that?" Hazel's faded blue eyes had a sly glint. "If I was able to tell him something that happened at Ms. Osborn's, maybe he'd be inclined to sort of pretend King just slipped."

"That depends." Skye didn't know what kind of bargain Wally would be able to make. "Was it something that happened recently?"

"The day before she was killed." Hazel straightened. "The chief will want to know this. You go ask him if he's willing to make a deal."

Skye figured there was a good chance Wally might be prepared to forget that King had attacked him, but she was positive he couldn't let Housley skate on the fake disability claim. That was fraud, and it was costing the taxpayers a bundle.

After telling Hazel that she'd be right back, Skye went outside and asked Wally to handcuff his prisoner to the porch swing so they could speak privately. Once Housley was secure and they were out of earshot, Skye informed Wally of Hazel's offer to exchange information for her husband's freedom.

Before Wally could respond, Skye took a breath and added, "Obviously we need to keep King and his wife separated since she's unaware we know he isn't really injured."

"We can take them both to the station." Wally reached for the radio attached to his shoulder. "I'll call for an additional squad car."

"My professional opinion is that you shouldn't wait for another officer to get here. If you don't act right now, before Hazel has a chance to think it over, she might change her mind." Skye paused, then continued. "Remember, it looks as if Housley has an alibi for the murder, so his wife may figure that he can wiggle out of the attempted assault charge, too. And there was some reason she didn't initially come forward with this info."

"Most likely because she didn't want to get involved." Wally shrugged. "A lot of people don't."

"Maybe." Skye considered his explanation. "Still, if you want to make a deal with her on the attempted-assault charge, you probably should do it now." She raised a brow. "What's the old saying? Strike while the wife is hot?"

"Cute." Wally glanced at the still ranting man. "But I don't think it's wise to leave him alone. He could slip the cuffs and take off."

"I'll keep an eye on him." Skye studied King's posture. "I think he's wearing himself out."

"Well." Wally hesitated, then reached down to his ankle holster and handed Skye his backup weapon, a Ruger .357 compact revolver. "Do you remember how to use this?" When she nodded, he added, "Stay out of his reach and yell for me if there's a problem."

"Got it." Skye tried to recall the afternoon that Wally had taken her shooting. "Go ahead." She really did need to start going to the gun range with him, and not just to protect him from Emmy.

Once Wally had disappeared into the house, King abruptly settled down, took a seat on the swing he was cuffed to, and asked Skye, "You and him think I killed that nosy woman next door, don't you?"

"No," Skye answered honestly, although she wasn't about to admit she knew he had an alibi. "But I'm curious what you two fought about."

"Why?" King squinted. "You another meddlesome busybody like her?"

"I just like to understand things." Skye shrugged her shoulders. "It's sort of what a psychologist is all about. Was it because she suspected you weren't really injured and threatened to turn you in?"

"That sounds like a motive for murder." King's expression turned guarded. "You trying to railroad me into a confession or something?"

"Not at all." Skye lowered herself to the front step, turning toward King so that she still had a direct line of fire. Then, assuming her best counseling air, she said, "I want to catch the real killer."

"Sure. And I've got a genuine diamond ring to sell you for twenty bucks. I'll throw in the earrings for free." When Skye didn't react, he asked, "Hey, why does a one-horse town like Scumble River have a fancy psychologist on the police payroll anyway?"

"Good question." Skye wasn't sure how to answer, so she tried humor. "One the mayor asks all the time, even though he is my uncle."

Housley didn't crack a smile.

"I guess because in the past I helped solve a few murder cases." Skye shrugged and added, "And my services come cheap."

"Cheap always works." King twitched his shoulders. "At least for most folks." He looked at Skye for a couple of seconds, then seemed to come to some sort of decision. Exhaling noisily, he said, "The witch next door might have seen me out working on my truck. And she might have said something about me not really being hurt. But she didn't have any proof because after that I was real careful that she wasn't around before I did anything outside. Plus, since she was moving away next month, I had no reason to kill her."

"That's a good point." Skye leaned forward, thought a moment, then asked, "Were you the one who phoned into the *Star* saying that Ms. Osborn better mind her own business or she'd regret it?"

"Yeah." King hunched his head into his chest. "I got liquored up after I caught her spying on me and called. It was dumb."

"Alcohol seems to have that effect on a lot of people," Skye sympathized.

"Ain't that the truth?" Housley was silent until Wally emerged from the house; then he said, "So, what did the old lady say?"

Wally ignored him and asked Skye, "You okay?" When she nodded, he whispered in her ear, "King's alibi checks out. I called the minister, and he verified that the Housleys were with him during the relevant time period."

"Good." Skye wasn't sure if she was happy or disappointed.

Wally held up a small key. "Martinez is at the end of the lane. You keep an eye on Housley and I'll walk down and let her in."

Ten minutes later, two Scumble River squad cars pulled up. Martinez got out of one and Wally exited from the other. While he transferred King into the young officer's custody and instructed her to hold the prisoner at the PD until he arrived, Skye got into Wally's cruiser.

Skye waited until Wally finished with Martinez, then got into the car and phoned the city attorney and the mayor to inform them about King's scam before she asked, "So did Mrs. Housley say anything that might help us find the killer?"

"Possibly." Wally flipped open his notepad and read, "Last Saturday afternoon, she was walking in the woods between her land and the vic's property and witnessed a man park what she described as a big fancy SUV in Yvonne Osborn's driveway and walk toward her front door. When the vic stepped outside, the guy started yelling and waving a crowbar at her."

"Did the man attack her?"

"The vic had a shotgun and forced the guy to leave." Wally started the Caprice.

"Was he Yvonne's husband?"

Wally shrugged. "Mrs. Housley said he had on a baseball cap and sunglasses, so she could only describe him as white and sort of bulky. She has no idea of his age or if his hair was gray or even his height. She said from the distance she was at, she just couldn't tell if he was short or tall."

"Neil Osborn is fairly muscular."

"Yes, he is."

"What was the man shouting at Yvonne about?" Skye put her hands to the car's vents. She'd gotten chilly being outside for so long.

"Mrs. Housley was too far away to hear what he was saying." Wally turned up the heat.

"What year was the guy's SUV and what color was it?"

"All Mrs. Housley could say was that it was new and white. So—" Wally was about to continue, when his cell phone rang. He answered it, listened, and said, "Okay. Thanks. But he'll be there tomorrow? Great. Thanks again." He hung up and put the phone in his pocket. "That was Neil Osborn's secretary," he told Skye with a scowl. "Her boss just called her from the development site to say he has to go into the city for something."

"So he won't be in Lawnton." Skye pursed her lips. With Hazel's information about some guy threatening Yvonne, Wally would be even more anxious to talk to Neil. "Did he say where in Chicago he's going?"

"Unfortunately, no." Wally put the squad car in gear. "I guess we'll have to wait and talk to him tomorrow morning."

"At least you can take care of the Housley situation ASAP." Skye tapped Wally's arm. "You can meet Uncle Dante and the city attorney at the PD right away and get the whole matter settled. You won't have to keep the mayor waiting."

"Always a good thing." Wally smiled at her. "And it looks as if you can make your nail appointment after all."

CHAPTER 18

Chapter and Verse

Skye was in luck. The Scumble River Spa hadn't re-booked her mani/pedi slot, and she was able to reclaim her original appointment. It was heavenly to relax while her feet and hands were being pampered, and she didn't once think about the murder investigation. Instead, she chilled out, daydreamed about her wedding day and honeymoon, and thoroughly unwound.

By six fifteen, her fingernails gleaming a pale pink and her toenails sparkling a deep berry, Skye headed home. Trixie, Frannie, and Loretta were picking her up in half an hour, and she had to feed Bingo and change clothes before they arrived.

Because neither Wally nor Skye was interested in going to a club or seeing exotic dancers, they had asked their best man and matron of honor to combine the bachelor and bachelorette parties and hold the event at a PG-rated location. Quentin had been happy to oblige and offered to cover the cost of both. Trixie had pouted for several weeks because she'd wanted to rent a male stripper, but she had eventually come around and taken over the planning for the whole extravaganza.

The invitations had instructed everyone to wear green

if they were romantically available, red if they were un-available, and yellow if they weren't sure. Skye's dress was scarlet. She'd selected it because of the flouncy ruffle that hung in a vee from the scoop neck to the waist, which added a bit of oomph while camouflaging any figure flaws.

The parties were taking place at Scumble River's Ju-piter Movie Theater, which had been built in 1939. At the time, the structure had been state-of-the-art construc-tion with masonry and plaster walls over steel, steam heating, and even air-conditioning. The Jupiter had closed in the midseventies and reopened only last Sep-tember.

The stage, ceiling, entrance, and ticket booth, along with the architectural fixtures, remained unchanged, but the theater was now divided into two. On one screen, the guys would watch *X-Men: The Last Stand,* and on the other, the women would view *The Devil Wears Prada.* Trixie had assured Skye that both movies were the year's hottest releases.

Afterward, the guests would adjourn to the huge lobby, where Trixie had arranged for rented lounge fur-niture to be set up. She'd also booked a jazz quartet, or-dered food, and hired a bartender. Evidently, Quentin's budget for the event had been nearly bottomless. Either that or Trixie hadn't presented him with the bills yet. Skye tended to believe the former, considering what she knew about Wally's family.

All thoughts about the cost of the party flew from Skye's mind when she and her attendants arrived at the Jupiter and saw that the marquee read: LOVE, LAUGHTER, AND HAPPILY EVER AFTER. STARRING WALLY BOYD AND SKYE DENISON. Fighting joyful tears, she thanked her friends. It had taken her a long time to figure out what she wanted from life. Wally and a home in Scumble River was the dream she'd been pursuing all along but could never quite articulate. Now that she knew, she would never let go.

After several rounds of hugs, Trixie, Frannie, Loretta, and Skye made their way into the theater. Before they could even shed their coats, the other guests started to arrive and the seats began to fill up.

Initially, the bachelorette party had been comprised of only Skye's closest friends. But once Trixie rented the theater, she exponentially expanded the invitees, which now included Skye's mom, aunts, cousins, and quite a few of her coworkers from the school district. Skye hadn't seen the bachelor party's guest list, but she was fairly certain it had increased, too, and now contained her father, uncles, male cousins, and the entire police force.

A half hour later, after Skye had greeted everyone and the lights began to flicker, indicating that the show would begin in a few minutes, she decided she'd better visit the little girl's room before she settled in for the movie. She hated having to get up in the middle.

Wally must have had the same idea because he was leaving the men's room when she hurried into the alcove where both restrooms were located. They exchanged a quick kiss, and Skye asked, "How did it go this afternoon with King Housley?"

She hadn't had a chance to talk to Wally since Housley had been brought to the police station, and she was anxious to know how the situation had been resolved. Disability fraud was both a criminal and a civil matter, and Wally hadn't been sure which case the city attorney and the mayor would choose to pursue or what kind of deal they might make with the maintenance worker.

"In exchange for not pressing charges against him, the city attorney and the mayor gave Housley the option of testifying against Dutch and Artie and repaying all the cash he's defrauded from the town."

"And?"

"He snapped up the offer almost before the attorney put it on the table. He claimed that Dutch had figured out how they could fake an accident and pretend to be hurt." Wally snorted his skepticism. "Apparently, Housley was just a pawn."

"Sure." Skye wrinkled her nose in disbelief. "Oh, well.

At least this way the taxpayers get their money back and don't have to pay for a long trial or foot the bill for his jail time."

"That is something." Wally blew out a puff of exasperation. "But I really hate to let criminals off like that."

"Me too. But it's out of both our hands." Skye kissed Wally again, then said over her shoulder as she pushed open the door of the restroom, "Gotta go. The movie's going to start any second, and I don't want to miss the beginning."

The show was great and everyone was laughing and talking afterward as they trooped into the lobby. Even though Skye had eaten a tub of popcorn only slightly smaller than a Tilt-A-Whirl car and a box of Junior Mints bigger than her head, her stomach growled when the aroma of pepperoni pizza, Buffalo wings, nachos, and onion rings enveloped her.

The men were already crowding the buffet, but the women elbowed their way in and filled their plates. Once everyone had their food, most of the guys drifted over to the left side of the lobby, where a poker table, a golf simulator, and Skee-Ball machine were available. The majority of the women headed to the opposite end, where couches and chairs had been arranged to resemble a nightclub.

Skye piled her plate with goodies, refusing to think about how tight her wedding dress might be if she ate everything she took; then she joined Frannie, Trixie, and her twin cousins, Gillian and Ginger. Both cousins were married and were dressed in red, but Frannie wore a bright yellow sweater and a pair of black jeans.

Skye had noticed Frannie's choice of color earlier but hadn't had a chance to say anything to her. Recalling their earlier conversation about where Justin would live once he went to college, she wondered if he and Frannie were on the outs.

While Skye pondered a way to bring up the subject, Ginger said, "This is such a great party. It had to have cost a bundle."

Shoot! Skye hadn't asked Wally how he wanted to handle this issue. He'd always been careful not to let anyone in Scumble River know about his well-to-do background because he didn't want people to treat him any differently than they would a regular small-town police chief. He lived modestly and refused to take money from his millionaire father. As far as Skye knew, only she and his ex-wife were aware of his family's extreme fortune.

Glancing at Trixie, Skye held her breath. What would she say? Come to think about it, did her friend have any clue just how wealthy Wally's father and cousin were? Since other people were bound to notice Carson's and Quentin's elaborate spending during their time in Scumble River, Skye needed to consult with Wally as soon as possible. If he wanted his family's affluence to stay a secret, they needed to come up with a story pretty darn quickly.

Trixie finished her bite of pizza and beamed at Ginger. "I'm so glad you're having a good time. When Skye said she didn't want to go to a Chicago bar or to see male strippers at a club, I really panicked." Trixie giggled. "Do you know that she suggested we hold it at the bookstore café?"

Everyone howled, and Skye smacked Trixie on the arm. "What? You love books, too, and the café's pastries are to die for. It would have been fun."

"Yeah." Frannie rolled her eyes. "If you're a hundred and two and a cloistered nun."

"Or Amish," Gillian added. "We might as well have had the party at the church hall and brought our knitting. Father Burns could have given us an inspirational talk about the sanctity of the marriage bed."

"Okay, you guys." Skye laughed along with everyone else. "You're right. This is much better." When they all simultaneously replied with the word *duh*, she added, "But my thinking was that Trixie and I work for the school district, so we have to be a lot more careful of our reputations than people in other professions. No one wants their kids to be educated by someone who gets drunk and watches men take off their clothes."

"Well . . ." Trixie trailed off. "I guess you have a point there, and poor Wally is in the same boat." She looked over to where the guys were whooping at someone's Skee-Ball prowess. "No one wants a police chief with a hangover and some bimbo's panties in his pocket."

"Except maybe Uncle Dante," Ginger said, gnawing on a hot wing.

"Why would he want that?" Skye was relieved that the cost of the party had been forgotten. "I mean, I know Uncle Dante isn't a big fan of Wally's, but he wouldn't want any bad publicity for the town. His biggest ambition is to make Scumble River a destination for daytrippers. Look at his last scheme to turn it into the Branson of Illinois."

"The tourist attraction idea is old news." Gillian took a swallow of her chocolate martini. "I heard Uncle Dante talking to Mama, and he wants to do away with the police department and use the money we'd save to build a big incinerator at the edge of town."

"Incinerator?" Trixie nearly choked on the onion ring she'd stuffed into her mouth. "What in God's green earth do we need with an incinerator? Scumble River doesn't have that much trash. Do we?"

"Uncle Dante's plan is to charge neighboring towns to use the incinerator." Gillian licked the foam from her upper lip. "He told Mama that it will pay for itself in a couple of years, then be a real cash cow for Scumble River."

"Cow patty is more like it," Skye muttered.

"And he wants to finance this moneymaking idea of his by eliminating the police force entirely?" Trixie asked with a look of incredulity. "So there would be no law enforcement in town?"

"Uncle Dante says we can contract for services through the county sheriff's department for a lot cheaper than what we spend on the police budget." Ginger wiped her fingers on her napkin. "He says we spend way too much for what we get since we don't have that much crime."

"Is the mayor on crack?" Frannie's mouth twisted into a sneer. "How about all the murders? According to my sociology class, the only reason a town like ours doesn't have more crime than it does is it has a good police force doing its job."

"Uncle Dante is like a lot of people." Skye tried to keep her voice calm, but the news of her uncle's plan had struck her like a blow to the stomach with a weed whacker. "Reality is what he wants it to be and has nothing to do with the true facts."

"If Uncle Dante succeeds"—Gillian crunched a nacho chip thoughtfully—"that would mean Wally would need a new job, wouldn't it?"

"I guess . . ." Skye's voice trailed off.

Gillian puckered her brow. "And you two would have to move away."

"Probably." Skye forced herself not to scream at her cousin. "Is this a recent plan?" Certainly, she'd been busy with the wedding and the holidays, but surely, someone would have mentioned Uncle Dante's proposal. Say, for instance her mother, Dante's sister. May should have been having a fit at the idea of Skye leaving town. "I wonder why I haven't heard anything about it."

"Oopsie! Guess I'm the big mouth." Ginger winked. "I forgot. Mama said it's a huge secret and Uncle Dante wants to sneak the whole thing through the city council in executive session without giving any of the townspeople a chance to object."

"Ah." Skye finally smiled. "Did Aunt Minnie suggest you might want to slip up and tell me about it?" Aunt Minnie, May's younger sister, wouldn't have the guts to go against Dante, but she'd be okay with having her daughters play the dumb-blonde card in order to warn Skye. "Or were you supposed to drop a hint to my mother?" Minnie was a lot smarter than most people gave her credit for being.

"Of course not," Gillian protested halfheartedly. "Mama

would never break Uncle Dante's confidence like that. She'll be so upset with us."

"Don't worry," Skye assured her cousins. "I won't let on how I came by this piece of news." She pasted an innocent expression on her face. "You know how hard it is to pin down a rumor in this town."

They all agreed that gossip was like small change; you never could remember where you picked up a certain dime or penny. After that, they switched the subject to something lighter, and a few minutes later Skye excused herself, saying she needed to mingle.

As soon as she was out of sight, she made her way over to where the guys were eating. As she'd suspected, Trixie had invited Skye's dad, uncles, and male cousins, as well as Wally's officers. Jed and his brother, Wiley, were in a corner drinking beer and mostly ignoring a NASCAR race on a big-screen television set, but almost everyone else was playing various games.

Skye scanned the rest of the guys, noticing Dante when he chortled triumphantly while pulling in a towering stack of multicolored chips. Uncle Charlie sat next to the mayor, a thoughtful expression on his face. He eyed the other three men at the table as he picked up the deck, shuffled, and dealt the cards.

Uninterested in the poker game, Skye glanced toward the golf simulator. Her brother, Vince, her cousin Hugo Leofanti, and officers Roy Quirk and Anthony Anserello were competing in a tournament. The four of them frowned in concentration as they putted.

Justin, Ginger's husband, Flip, and Gillian's husband, Irvin, were taking turns at the Skee-Ball machine. As the device spit out tickets, the three guys stuffed their winnings into their jeans pockets. The vouchers could be redeemed for prizes displayed on a table in the rear.

Skye didn't see Wally anywhere in the gaming zone and he hadn't been over in the lounge area, so where was he? Swiveling her head, she finally spotted him off to the side of the lobby, talking to his father and a man who had to be Quentin. Carson was a distinguished-looking older version of his son, and Wally's cousin could pass as his younger brother.

Carson was gesturing emphatically and appeared to be attempting to convince his son about something. And although Quentin nodded his agreement, his expression belied his concurrence.

Skye was trying to decide whether to interrupt the men when Bunny Reid tottered over to them in five-inch rhinestone and marabou-feathered stilettos. She was known for her outlandish fashions, and tonight she had outdone herself. She had on a bright green lace mini-dress that would have been better suited to a woman of twenty-eight than fifty-eight.

Bunny wound her arm through Carson's and tossed her red curls. He smiled down at her and she patted the deep vee of her neckline, drawing his eyes down to her cosmetically enhanced boobs. Once she had his attention, she whispered something in his ear. He shook his head, but she leaned closer and whispered again.

Skye couldn't hear Carson's reply, but Bunny's voice carried. The redhead sniggered and said, "I don't care about top or bottom; my favorite position for a man is CEO."

Carson chuckled and murmured something else that Skye didn't hear, but Bunny swept her hands over her hips and said, "Thank you, kind sir. I *have* indeed found the fountain of youth. Turns out it was in a tequila bottle all the time."

With that, Carson shrugged at Wally and Quentin and allowed himself to be pulled away.

Trust Bunny to zero in on the richest, most eligible man in the place. Skye wondered what had happened to the not-quite-divorced, over-the-hill TV star Bunny had been dating. Maybe he'd gone back to his wife. The ditzy redhead didn't seem to have much luck with men. Which was a real shame, since she'd been desperately seeking a husband for as long as Skye had known her.

Originally, Skye had debated whether to include the flamboyant redhead and her daughter, Spike Yamaguchi, in the wedding events. Although Skye considered both Spike and Bunny friends, it was sometimes awkward having the mother and half sister of her ex-boyfriend around. And the last thing she wanted was for Simon to show up with the excuse that he was Bunny or Spike's plus one.

However, in the end, Skye had decided that it would hurt both women's feelings if they weren't part of the festivities. So, much to her mother's dismay, since May wasn't a fan of the redhead, Skye had added Bunny and Spike to the bachelorette party and wedding guest lists.

Now, as she watched Wally's father laugh at something, then lead the flirtatious redhead over to the tiny area in front of the jazz quartet and start to dance with her, Skye was glad she'd chosen to include Bunny. Especially since it looked as if Wally was relieved to have his father distracted from whatever point the older man had been trying to make.

As soon as Carson and Bunny left to dance, Quentin thwacked Wally's arm and wandered over to the golf simulator. He shook hands with Vince, and the two men immediately struck up a conversation. While Skye wondered what a big-shot oil executive found to talk about with her brother the hairstylist, she was happy to see the guys bonding.

Wally was now standing alone, but before Skye could get to him, a blonde wearing a long sequined gown joined him. Skye froze. What was Emmy doing here? Skye certainly hadn't invited her. Had Wally put her on the guest list? Who else would have? Only Trixie, Quentin, Skye, and Wally were supposed to have added names. Surely, when Skye had had her meltdown earlier in the day, Trixie would have mentioned if she had invited the dancer, and Quentin didn't know anyone in Scumble River, so it couldn't have been him.

Skye edged behind a column. Part of her was fuming,

but her cooler, more rational self was wondering when she'd become such a shrew. That part of her urged her to either join Wally and Emmy or walk away. It lectured her that it was childish to hide and spy on them. Still, she couldn't make herself move into view.

Suddenly, Emmy nodded to the quartet, and the musicians stopped playing "Come Fly with Me" and swung into a sexy rendition of "Let Me Entertain You." Emmy pulled Wally into the center of the lobby.

Once everyone at the party had gathered around, the blonde started to dance to the song. Slowly, she removed one of her elbow-length gloves and trailed it over Wally's chest in time to the sensuous beat of the burlesque music. Finally, she threw it into the crowd, where Vince nabbed it, earning him a frown from his pregnant wife.

Emmy's second glove was caught by Justin, and Skye quickly glanced at Frannie, whose expression now matched Loretta's. She noticed that Bunny had a firm grip on Carson's hand, and other women were moving in to stake a claim on their own men. Skye was comforted to see that she wasn't the only one with a jealous streak.

By the end of the song, Emmy was down to a black satin corset with a short tulle tutu. She had divested herself of the sequined gown, a pair of thigh-high stockings, and a red ribbon garter. After the applause died down, she kissed Wally on the cheek, gathered her discarded clothing from the various men who had captured the items she'd tossed, and then ran for the front door.

Skye chuckled, relieved at the outcome. Apparently, someone had hired Emmy to do an extremely tame version of a striptease. Skye's gaze raked the throng, searching for the culprit. A second later, she spotted Quentin following the blonde. He stopped Emmy just before she exited and handed her an envelope. She stuffed it into her décolletage, hugged Quentin, and left with a wave of her hand.

Hmm! Skye wondered if Simon was aware that his new girlfriend performed burlesque at bachelor parties.

Not that Skye was about to tell him, but this was Scumble River, where news traveled fast. Then again, maybe he'd just be happy it wasn't his mother stripping.

When Skye looked back, Wally was surrounded by all the men, laughing and talking. Should she pull him away and tell him about Dante's plan regarding the police force now or wait until tomorrow? Tomorrow would be soon enough, she decided. She'd let him have a good time tonight. After all, there was nothing he could do about the mayor's scheme right this minute.

On the other hand, there was something Skye could do. The last person Dante would want knowing about his plot would be his sister May. Not only would it mean she was out of a job, since no police force meant no police dispatchers, but May had finally gotten her daughter back home and nearly married. She would not be pleased that her brother was about to ruin everything.

So, feeling a little like a five-year-old, Skye went to tattle on her uncle.

CHAPTER 19

Leave No Page Unturned

After Emmy's burlesque act, most of the men and women remained together, and when the jazz quartet struck up the Ronettes' version of "Be My Baby," several couples drifted onto the dance floor, with Carson and Bunny leading the way. Soon Trixie and Owen joined them, then Quirk and Spike, with Anthony and Judy Martin following closely on their heels.

Watching the part-time officer and the library director sway to the music, Skye wondered if Wally had ever talked to Judy about Yvonne. He'd never mentioned interviewing her, and there hadn't been any notes about it in the file.

Thinking that Judy might have some information about the substitute librarian, Skye decided to have a chat with her before the evening ended. Maybe she knew about someone Yvonne had ticked off during her tenure at the Scumble River Library of whom the police were unaware. After all, it never hurt to have another suspect, especially when so many of their original ones seemed to have airtight alibis.

As Skye searched for her mother, she spotted Frannie and Justin playing Skee-Ball. The young couple appeared to be getting along fine, but Frannie's clothing choice of yellow and Justin's of red were at odds. Something was up with those two, and Skye wanted to know what. They were both extremely competitive, and now that Justin would also be in the University of Illinois's journalism program, they'd be vying with each other for grades, internships, and the attention of their professors. That kind of rivalry might not work out very well in their personal relationship.

Skye's gaze moved to the poker game. Uncle Charlie was gone and Loretta had been dealt in. Dante was no longer smiling. In fact, the only man at the table who looked happy was Vince. He was leaning on the back of his wife's chair and grinning as she gathered in a huge stack of chips.

Where in the heck was May? Skye scanned the lobby again and frowned when there was no sign of her mother. May was usually in the thick of things. She adored being the center of attention and withered if she felt neglected. Was she off pouting somewhere because Jed refused to dance and no one was making a fuss over her?

Maybe May was in the bathroom. As Skye headed toward the corridor where the restrooms were located, she passed the door to one of the two theaters and heard her mother's voice. What was May doing sitting in an empty auditorium when there was a party going on?

Skye was about to walk inside when she heard Uncle Charlie's booming baritone say, "May, honey, tell me what's wrong."

Charlie Patukas was Skye's godfather. He'd never married or had any children of his own, and he had been like a father to May, whose real dad had died when she was young.

"There's too much happening, and I feel like I'm missing something." May's voice quavered. "Between the holiday rush, Vince and Loretta's pregnancy and their new house, and the cruise Jed and I are taking with my knitting group, it seems as if everything is passing by too fast. What if I forgot something for the wedding?"

Her parents were taking a trip? When were her folks going?

Skye didn't remember May mentioning a cruise. Was her mother keeping it a secret? Skye pursed her lips. Why would she do that?

Skye needed to find out, but it wasn't easy to get information from May, and Skye didn't have time to go into a lengthy interrogation right this second. Probably not tomorrow either, since she was booked solid with the murder investigation, the rehearsal, and the dinner. And the day after that was her wedding. She'd have to wait until after she got back from her honeymoon to find out more about her mother's cruise plans.

As Skye moved down the aisle, Charlie said, "I'm sure Skye's got it under control. That girl was born organized."

May and Charlie sat side by side facing the movie screen. With their backs toward Skye, she noticed how tiny her mother seemed next to her godfather's six-foot, three-hundred-pound frame.

"That she was." May's voice held a smile. "She used to hang all her Barbie clothes according to color and length, not to mention lining up Vince's Matchbox cars by their make and model."

"See." Charlie patted May's back. "Everything will work out fine."

"I hope so." May sighed. After a few seconds, she seemed to shake off her qualms and changed the subject. "Did you taste that meatless lasagna? It was really good."

"I'll eat vegetarian pasta when Italian sausage starts growing on trees."

"Oh, Charlie." May giggled.

"But that reminds me: Did you notice how much money Wally's father and cousin seem to be throwing around? This party alone had to cost a pretty penny, and I heard the cousin paid for it all," Charlie said. "What do they do for a living?"

"Wally said they're both in the oil business and the CEO of the company they work for is very generous." May's voice reflected her pride. "Their boss is footing the bill for this party and the rehearsal dinner, and he even let Carson and Quentin borrow the company plane to fly here."

Skye smiled to herself. Apparently, Wally had already put out a smoke screen regarding his family's wealth. Telling May that his dad and cousin worked for the business rather than owned it had been a brilliant move. Anyone curious about Carson and Quentin's spending habits would eventually ask Skye's mother, who would tell them the cover story Wally had concocted. And it had the advantage of being close to the truth.

"Well, that explains a lot."

"And speaking of flying—" May broke off as she saw Skye, narrowed her green eyes, and demanded, "How long have you been standing there?"

"A minute or so." Skye narrowed her own matching emerald eyes. "Why? Are you two discussing something that I shouldn't know about?"

"Of course not," May huffed. "I don't have any secrets from you."

"Right." Skye believed that about as much as she believed in Santa Claus.

"So why aren't you at your own party?" May asked. "I hope you aren't sulking because of that stripper."

"Actually, considering everything, her act was pretty tasteful." Skye looked her mother in the eye. "I was looking for you."

"Why?" May tensed. "What's wrong? You're not calling off the wedding, are you?"

"Not in a million years." Skye shook her head vehemently, but when her mother relaxed, she said, "Although you might think this is worse." She glanced between May and Charlie. "Have you two heard what our esteemed mayor is up to now?"

As soon as Skye finished telling them about Dante's plot to do away with the Scumble River Police Department, May exploded, using words few of her friends or family would have ever guessed she even knew. She sputtered on and on, calling her brother names that questioned his parentage and his eternal salvation.

Finally, running out of obscenities, May turned to Charlie and said, "That little weasel. I looked the other way when Dante fiddled with our mother's trust fund to buy new 'toys' for his own farm, and I forgave him for trying to steal her estate away from the rest of us when she passed, but this is too much. We have to stop him. I will not let him wreck my daughter's life."

"There's no way that snake will get away with this." Charlie ran sausagelike fingers through his mane of snow-white hair. "Did he forget that I'm the president of the city council this year?"

"I doubt Uncle Dante forgot that. He must have some scheme worked out." Skye wrinkled her brow and asked, "When's the next meeting?"

"Son of a buck!" Charlie's thick white brows almost disappeared into his hairline, and he jumped up from his seat. "It's tomorrow night."

"When we'll all be at the rehearsal dinner." Skye slapped her forehead with her palm. "He planned it for when you wouldn't be able to attend. And right before New Year's Eve, when a lot of townspeople wouldn't be there either."

"Fu—" The color of Charlie's complexion was somewhere between beet and lobster. "He must have been plotting this for months."

"Do you think he's telling the truth about the incinerator being a moneymaker for Scumble River?" Skye bit her lip. "A lot of people might be willing to sacrifice the police department if they think their taxes will be lowered."

"To misquote Winston Churchill," Charlie deadpanned, "Dante occasionally stumbles over the truth, but when that happens, he picks himself up and hurries away as if nothing happened."

"How many votes does Uncle Dante need from the council to pass this?" Skye asked.

"Four. A simple majority." Charlie's blue eyes were frosty. "Which he might be able to swing if the representatives are allowed to vote in a closed session by secret ballot rather than roll call."

"Well, I can make sure everyone knows what he's up to." May patted her perfectly coiffed salt-and-pepper hair.

"And I can ensure we don't vote in executive session." Charlie looked at Skye. "But I'll have to miss your rehearsal dinner."

"Don't worry about that." Skye hugged her godfather. "Just save all our jobs."

May sprang to her feet and announced dramatically, "I need a telephone and my address book."

"I want to make a few calls, too." Charlie kissed both women's cheeks, then disappeared up the aisle, yelling goodbye over his shoulder.

"Let's go." May seized her daughter's hand and stomped out into the lobby, where she hugged Skye and said, "You have a good time and don't worry about a thing. Charlie and I will fix Dante's wagon. He'll never know what hit him."

May marched over to where Jed was sitting, grabbed her husband's arm, and spoke rapidly into his ear. Skye's father shook his head, but when May's voice rose, he hurriedly chugged the rest of his beer, struggled to his feet, and fetched his and his wife's coats from the rack. Within seconds, the couple was out the door.

Skye had no idea exactly who her mom was planning to telephone. However, she *was* certain that by tomorrow morning most of Scumble River would know about Dante's latest scheme. Thankfully, the rest of the bachelor/bachelorette party was uneventful and a lot of fun. It was well past midnight when Skye got home. And although she was tired, she immediately turned on her laptop—Wally had given her his old one when he bought himself a new model. She was determined to find out as much as possible about towns that had built incinerators.

While she waited for the ancient machine to boot up, she fussed over Bingo. The black cat hadn't been getting his usual quota of attention and pouted until she brought out his favorite treats. He pounced on the Whiskas Temptations that Skye scattered across the sunroom floor; then, after he'd found the last crunchy nugget, he hopped next to her on the love seat and purred.

Finally, the monitor blinked into life and Skye clicked on the AOL icon. And clicked. And clicked. *Crap!* The Internet was down again. As with cell phone coverage, Scumble River's wireless service was iffy at best, and apparently, tonight wasn't her lucky night.

After several attempts at other locations in the house, including the second-story balcony, Skye admitted defeat and switched to plan B—trying again in the morning.

Skye and Wally had agreed that they'd spend the two nights immediately before their wedding apart. She had wanted some time to herself before the big day and thought it would be good for Wally to have a little alone time, as well. This would give them both a chance to say goodbye to their single lives, contemplate the step they were about to take, and anticipate their future together.

Thinking about how Dante's scheme could change that future, Skye put on her flannel pajamas, washed her face, and went to bed. She was sound asleep within seconds of lying down and dreamed of billows of smoke blowing away all her hopes and aspirations as Scumble River burned.

Skye was up before six, feeling edgy and unrested. Aiming to lighten her mood, she selected a cheery butter yellow twin set to wear with brown wool slacks and her new suede ankle boots. Once she was dressed, she fed Bingo, gave him fresh water, and cleaned his litter box. As she drank a cup of coffee and ate a bowl of Special K, she tried once again without success to access the Internet.

She had promised to meet Wally at nine at the police

station in order to drive to Lawnton to reinterview Neil Osborn. Neil's secretary had said that her boss rarely got to the jobsite before ten, and Wally wanted to arrive shortly after Yvonne's ex.

But before Skye resumed her role as psych consultant, she really needed to go online. As she finished the last of her coffee, she pondered her options. The library wasn't open until later, and she didn't want to use the PD's computers in case Dante had somehow bugged them. She had no idea if that was even possible, but why take chances? Was there anywhere else she could go?

A moment later, Skye silently yelled *Eureka!* The one place in town that always seemed to have a signal was Tales and Treats Bookstore. And, thank goodness, the bookstore's café had started opening at six in order to supply the before-work crowd with their much-needed fix of caffeine and sugar. She'd indulge in a cappuccino, log on, and dig up some facts about the profitability or, she hoped, losses of municipality-owned incinerators.

Feeling slightly more optimistic now that she had a strategy, Skye headed out the door. She had a lot to accomplish within the next twenty-four hours, and she was determined to get it all done before her wedding.

When the bookstore was open, customers entered Tales and Treats through the main doorway. But during the early-morning hours, when only the coffee shop was doing business, patrons came in through the side entrance that brought them directly into the café. As Skye turned the corner into the alley and saw that the line went all the way to the sidewalk, she hesitated. Did she have enough time to wait?

Shrugging because she really had no other option, Skye joined the queue. What seemed like an eternity later, she finally greeted Orlando Erwin, the co-owner of Tales and Treats, and placed her order.

While Orlando made her cappuccino, she looked around. Most of the small tables were already occupied, and several people were tapping away on their laptops.

Relieved, Skye paid for her drink and reluctantly declined his offer of a muffin. After she'd stuffed herself the night before, it wouldn't be wise to indulge in the calorie-laden treat. At least not if she wanted to fit into her wedding dress.

Skye found a seat and had been surfing the Web for several minutes when she struck pay dirt. A city out east had built an incinerator, expecting to use the fees to pay off the construction loan and then, once it was free and clear, gradually make a profit. Instead, the town was now millions of dollars in debt.

Their problem was that the machinery had never worked correctly and they'd needed to refurbish it several times, borrowing more and more money to fix the faulty mechanisms. Who was to say that Scumble River would have any better luck with their equipment?

Skye made a note of the URL where she'd found the article, then started her second search. This time she was looking for crime statistics on towns that had eliminated their police force and relied solely on the county sheriff's department for protection.

An hour later, Skye had her facts compiled and left the café. Her next stop was the local newspaper. The *Star*'s owner and editor, Kathryn Steele, lived above its offices, and she was known for being on the job nearly 24-7. Kathryn and Dante had had many disagreements, so Skye was betting the journalist would be open to printing a special edition with the story about Dante's plans for Scumble River.

The newspaper's front counter was vacant when Skye entered the building. The space had a dusty, slightly deserted feeling to it, and the odor of ink made Skye's nose wrinkle in anticipation of the sneeze she could feel threatening the back of her throat.

The jingle of the bell above the door must have alerted the owner because Skye heard Kathryn call out, "If you have a story for me, I'm in my office. Anything else, come back at nine when Nan gets here."

"Hi, Kathy," Skye called as she made her way toward the sound of the woman's voice. "I hope it's not too early for me to stop by."

"Depends." Kathryn was seated behind a desk overflowing with papers. "Have you and that hot police chief of yours found Yvonne Osborn's killer?"

The newspaper owner was an attractive woman in her thirties. Her dark hair was held back with a large gold barrette, and diamond studs twinkled in her ears. Skye had always wondered about Kathryn's background and apparent wealth. She'd arrived in Scumble River four years ago, purchased the *Star*, and changed its content from mostly advertisements and local sports statistics to actual news.

Realizing she'd been lost in thought and hadn't answered Kathryn's question, Skye said, "Not quite yet, but we're hoping to make an arrest soon." She indicated the visitor's chair. "Mind if I sit?"

"Be my guest." Kathryn leaned forward. "What can I do for you?"

"Have you heard about the mayor's plan to eliminate the police department in order to fund the construction of an incinerator at the edge of town?" Skye asked, pulling her notes from her tote bag while she closely watched the newspaperwoman's expression.

"Not in so many words." Kathryn adjusted the lapel of her exquisitely tailored red suit. "Why don't you tell me all about it?"

Skye outlined Dante's scheme, then summed up the articles she'd researched on incinerators and towns that had eliminated their police forces. While Skye talked, the newspaperwoman scribbled furiously on a yellow pad she'd pulled from one of the towering piles on her desktop, pausing occasionally to ask a question.

After providing Kathryn with the Web addresses of the articles to back up her claims, Skye said, "So you didn't know anything about Dante's plans?"

"Well . . ." Kathryn said slowly, plainly considering how

much she would share with Skye. "Someone did mention the idea of using the sheriff's department in place of local police. And on a separate occasion this person also asked what I knew about town-owned incinerators."

"But you didn't connect the two or investigate it as a story?"

"No." Kathryn pursed her lips. "The conversations took place several days apart, and at the time, I thought the person was referring to articles that she had read and just wanted my opinion."

"Who was it?" Skye twisted the strap of her tote bag into a knot. "Clearly that person knew about the mayor's scheme."

"Sources are confidential." Kathryn tapped a perfectly manicured nail on a folder. "But I guess since she's deceased and wasn't really a source . . ." She trailed off, then seemed to make a decision and said, "It was Yvonne Osborn who brought up both topics."

CHAPTER 20

Out of Circulation

As Skye drove to the police station, a new anxiety gnawed at her. Had her uncle been involved in Yvonne's death? It appeared that the substitute librarian had been aware of the mayor's scheme. What if she had confronted him? Could Dante have been behind the wheel of the vehicle that forced Yvonne's car off the bridge? Although he didn't own an Escalade, he was partial to Cadillacs. If he were going to steal an SUV, he'd be drawn to his favorite brand.

Pushing the concern about her uncle's possible homicidal actions aside, Skye focused on another worrisome issue. The more she thought about it, the more she suspected that she should have told Wally about Dante's scheme the night before.

At the time, she'd convinced herself that she didn't want to ruin his evening. There really hadn't been a good moment during the party to drop the bombshell on Wally that his career was about to go up in smoke. Then they'd left the theater separately, so she hadn't been able to speak to him about the situation afterward either.

At least that's what she told herself, but in truth, she'd been afraid to admit to Wally that another one of her family was about to cause him problems. She was related to half the local population, so it was inevitable that her relatives would have some run-ins with the police. But how many fiascos could Wally take before he decided Skye was more trouble than she was worth? Or maybe he'd give in, do what his father wanted—move to Texas and take over CB International.

Wouldn't that be the ultimate irony? A few years ago, Skye's most fervent wish had been to escape her hometown. But slowly and surely, Scumble River and its citizens had won her over and carved a place in her heart. Now the last thing she wanted to do was leave. How could she tell Wally what her uncle was up to?

As soon as Skye turned onto the block that held the PD, city hall, and library, she realized that informing Wally about Dante's plans was now out of her hands. She watched in astonishment as an undulating wall of humanity marched in front of the building holding anti-incinerator picket signs.

The parking lot was packed, and Skye had to drive several blocks before she found a space for the Bel Air. Hiking back toward the station, she heard rumbling that she thought was thunder, but as she got closer, she realized it was angry voices.

A few more steps and she made out the words being shouted, "Hell, no! The police shouldn't go!"

Apparently, May had been able to rally a huge number of supporters with her calls. Skye had to give her mother and the grapevine credit; there were at least a hundred and fifty people marching, holding placards, and chanting. Quite a feat for a community with a population of just over three thousand. And all achieved in a little less than twelve hours.

Skye stopped in front of the throng to admire some of their signs. Miss Letitia, the ninety-year-old president of the Scumble River Historical Society, held a poster that read: BURN THE MAYOR, NOT THE TRASH. Jess Larson, owner of the Brown Bag Bar and Liquor Store, had one that said LESS COPS = MORE CRIME. And Risé Vaughn from Tales and Treats carried a notice with ANOTHER IDIOT IDEA BROUGHT TO YOU BY THE BUREAUCRATS blazing in red letters across a white background.

Edging through the mob, Skye recognized most of the protestors. Everyone she passed patted her on the back and told her they were a hundred percent behind Wally and his officers. She thanked them and kept moving, intent on reaching the door.

At the front of the building, she noticed Judy Martin standing by the door that led to the stairway up to the library. Last night, Skye had never gotten a chance to talk to Judy, so she walked over to her and said, "Quite a turnout, isn't it?"

"Yeah." Judy shook her head, her sandy brown ponytail swinging. "I'm a little shocked that so many people support the police department and are willing to show it." She wrinkled her freckled nose. "It sure makes me proud to live here."

"Do you have a minute?" Skye asked, admiring the petite brunette's vintage purple swagger coat with its oversize moonstone plastic buttons. "Has Wally talked to you about Yvonne Osborn?"

"No." Judy furrowed her brow. "Why would he? I really didn't know her."

"You hired her though, right?" Skye said, and when Judy nodded, she asked, "Did you work with her at all before you left?"

"We spent a day together while I showed her the ropes, but that's all."

"I assume you thought she was a good librarian or you wouldn't have chosen her, but what was your impression of her as a person?"

"Well . . ." Judy hesitated, sticking her hands in the coat's deep pockets. "It was clearly important to her to do the right thing, not just what was easy or expedient." Judy hunched her shoulders. "Yvonne lost her previous job because she blew the whistle on a shady deal that the library director had made with a supplier. She was willing to take the consequences of her actions and didn't try to sugarcoat what she'd done."

"That's pretty much what we've heard about her," Skye agreed. "I know there were probably a lot of people who disliked her for taking the moral high ground, but have you heard about anyone who was seriously threatened by or angry with her about her ethics?"

"She left me a folder with some of her concerns." Judy bit her lip. "In fact, I just discovered it this morning in the computer files. Evidently, she had planned on e-mailing it to me at the conclusion of her employment, but she must have been killed before she had the chance to send it." Judy sighed. "Yvonne was supposed to be on duty this week. I wasn't scheduled to go back to work until January second."

"The police will need a copy of that file."

"I already printed out Yvonne's report and dropped it off with the dispatcher." Judy glanced at her watch. "I'd better get going. It's almost time to open up the library."

"Was there anything she'd written in her notes that we should check into right away? Maybe somebody who frightened her?"

Judy opened the door, then turned and said, "There was one person Yvonne seemed more intimidated by than the others." Judy gazed at the protestors. "She had somehow found out about the mayor's plan to eliminate the police department and put up an incinerator—probably because when Dante's talking on the phone, you can often hear him through the heating vents that connect his office to mine."

"Oh?" Skye tucked away that piece of info in case she ever wanted to eavesdrop on her uncle. "Was the mayor aware that Yvonne knew about his scheme?"

"Yes." Judy nodded. "She gave him an ultimatum. If he didn't come forward and inform the townspeople about his plan before Yvonne left Scumble River, she was going to the newspaper with the information."

"Thanks, Judy." Skye waved as the young librarian disappeared up the stairs.

For a long time, Skye stood staring into space as her thoughts raced. Her fears had been confirmed. Dante *was* a viable suspect. There was no way for her to deny that her uncle had an excellent motive to murder Yvonne. Finally, she turned and walked slowly toward the police department's door.

Skye had just stepped into the station and was thinking how awkward it would be to have Dante at the wedding if she and Wally were investigating him for murder when another thought popped into her head. *Shoot!* The cake topper had to be at the bakery by two thirty today.

As promised, Isla had delivered it to the PD Wednesday night and Skye had picked it up yesterday, but she hadn't had a chance to get it to Tom Riley. And between the Dante situation and reinterviewing Neil Osborn, there was no guarantee she'd be able to make it to Laurel anytime soon.

Whom could she ask to run it over to the bakery? Skye had tried really hard not to be a demanding bride who expected her attendants to drop everything and be at her beck and call, but this was an emergency. She pulled out her cell and dialed, praying that Trixie was free.

When her friend agreed to handle the delivery, Skye heaved a sigh of relief. She quickly told Trixie where her spare house key was hidden and that the cake topper was on the dining room table, then said goodbye and went to look for Wally.

Figuring he'd be in his office, Skye made her way to the back of the station and hurried up the stairs. Pausing on the top step, she glanced uneasily to her right. A year ago, Dante had had an opening cut between the city hall and the police department, and she was always half afraid her uncle would pop out through the archway like an ax murderer in a horror flick.

When she saw that Dante's door was closed, she let out the breath she hadn't realized she'd been holding.

However, since there was a light coming from underneath the mayor's door, she tiptoed past the entrance to his lair and down the hall toward Wally's office. She knew they'd eventually have to confront her uncle, but she wasn't ready to deal with him yet. First she needed to talk to Wally.

She found him behind his desk surrounded by his officers, all of whom were speaking at once. Skye waited a few seconds, hating to interrupt, but when they continued talking, she signaled Wally with a jerk of her head that she needed to see him alone. He nodded, murmured something to Quirk, and joined her in the hallway.

Once he closed the door, Skye launched into a blow-by-blow account of what had happened since she'd learned of her uncle's scheme. She finished with, "And I'm so sorry that once again someone in my family is a pain in your rear end."

"There's nothing to apologize for." Wally hugged her. "None of this is your fault." He paused. "Except for not telling me about it last night, and I understand that you didn't want to ruin my evening."

"I should have known better. It's never a good idea to try and save someone from bad news."

"Not when that person will hear about it eventually anyway."

"Right." Skye jerked her thumb at the closed door of Wally's office. "I take it the whole force has heard about Dante's plans?"

"Oh, yeah." Wally made a face. "They all got phone calls."

"And?" Skye asked.

"And I assured them no one will be losing their job." Wally grinned. "Between the protestors and your mother, the mayor doesn't stand a chance in hell of passing his proposal at the meeting tonight."

"I sure hope not." Skye bit her lip, still not convinced everything would be okay. "You know Uncle Dante can be pretty tricky."

"I just got off the phone with Charlie and he said there isn't one city council member who is voting with Dante on this matter."

"Phew. I guess we don't need the special edition of the *Star* after all. But since it is breaking news, Kathy will probably go ahead with the story anyway." Skye exhaled loudly. "I'm glad the incinerator versus the police force issue is settled, but there's still the fact that Dante might have murdered Yvonne to keep her quiet about the whole thing."

"That is definitely the next problem we need to tackle." Wally kissed Skye. "So, who should we talk to first, the vic's ex or the mayor?"

"Dante," Skye answered immediately. "I really don't think I can concentrate on Neil Osborn until we hear what my uncle has to say. The light in his office is on. Shall we beard the lion in his den right now?"

"Give me a second." Wally stuck his head into his office, shouted until he got his officers' attention, and ordered them all back to work. Then he put his hand on Skye's waist and said, "Shall we?"

When Wally knocked on the mayor's door, Dante yelled, "Go away!"

"It's Chief Boyd," Wally called through the wood. "I need to speak to you."

"I have nothing to say to you." Dante's voice vibrated with outrage.

"He must be pouting because his scheme's been exposed," Skye said under her breath.

Wally shrugged at Skye, then announced, "Official business. Let me in."

"Leave me alone!" Dante screeched. "You're all out to get me."

Wally grabbed the knob, and Skye was surprised when it turned. She'd half expected her uncle to have locked himself in. Motioning for Skye to stay behind him, Wally entered the mayor's office.

"Get out!" Dante squawked like the penguin he resembled. "Get out! Get out! Get out!"

"Calm down, Mr. Mayor." Although Wally's tone was relaxed, his shoulders were tense. "We just need to ask you a few questions."

Dante shoved his chair back so hard, it hit the wall behind him, causing his skull to ricochet off the headrest. Blinking rapidly, he leaped to his feet, shaking his fist and screaming like a two-year-old having a tantrum. "Haven't the pair of you caused enough trouble?"

Skye stepped around Wally and confronted her uncle. "We're not the ones who tried to pull a fast one on the whole town. That would be you."

"You ungrateful little witch." Dante advanced on Skye. "You and your mother have never appreciated what I've sacrificed for our family."

"We're perfectly aware of what you've done." Skye put her hands on her hips. "Like stealing funds from Grandma Leofanti's trust and trying to grab control of her estate when she passed away."

"I never . . . That money was used for farm equipment. . . . May and Minnie understood . . ." Dante sputtered to a stop and stared into space.

Wally whispered to Skye, "Did he just have a thought, or did his brain overheat?"

Before Skye could answer, Dante clutched his chest. "I . . . I . . ." The blood drained from his face, his eyes rolled back in his head, and he toppled to the floor as if someone had yelled *Timber!*

CHAPTER 21

Easier Read Than Done

From the doorway, Skye watched as two paramedics shifted her uncle onto a gurney, fastened straps around his torso, and slid the side rail into position. One paramedic grabbed the foot of the stretcher and the other picked up the head, lifting in unison until the legs extended.

As the mayor was rolled feetfirst over the threshold, Skye asked, "Is he going to be okay?" A big ball of guilt had settled in her stomach. Had she really just given her uncle a coronary?

"He seems fine," the female paramedic answered. "His heartbeat is regular, his pulse is good, and his blood pressure is high average."

"But you're taking him to the hospital." Skye followed the gurney down the stairs. "If he's all right, why are you transporting him?"

"Mayor Leofanti says he still feels light-headed," the male paramedic explained. "And we can't rule out a transient ischemic attack."

"That's a mini stroke, right?" Skye asked, a new wave of worry washing over her. "What are the signs for one of those TIA thingies?"

"Being unable to move or feel on one side of the body, speech and vision disturbances, confusion, difficulty speaking, and the inability to follow commands," the woman answered.

"Dizziness, loss of balance and coordination, and trouble walking," her partner added.

The paramedics started toward the rear exit, but Dante pulled down the oxygen mask that he'd insisted on having and ordered, "Go out the front." When they hesitated, he lifted his head, narrowed his beady black eyes, and barked, "Move it, you morons!"

Wally had been calling Dante's wife, Olive, and May, but as he joined Skye in the city hall's lobby, he murmured in her ear, "He wants the protestors to see him and feel sorry for him. He's going for the sympathy vote, which is probably the only way he'd be reelected at this point."

"Ah." Skye's shoulders relaxed. "How did Mom take the news of Uncle Dante's collapse?"

"I would say she's concerned, but calm," Wally reported. "May's picking up Olive and driving her to the hospital in Laurel."

"Trust Mom to be there for her brother even though he just tried to pull a fast one that would have put her out of work and forced us to leave town." Skye's voice held a touch of admiration. "Of course, if it turns out Dante killed Yvonne, Mom might reconsider. Even she won't be able to forgive murder."

"I don't think May has to worry about that." Wally's expression was a cross between relieved and disgusted. "Olive told me that she and Dante were at the mall in Kankakee shopping between four and five thirty, then drove straight to your folks' place for the family Christmas Eve party. Do you recall when they got there?"

"They were already at the house when I walked in at six." Skye paused, searching her memory about that night. "Their Cadillac was right by the garage, with three or four cars parked behind it, so they had to have been among the first to arrive. And it's a good half hour to drive from Kankakee to Scumble River."

"Olive said that Dante caused a scene at Bath & Body Works because someone cut in front of them in line, so the people who work there will probably remember them." Wally rubbed the back of his neck. "She still has her receipt, and she says the time stamp should be around five thirty. I sent Martinez to Kankakee to talk to the clerks and check the store's security tapes."

"Which leaves us with Neil Osborn. The only one of our suspects with a motive and no supportable alibi."

"Yep." Wally took Skye's arm and steered her toward the garage. "We need to head to his development site right now. It'll take us at least an hour to get there."

"Okay." Skye quickened her pace to keep up with Wally's long strides. "Did you read that file Judy Martin dropped off with the dispatcher this morning?"

"Uh-huh." Wally opened the squad car door. "It listed King Housley's fake injury, Earl Doozier's improper control of his dog, and Dante's transgressions, as well as a few library infractions—cutting pages from books, going to forbidden Web sites, et cetera."

"So, nothing new, huh?" Skye asked as she slid into the Caprice.

"Not a darn thing." Wally pulled the Chevy into the street, waving at the protestors who were shouting words of encouragement and brandishing their signs in support of the police department.

Skye and Wally discussed wedding details for most of the drive—what time he'd pick her up for the rehearsal that night, when she wanted him at the church the next day, and if he should stop by Vince's for a haircut. Then, just as they were turning off the highway, "Mama Told Me Not to Come" sounded from Skye's tote bag.

She dug out her cell, flipped it open, and said, "Hi, Mom. How's Uncle Dante?" She turned on the speaker so Wally could hear the conversation.

"He's fine." May sounded annoyed. "I think he faked the whole thing."

"Oh?" Skye was more than half convinced her mother was right.

"The ER doctor said that for an overweight, older man with a type A personality, Dante is in remarkable shape." May *tsk*ed. "Even as a boy, he'd pretend to be sick if Mama or Daddy caught him being bad."

"Still, it's a relief he didn't have a stroke." Skye saw a sign that read THE GREENS OF LAWNTON, AN ENVIRONMENTALLY FRIENDLY ESTATE COMMUNITY and said quickly, "Thanks for letting me know Dante's all right, but I've got to go. Wally and I are about to talk to a suspect. See you tonight at the rehearsal."

"Glad your uncle is okay." Wally patted Skye's knee, then gestured to the huge stone columns at the entrance. "This place looks pretty ritzy."

"Yes, it does." Skye gazed at the spectacular custom homes situated on one-acre lots. "I thought Tom Riley said that Neil's original plan was to build ecofriendly housing for middle-income families."

"But he also said that Osborn had been corrupted by the money and being environmentally responsible turned into a scam for him." Wally stopped the Chevy in front of a construction trailer with a sign that read OSBORN & GASKIN BUILDERS. "I wonder what he meant by that."

"My guess is that Neil no longer believes in the cause, but he's making money off of his customers' desire to live green."

"Maybe." Wally walked around to Skye's side, and when he opened her door, he added, "But it could be something shadier."

"True." Skye noticed that they were parked next to the same Honda Civic that Hank Gaskin had been driving the day they saw him at Neil Osborn's house. She touched Wally's arm and said, "Did Neil's partner strike you as the type of man who would drive an economy car?"

"I hadn't thought about it." Wally shrugged. "Maybe it's his work vehicle."

"But—"

"Look over there," Wally interrupted, pointing to his left. "This property is located between a golf course and a forest preserve."

"A perfect way to ensure that nothing will be built next to the subdivision."

"So Osborn can boast that his homes are adjacent to boating, fishing, and hiking and biking trails." Wally whistled. "Plus, I noticed a commuter train station nearby."

"These houses have to be going for more than a million each." Skye looked around, then revised her estimate. "Maybe a million and a half."

As they were chatting, the door to the trailer swung open and Hank Gaskin stepped out onto the metal stairs. He wore expensively tailored slacks and a cashmere sweater, and a Rolex glinted on his wrist.

Hank smiled and said, "Come on in." Waving at them, he continued. "What kind of house are you interested in? We have several plans available that you can customize, or we can work from your architect's diagrams. Whichever way makes you feel most at home."

Skye slid a glance at Wally. Considering he was in uniform and they had arrived in a squad car, did Hank really think they were potential buyers? How much did the cops in Lawnton make?

Wally winked at her, then said, "I'm Chief Boyd from the Scumble River Police Department, and this is our psychological consultant, Ms. Denison. We're here to talk to Neil Osborn. Is he inside?"

"No." Hank jerked his thumb to the right. "He's at the playground we're putting in. I handle the land acquisition and sales end of things and Neil's the construction guy."

"Okay." Wally nodded his thanks, then commented, "I guess it's a good thing the winter's been so mild. I'm a little surprised you're still able to work this late in the year."

"We've been lucky. The ground's not even frozen yet." Hank shuffled from foot to foot, then said over his shoulder as he scooted back inside, "Neil's over that way. Just follow the path through those trees."

"Got it." Wally took Skye's arm and said in a low voice, "I wonder why Gaskin was so anxious to get rid of us." He chuckled and guided her over a root. "I guess because he figured out we weren't buyers."

"A lot of people are nervous around police officers or psychologists. Or both."

Skye and Wally emerged onto a large expanse of lush green grass. In the center, Neil Osborn was directing a group of workers who were assembling a huge complex of slides, swings, climbing nets, and a gigantic artificial oak tree with two decks built into its fake branches.

Skye poked Wally and whispered in his ear, "Shouldn't an ecofriendly community have real trees, not plastic or concrete ones?"

"One would think." Wally nodded, then raised his voice and called out, "Mr. Osborn."

Neil looked toward them, frowned, and said something to one of his men. His expression smoothing out as he sauntered over to where Wally and Skye stood, he asked in a pleasant tone, "What are you doing here, Chief Boyd? Have you found out who killed Yvonne?"

Wally ignored Neil's question and herded him out of earshot of the workers. "Did you really think you could get away with lying to us?"

"What are you talking about?" Neil's thick black brows drew together.

"You told us that you and your ex-wife had an amicable divorce, but that wasn't true." Wally's eyes were icy. "Was it?"

"I stand by my statement." Neil crossed his arms and attempted to stare down Wally. "Yvonne and I got along just fine."

"That's not what her new boyfriend told us."

"Of course he'd say that," Neil blustered. "Yvonne probably told him we didn't get along so he wouldn't be jealous. Or maybe he wants to implicate me in her murder, so you don't look too hard at him."

"He has a reliable witness who puts him an hour away from the scene at the time of her death." Wally leaned against a stack of two-by-fours. "And every one of Yvonne's friends and colleagues whom we've spoken with corroborates his statement about your relationship with your ex-wife while vehemently disagreeing with yours." Wally put his hands in his pockets. "So why did you lie to us?"

"I ... I ... I wasn't lying, exactly." Neil's shoulders slumped, and he looked every year of his age. "But maybe I was telling you how I wish it had been rather than how it ended up being." He exhaled noisily. "At one time, back when we were young, I really loved Yvonne, and I never wanted things to end up the way they did."

"Killing her, you mean?" Skye asked in a gentle voice. "Maybe it was an accident. Were you following her too closely and lost control of your car?"

"No!" Neil yelped. "I didn't. I meant the divorce and the fighting."

"But you can see how it looks," Skye continued, her tone understanding. "An ex-wife whom you don't get along with is murdered and you lie to the police. That isn't the behavior of an innocent man."

"Plus you don't have an alibi," Wally pointed out.

"But I do," Neil protested. "I was home with my wife." He looked at Skye. "Don't you remember me telling you that?"

"Sorry." Skye shook her head. "We have to assume a wife will lie for her husband. Either because of love or financial security."

"My partner came over about seven. You can ask him."

"The critical time is between four forty-five and five

fifty-five." Skye shrugged. "So a witness to your presence at seven is too late. At most, it's an hour's drive from Scumble River to Laurel."

"Even though Yvonne and I fought, I didn't hate her." Neil's voice cracked. "Don't you think you have to really hate someone to kill them?"

"There are a lot of motives for murder." Skye rubbed her hands, trying to warm them up. "Love, hate, revenge, money, jealousy."

"None of those apply to me." Neil straightened and his expression hardened. "Now, arrest me, or I have to get back to work."

They asked Neil several more questions, but he didn't crack, and without enough evidence to charge him, they had to let him go.

"Son of a buck!" Wally cursed as he and Skye walked back to the squad car. She was trying to think of something comforting to say when Wally's phone rang.

He answered it, listened briefly, then hung up and said to Skye, "That was Martinez. Dante's alibi checks out."

"I guess that's good news," Skye said as she examined her suede ankle boots. *Yuck!* They had green marks on the heels and toes. She must have gotten grass stains on them when she walked on the playground.

"I suppose." Wally turned the key and started the engine.

While she pondered whether the stains would come off her new shoes, a random thought popped into Skye's head. "Hey, I never asked if you searched Yvonne's house for clues. I mean, since she wasn't killed there, did you even think it would be a good use of your time?"

"We searched it the day we learned she was murdered, but didn't find anything helpful." Wally steered the squad car toward the highway. "What made you ask about that now?"

"I was thinking about the file she left for Judy on the library computer. Maybe she had something similar on her home PC."

"Hmm." Wally's expression was thoughtful. "We didn't find a computer at her house. I'll have to ask Phoebe if her mother owned one." He narrowed his eyes. "I also need to find out when the vic's wake and funeral are being held. They released the body this morning."

"Poor Phoebe. Since Yvonne didn't have any relatives, I hope Neil helps his daughter with the arrangements."

"I'm sure he will, if for no other reason than because it would look bad if he didn't." Wally glanced at Skye, then said, "We need to talk to Osborn's wife ASAP. It'll be faster if we go straight to Laurel from here to speak to her. Are you okay with that?"

She checked her watch. It was only eleven thirty. "Sure." They didn't have to be at the church for the rehearsal until five.

"Great." Wally patted her leg. "Let's go to a drive-thru and eat on the way to Osborn's house."

"Anything but McDonald's." Skye sighed. So much for healthy eating. "Since Mickey D's is the only fast food in town, sometimes it feels like I'm turning into a Chicken McNugget."

CHAPTER 22

Much Overdue
About Nothing

Kerry Osborn wasn't what Skye had been expecting. For some reason, she had pictured Neil's new wife as extremely young, with a centerfold body and a vacuously gorgeous face. The woman who answered the doorbell was none of the above. Instead, she appeared to be somewhere in her mid- to late thirties with an average figure and a mousy brown ponytail. In fact, Kerry looked a lot more like the media's stereotype of a librarian than Yvonne had.

While these thoughts were zipping through Skye's mind, Wally stepped forward, extended his hand, and said, "Mrs. Osborn, I'm Chief Boyd, and this is the police psych consultant, Ms. Denison. May we come in and speak with you for a few minutes?"

"Sure. Come on in. Excuse the mess." Kerry tucked a flyaway strand of hair behind her ear. "Is this about poor Yvonne?"

"I'm afraid it is." Wally stepped inside. "Last time we were here, you were ill so we didn't get a chance to talk to you."

"Neil told me." Kerry led them into the kitchen. "The baby is down for his nap, so I'm trying to get the prep work for dinner out of the way." She waved Wally and Skye to seats at the counter. "Neil's usually starving when he gets home, and I like to have the meal ready to hit the table as soon as he walks in."

"So you're feeling better?" Skye asked, climbing onto the stool.

"Thank goodness, yes. And thank goodness I was sick during winter break, not when school was in session. I'm a kindergarten teacher here in Laurel and having a sub for a week is a nightmare." Kerry picked up a paring knife and resumed mincing onions. "Luckily, Neil never came down with it, so he could take care of our son."

"That is fortunate. Speaking of your husband," Wally said in a deceptively casual tone, "Mr. Osborn told us that he had to run an errand on Christmas Eve, so he was gone from about four o'clock until nearly six."

"He did?" Kerry frowned. "He must be confusing that with a couple of nights before, because after we got home from church Christmas Eve, we never left the house."

Wally shot Skye a quick glance, then twitched his shoulders. She figured he was indicating that he'd struck out with his lie. She squeezed Wally's knee, asking for permission to take over.

When he nodded slightly, Skye said, "How odd that Neil misremembered."

"I think with the holidays, then me getting the flu, Neil is a little discombobulated." Kerry put the chopped onions into a Baggie and started slicing tomatoes. "He even brought home the wrong file the other day. That's why he had to go out Thursday night. He was so upset when he discovered that he didn't have what he needed and he had to run all the way back to Naperville."

"What a bother." Skye rested her elbows on the counter. "I thought most records were computerized nowadays." She smiled wryly. "At least that's what the kids always tell me."

"Neil's old-school." Kerry finished the tomatoes, went

to the refrigerator, took out a bunch of carrots, and started shredding them. "He and his partner like to work from hard copies."

"Is there anyone, besides you, who can confirm that Neil was home from four forty-five until six on Sunday evening?" Skye leaned forward with an encouraging look. "Maybe a neighbor?"

"No. Not that I can think of. Phoebe was supposed to be here, but you know about that." Kerry slowly put down the grater and frowned. "Surely you aren't thinking that Neil might have killed Yvonne?"

"We're trying to rule him out," Wally assured her, then added, "Just to tie up any loose ends. We have to look into the victim's ex-husband; otherwise when we find the murderer, his or her lawyer will say we didn't investigate all the possible leads."

"But . . ." Tears welled up in Kerry's hazel eyes. "He would never hurt the mother of his child." She swiped at the moisture on her cheeks. "Sure, he and Yvonne had their differences . . ." She trailed off. "But there was never anything violent between them."

"It's hard to imagine someone we love doing anything really evil," Skye sympathized.

"Shoot!" Kerry smacked the cutting board with her palm. "If only Hank had been on time, he could have seen that Neil was here."

"Your husband's partner was supposed to be at your house earlier than he was?" Skye asked.

"Uh-huh." Kerry nodded. "But he and his wife had some kind of tiff, and he ended up just dropping Phoebe's and Neil Junior's gifts off and leaving. Which is a shame since he lives in Chicago and that's a long round-trip for nothing. I think maybe Bobbie Sue might have kicked him in the shins, because he was limping pretty badly. She has a temper and Hank was in a real weird mood. He was sort of both excited and upset. Like one of those manic-depressive people."

"It is a shame he wasn't on time," Skye commiserated. "Is there anyone else?"

"No . . ." Kerry shook her head, paused, then cried out, "Wait a minute! I just thought of something. Since this is Neil Junior's first Christmas, we recorded the whole evening. I started the camera at four thirty and didn't shut it off until the baby fell asleep after Hank left at quarter after seven."

She ran over to the built-in desk, grabbed a laptop, and placed it in front of Skye and Wally. After powering it up, she clicked on an icon and fast-forwarded until the monitor was filled with Neil sitting on the floor with a ten-month-old that looked just like him.

A huge flat-screen television was on in the background, and Kerry tapped its image on the computer monitor. A meteorologist was reporting Santa Claus's progress. And in the bottom right corner, *5:20 P.M.* glowed in red.

There was no way that Neil could have forced his ex-wife off the bridge at four forty-five and been home in thirty-five minutes. Also, even if he left his house in the next second, he couldn't have made it to Scumble River before six o'clock. Unless the recording had been tampered with, Neil Osborn had an ironclad alibi.

"Shit! Shit! Shit!" Wally thumped the steering wheel. He'd been mute since leaving Kerry and Neil Osborn's house. "If that home movie is legitimate, our last suspect just bit the dust."

"Maybe Phoebe will have remembered something." Skye tried to keep the discouragement out of her voice. "She's had a few days to think things over." They were on their way to talk to Yvonne's daughter.

Wally grunted.

"It could happen," Skye insisted, sneaking a look at her watch. It was nearly two. The rehearsal was in four hours, and the wedding was the next day. They were running out of time. This might be a case they didn't solve. At least not until they got back from their honeymoon, and by then the trail would be stone-cold.

Wally snorted, then was silent during the rest of the drive. When they finally pulled into Yvonne's driveway, there was a moving van backed up to the front door. They got out of the squad car and hurried over to where Phoebe was directing two men carrying a sofa.

When she spotted Skye and Wally, she rushed toward them. Meeting them halfway, she asked, "Did you find out who murdered my mother?"

"Sorry." Skye patted the young woman's cold hand. "Not yet. Have you thought of anyone else who might have wanted to harm her?"

"Just the ones we already talked about." Phoebe's shoulders slumped.

"Did Tom Riley leave a message on your answering machine the night your mother died?" Skye asked.

"Yeah." Phoebe nodded. "A couple of them."

"But you didn't call him back to tell him what had happened to her?"

"It was a couple of days before I listened to the messages, and by then I figured he'd already heard about the accident." A tear ran down Phoebe's cheek. "Besides, I just couldn't talk about it."

"I see you're moving." Wally broke the silence that had fallen after Phoebe's last statement. "Where are you going?"

"The lease is up, so I'm putting everything in storage and moving in with Dad and Kerry until I go to college in the fall." Phoebe grimaced. "Not my first choice of living arrangements, but it's the only practical solution, and I can help out with Neil Junior."

"Have you arranged for your mother's burial yet?" Skye asked gently.

"She wanted to be cremated and have her ashes scattered in the wind." There was a catch in Phoebe's voice.

"Her motorcycle club will do that for her on their next run."

"No service?" Skye asked, knowing Wally would want one of his officers to attend to see if anyone acted suspiciously at the wake or funeral.

"No." Phoebe shook her head. "Mom wasn't religious, and I can't face the idea of standing there while people say all the stupid stuff they say at wakes and funerals."

"I understand," Skye said, her heart going out to the teenager.

"One more thing and then we'll let you get back to work." Wally gestured toward the moving van. "When we searched the house the day after your mom died, we didn't find any computers. I know you had your laptop with you. Did your mother have one of her own, or did she just use yours?"

"Mom had her own," Phoebe said. "But hers was at the repair shop when you went through the house. I got it back yesterday." She half turned. "It's in my car. Do you want to see it?"

"We'll need to borrow it for a while." Wally followed Phoebe as she took off at a trot toward the bright green cube-shaped vehicle parked off to one side. "I'll make sure you get it back as soon as we're done with it."

"No rush." Phoebe handed him a black canvas case. "I told Mom to just buy a new laptop and not even bother to get this one fixed. It's as old as the Rolling Stones and as useful as a piece of shit."

After Wally and Skye finished with Phoebe, they drove back to the police station, where they spent the next hour going over Yvonne's computer. Unfortunately, several files were locked. Despite numerous guesses, they weren't able to figure out the password, and when they called Phoebe, she said she didn't know it.

With all of Yvonne's possessions packed and in storage, it was unlikely that Phoebe would run across a list of her mother's passwords anytime in the near future, so Wally decided to try the crime lab and hope the techs could work on the laptop right away.

He dialed the lab, then pressed the speaker button to allow Skye to hear the conversation. After he explained what he needed, the tech said, "Sorry, Chief. Unless you have a suspect in custody, we won't be able to get to the computer until Tuesday at the earliest. With New Year's Day on Monday, most people around here already took off for the long weekend."

Skye had been more than half afraid that Wally would insist on taking the laptop to Laurel himself, so when she heard the tech's statement, she breathed a sigh of relief. Then, when she saw how frustrated Wally was with the situation, she was sorry for being so selfish and tried to think of a way to help him.

After a few seconds of thought, she said, "Since the lab can't do anything until January second, why don't we ask Justin to try to open the files? He's helped me out several times."

"I can't let a civilian hack into a computer." Wally crossed his arms.

"Hire him as a consultant. He's a real computer wizard, and he could use a few extra bucks for college. What do you have to lose?"

"That might work." Wally thought it over, then shook his head. "But I don't know if what he finds would be admissible in court."

"Can you check with someone?" Skye asked.

A short phone conversation later, Wally turned to her and said, "According to the city attorney, we might as well let Justin give it a try. Nothing on the computer would be allowed as evidence anyway because the laptop has been at the repair shop, where files could have been altered."

"Okay, I'll call Justin and see if he's available and thinks he can help us."

Justin answered on the first ring and agreed to Skye's

proposal, saying he'd be at the PD in five minutes. He cautioned her that it might take him several days to get into the files. Once he arrived, completed the paperwork for his temporary employment, and left with the laptop, Skye and Wally went over every bit of information they had on the case. They reread all the reports, trying to come up with some angle they hadn't yet explored. Finally, at four, Skye called a halt to their brainstorming session and decreed that they both needed to go home to get ready for the rehearsal.

Wally reluctantly agreed, and they walked out to the parking lot together. It wasn't that Skye didn't trust Wally, but she *did* watch to make sure he actually got into his T-bird and drove away from the police station before sliding behind the wheel of her own car. As she steered the Bel Air down the familiar road toward home, she had mixed feelings. While she was glad that both she and Wally were now officially off duty until they returned from their honeymoon, she was disappointed that they hadn't yet figured out who had killed Yvonne Osborn, or why.

With only forty-five minutes to shower, curl her hair, and reapply her makeup, Skye was just pulling on her clothes when she heard the front door open and Wally's voice announcing his arrival. She hurriedly slipped on her shoes, then caught a glimpse of herself in the full-length mirror and hesitated. *Yikes!* When she had purchased the dress for the rehearsal, she'd been afraid the skirt was a little short, and now, after two weeks of holiday overeating, the hem was well above her knees.

Not wanting to be late, Skye knew she didn't have time to change, so with a silent apology to the gods of fashion, she hurried down the stairs. As always, Wally was breathtakingly handsome in a charcoal gray suit, steel blue shirt, and red silk tie. He whistled when he saw Skye, and she ran into his arms. Maybe the dress wasn't too snug after all.

However, once the rehearsal was over an hour later,

Skye stood at the back of the church thinking maybe she should have put on something else, if for no other reason than to avoid the inevitable criticism from her mother.

May tugged at Skye's skirt and fussed, "This is way too tight on you." Leaning forward, she hissed in Skye's ear, "Have you gained weight? What if your wedding gown doesn't fit?"

"Thanks so much, Mom," Skye drawled. "You look real nice, too."

"I wish I hadn't let you talk me into this outfit." May frowned, yanking at the waist-length beige lace jacket she wore with a brown satin tank and matching slacks. "It's too fancy for me. Everyone will be saying, 'Who does she think she is?'"

Skye smiled, happy her mother's attention had been diverted from her daughter's clothing choice to her own appearance. Because although Skye's dress was more figure-hugging than her normal choice, and more of a mini than she usually preferred, she loved the soft red material shot with silver threads. And the boat neckline was both elegant and flattering. Most important, Wally loved her in it.

Realizing that May's mind had wandered and she was now complaining to her son that he had ruined her hair, Skye looked around. The rehearsal had gone smoothly, and the bridal party and their significant others were waiting in the narthex for Wally's father to appear and tell them where the dinner was being held.

Quentin had cornered Wally as soon as the priest dismissed them, and the two men were having what appeared to be a serious discussion off to one side. Wally caught Skye's gaze and twitched his shoulders, indicating that he was trapped and she nodded her understanding.

Looking away from where her fiancé and his cousin stood, she glanced nervously toward the entrance. Where was Carson? Should she interrupt Wally and Quentin to ask what was going on? Before she could decide, a huge white limousine pulled up in front of the building.

Skye watched through the church's glass doors as Carson Boyd emerged from the rear of the limo, strode inside the building, bowed to Skye, and said, "Your carriage awaits, darlin'."

"Wow!" Skye was as close to speechless as she ever got. "All I can say is wow." She grinned at her future father-in-law and shook her head. "I guess when I said that I didn't want people to have to drive too far for the dinner, you took me seriously."

"I certainly did, sugar." Carson beamed. "I knew you were worried about people driving home under the influence." He dusted his hands together. "I thought a limo would solve that problem and still let us eat at a decent restaurant."

"Where are we going?" Skye asked, excited to learn Carson's choice.

"Tallgrass in Lockport." Carson took her elbow. "Have you been there?"

"No."

"*Chicago* magazine named it one of the top-twenty restaurants and *Zagat* gave it a twenty-eight out of thirty rating." Carson's Texas twang increased as he spoke enthusiastically about the restaurant.

"That sounds wonderful." It was a good thing Wally had given May a cover story for his father's spending habits. "But it may be a little extravagant for my friends and family." Skye worried her parents and attendants might be uncomfortable. Their taste ran more to the Lone Star Steakhouse than to fine dining.

"Trust me." Wally joined them, putting an arm around Skye. "It's not a little extravagant." He rolled his eyes at his father. "If Dad picked it, the place is over-the-top."

CHAPTER 23

Many Happy Book Returns

When they first arrived at Tallgrass, Skye felt a flicker of disappointment. The stone-and-brick Victorian building wasn't what she'd envisioned when Carson had described the top-rated restaurant. And as her future father-in-law escorted her down an uneven flight of concrete stairs, she glanced uncertainly at Wally, who shrugged as he opened the door for her.

Stepping over the threshold, Skye heard her mother mutter to Uncle Charlie, "Why do we have to come in through the basement?"

Uncle Charlie's answer was lost when the hostess greeted Carson, Skye, and Wally and took their coats. Once the rest of the bridal party had assembled and been divested of their outerwear, the woman showed them into an area to the right of the lobby. Here the cherrywood wainscoting and antique gas chandeliers were more what Skye had been expecting.

The large room was empty of any other diners, and three long tables were positioned in a U-shape to accommodate the fourteen people in their party. Cut-crystal goblets and wineglasses sparkled next to beautiful china, and polished silver was nestled on snowy-white napkins, creating a stunning setting.

As Skye gazed at the vacant tables scattered around the rest of the space, the hostess came up to her and murmured, "We usually do private events at the Tallgrass Loft in the Norton Building, but that was already booked, so Mr. Boyd purchased the entire second seating."

"Wow." Skye smiled at the woman's awed tone. "How thoughtful of him."

Once everyone had taken their places, three servers appeared and handed out specially printed menu cards that had WALLY AND SKYE in a heart on the top. As she studied the choices, her mouth watered. This could very well turn out to be the best meal she'd ever eaten.

To Skye's right, Trixie and her husband conferred over the selections. While Trixie seemed delighted, Owen's brow was wrinkled in confusion. Glancing around, Skye noted that her parents, Uncle Charlie, and Justin shared Owen's bewilderment, but Loretta, Vince, Frannie, Grandma Denison, and Father Burns were on Team Trixie.

After drinks were served, Wally and Skye got to their feet, and Wally said, "Skye and I would like to thank all of you for being not only a part of our wedding, but also a part of our lives. And for giving us your time and energy to help make our big day special."

Wally and Skye lifted their wineglasses, and she saluted, "To our friends and family."

Carson rose, turned to Wally and Skye, and said, "May you always work as a team. Because if you don't pull in the same direction, you'll be hanged by the rope."

Quentin advised, "May you always be partners, friends, and lovers." He winked. "But not necessarily in that order."

Trixie popped up next and giggled. "May Wally be a man who will mess up your hair, not your mind."

Before anyone else could come up with a toast, the first course was served. Skye had chosen the trio of soups, and she was amazed to see that the snap pea/fennel, potato/mushroom, and watercress/sweet onion were all in the same bowl, but somehow separated into three distinct sections.

As Skye sampled her soup, she checked out the other guests' responses to their appetizers. While she watched, Owen picked up a sprig of watercress from his salad, examined it as if it were a foreign object, then chomped off the end like he was biting off a wad of chewing tobacco. Trixie followed Skye's gaze and swatted her husband's shoulder. He grinned and snatched a morsel from her plate.

To Owen's right, Justin was inhaling his butter-poached wild prawns as if he were a surgeon who had to get back to a patient he'd left on the operating table. Suddenly, he stopped and poked suspiciously at the balsamic bubbles on top of the shishito peppers; then, apparently deciding they weren't poisonous, he shoveled a forkful into his mouth.

Jed and May had different methods of attacking the unfamiliar food. Jed popped a whole crab beignet into his mouth; then, with his jaw moving as speedily as a sewing machine needle, he chewed and swallowed the delicacy. After a moment, he grunted his approval and reached for another beignet.

May, on the other hand, approached her sweet red pepper panna cotta like a finicky feline presented with a new cat food. Using her spoon, she broke off a tiny piece of the custard, then took rapid little bites like a chipmunk eating an acorn. Once she had sampled the dish, she switched to her fork and dug in.

Ten minutes later, Charlie finished his bruschetta salad, wiped his mouth on his napkin, and said, "For fancy crap, that was pretty darn good."

After Charlie's pronouncement, they progressed through the remaining three courses without incident, and even those who had seemed daunted by the menu were *ooh*ing and *aah*ing over the food. Conversation was lively, and everyone appeared to be having a great time.

Two hours later, dessert was served. Skye gasped when hers was placed in front of her. Four dark chocolate walls bordered a flourless chocolate cake foundation, and the entire towering structure was filled with raspberries and whipped cream. Her plan to take just a tiny taste flew out the window at the first spoonful. Lord have mercy, she hoped she could get into her wedding dress the next day.

Most of the party had finished eating when Skye and Quentin simultaneously excused themselves to freshen up. They chatted as they walked toward the bathrooms, and Skye found herself enjoying Quentin's company. She wondered about his relationship with Wally and hoped that after spending time together during the wedding activities, the two men would become closer.

As Skye and Quentin paused outside the restrooms, she said, "I'm so glad Wally asked you to be his best man. It's nice that he has his family to support him tomorrow. Sometimes I feel bad that there's no one who lives closer to him since I have so many relatives within a five-mile radius."

"That's his choice." Quentin's expression was hard to read. "He could be in Texas working at CB International with me and his dad. His father has been trying to persuade him to do just that ever since we got here."

Skye was about to defend Wally's choice when something clicked, and instead she said, "But you wouldn't want that, would you?"

"Truthfully?"

Skye nodded.

"No. And not because he'd be stepping into my shoes." Quentin made a face. "I just don't think he's cut out for that kind of job, which is what I was telling him after the rehearsal."

"Why do you say that?"

"He's too honest." Quentin raised a brow, clearly daring Skye to make a comment. When she didn't, he continued. "Wally is too much of a Dudley Do-Right. There aren't a lot of shades of gray in his world."

"I see." Where had Skye heard that before? "And that would be a problem why?"

"Because it would threaten the business. Which means not just the Boyds but thousands and thousands of employees and their families."

"Can't you do the right thing as a company?"

"Not always." Quentin shook his head, a stubborn look on his face. "Sometimes you have to do what you have to do to keep the business in the black and beat your competition."

"And Wally would never be comfortable cutting those kinds of corners."

"Forget comfortable." Quentin laughed. "He just plain wouldn't do it."

"True. And he wouldn't allow you to do it either." Skye narrowed her eyes. "Which would be the real problem, right?"

"Absolutely." Quentin thrust out his jaw. "And I could never allow him to threaten our company. So it's just as well that he keeps turning down Uncle Carson."

Skye contemplated Quentin's words while she used the facilities. Something about what he had said niggled at her subconscious, but when she returned to the table, Grandma Denison struggled to stand in order to give one last toast before the group left the restaurant, and her words pushed aside what Skye had been pondering.

Cora Denison was Skye's only remaining grandparent. At eighty-six, she had buried a husband, two stillborn babies, and a teenage grandson. Up until a year ago, she'd made a batch of her famous Parker House rolls nearly every Sunday, but she had been failing for quite a while, and Skye was thrilled that her grandmother had felt well enough to attend the rehearsal. Now she gazed tenderly at the old woman who was such an important part of her life.

Cora leaned heavily on her cane, but her voice was strong. "Skye and Wally, my wish for you is a long and happy life, with few cares and sorrows and many friends who are faithful and true." She paused, then added, "And may your voyage through life be as happy as the dancing waves on the deep blue sea."

At Cora's last few words, May snickered and Skye looked at her mother. What was so funny about that?

A little before seven a.m. Saturday morning, Skye bolted upright in bed. Yawning and stretching, she quickly glanced out the window. Although all the local meteorologists had promised it would reach fifty degrees today, with only a slight chance of drizzle, she was beyond reassured to see that there was no snow falling or ice crystals coating the glass.

For the past six months, May had been hyperventilating about a blizzard shutting down the wedding. After hearing her mother's dire prediction so many times, Skye had almost begun to believe it would come true. But May had been wrong. The weather would be just fine. In fact, it might be a tad too warm for the bridal gown Skye had chosen, which was something she could deal with in exchange for a nice day.

Once Skye had showered and put on her favorite blue tracksuit, she strolled downstairs. Bingo was waiting in the kitchen by his food bowl, and before she put the kettle on to boil, she took care of his needs. As she sipped a cup of tea, she realized that it felt funny not to be rushing somewhere. But as far as she could tell, everything was ready. She had nothing to do for nearly two hours, until her hair and makeup appointment at nine.

Still full from last night's amazing dinner, Skye was trying to decide if she should eat something despite her lack of appetite when the doorbell rang. Setting her mug on the table, she headed down the hall. Her aunt had picked up the ceremony and reception boxes yesterday, so she wasn't expecting anyone. A ripple of apprehension flashed down her spine as she peered out the window and saw Frannie and Justin on her porch. What in the heck were *they* doing here?

"You've got to see this." Justin rushed inside as soon as Skye opened the door.

"Sorry," Frannie apologized. "I know this is probably the last thing you want to do the morning of your wedding, but Wally's not at the police station and we felt kind of funny going to his house."

"Look what I found." Justin thrust the laptop at Skye and kept talking as she squinted at the small screen. "I finally got into the files this morning, and I totally understand why she had them password protected."

"Let's go sit in the kitchen." Skye gave up trying to read the wobbly monitor. "I have a feeling I'll need coffee for this."

Once they were settled around the table with cups of French Roast at their elbows, Skye studied the documents that Justin had brought up on the computer. She read each page several times before she fully understood what she was seeing. According to Yvonne's notes, Neil Osborn's so-called ecofriendly housing development was built on contaminated acreage.

"Now, this is something that a person would kill over," Skye muttered half to herself.

"That's what we thought." Frannie reached across Skye and brought up another file. "See, here it says that Yvonne gave her ex-husband until the day after New Year's to own up to what his company was doing or she was going to the authorities. She states that he claimed she was mistaken about the property being polluted, but she thought he was just trying to wiggle out of taking responsibility for what he'd done."

"I wonder how she found out about the tainted land," Justin said, taking a sip of coffee.

"I bet I know." Skye got up, ran upstairs, then returned with the suede ankle boots she'd been wearing when she and Wally had visited the development. "I thought these were grass stains on my shoes, but I bet they're some kind of dye Neil was using to make the turf look green."

"Why do you think that?" Frannie asked.

"Because the lawn around the construction trailer was brown. Only the playground and the finished houses had green grass." Skye scraped a fingernail along the marks and sniffed. "This smells like chemicals."

"There was an exposé that I used for a talk in one of my journalism classes about a developer who built on a contaminated site and it was discovered because the grass would never grow right." Justin wrinkled his brow. "In fact, I made Xeroxes of the article at the Scumble River Library a month or so ago to include in my handouts. I was one short, so maybe I left it in the copy machine."

"And Yvonne could very well have found the article, read it, and remembered it when she visited her ex's development." Skye tapped her mug with her spoon. "And I know she was there a couple of weeks ago because her daughter said they drove out together to show Phoebe's father her college acceptance letter."

"So Neil Osborn had a zillion-dollar motive to shut up his wife," Frannie said excitedly.

"There's only one problem. He has an alibi." Skye explained about the recording. "Unless it was somehow altered." She turned to Justin. "Can that be detected?"

"Yes." Justin nodded, then added, "But faking something like that would be pretty difficult. You'd have to have really sophisticated computer graphic equipment and know how to use it."

"Most likely not something a kindergarten teacher or a contractor could do without help." Skye sagged in her chair.

"Sorry. No." Justin shrugged. "Not unless they had a digital recording background. And anyone they asked to do it for them would probably want to know why."

"Yeah." Frannie put her chin in her hands. "Would they trust someone to keep quiet? Especially after the murder made the news?"

"That's a good point." Skye checked the wall clock and was surprised to see it was only quarter to eight. "I'd better let Wally know what we've found."

When Wally didn't pick up his home or cell phone, she left a message for him to call her back. Then Skye checked with the PD, but the dispatcher said she wasn't expecting him. Realizing she'd just have to wait for Wally to return her calls, Skye pulled up a chair and asked Frannie about college.

"I really like it at U of I." Frannie beamed. "And it will be even better next year with Justin there."

"Oh?" Skye glanced between the two young people. "I'm glad to hear that. You know, earlier I had the distinct impression that there was some kind of problem. Has it been settled?"

"Well . . ." Frannie snuck a peek at her boyfriend, who gestured for her to go ahead. "The money Justin was counting on for school didn't come through, and since his folks can't afford to help him, it looked as if he might not be able to go."

"So what happened?" Skye was well aware that Justin's parents could barely manage their own bills. Mr. Boward was in constant pain, and his wife suffered from a debilitating depression, which meant neither was able to hold down a job.

"Uh . . ." Frannie bit her lip. "Uh, someone agreed to pay for his next two years."

"Great!" Skye smiled. "Who?"

"Uh . . ." Frannie hesitated again.

"Simon," Justin blurted out, then said a little defiantly, "I know you didn't pick him, but he's still a nice guy."

"Of course he is. And although I don't feel about him the way I do Wally, I still love him as a friend." Skye patted Justin's hand. "I'm just surprised he has that kind of ready cash. He's not superrich."

"No, he isn't," Frannie said. "But he makes quite a bit of money from the funeral home and earns a salary as the coroner, too, so he's better off than most people around here."

"Still, even though I agree he's a nice guy and has the money, why would he pay Justin's tuition?" She turned to the young man. "You're not related to Simon, are you?"

"I wish," Justin muttered, then explained, "Simon told me that he'd done really, really well in the stock market the last few years and he'd been considering setting up a scholarship for local kids. So when Frannie told him my problem, he decided that I would be the first recipient. His only condition is that I earn at least a B average, and when I graduate, I have to mentor another Scumble River student who wants to attend U of I."

"That's just incredible." Skye was overcome at Simon's altruism. "I had no idea he was so generous."

"Well, he is." Frannie thrust her chin out. "And he feels bad that you didn't invite him to the wedding. Why didn't you?"

"It would have been awkward," Skye explained. "Are you sure he would want to come?"

"Yes. That way he can show everyone he's not a loser and you two are okay." Frannie ducked her head. "And I think his new girlfriend really wants to go, so he feels bad he can't take her."

"Why would Emmy want to come to my wedding?" Skye asked, confused.

"Duh." Justin grunted. " 'Cause it's the place to be."

Frannie translated her boyfriend's observation. "She's new in town, and she wants to be accepted as part of the community. Being at your wedding would give her a chance to meet people and mingle."

"I see." Skye thought about what Frannie and Justin had said and something clicked in her head. Simon and Emmy both had a similar motive for wanting to attend her wedding, although Emmy's was less obvious.

"You could still invite him," Frannie prodded. "I could let him know right now." She whipped out her cell, her fingers flying over the tiny keyboard.

"Sure," Skye murmured absently, still thinking about motives. Who else, besides Neil, would lose millions if Yvonne revealed the company's use of contaminated land? "Oh, my God!" Skye squealed.

"What?" Frannie and Justin asked simultaneously.

"Hank Gaskin." Skye reached for her phone just as it rang. "Hank Gaskin killed Yvonne."

CHAPTER 24

If Books Could Kill

"So you see, he had as much motive as Neil." Skye had explained to Wally about the polluted property, and now she was making her case for Hank Gaskin as the killer. "Plus, he was late getting to the Osborns' on Christmas Eve, he was limping when he arrived, and Kerry described his mood as weird." Her words poured out faster and faster as all the pieces fell into place. "I bet he hurt his leg in the crash. I wonder if he has a white 2006 Escalade or—"

"Whoa," Wally broke in. "You've made a lot of good points. But before we get ahead of ourselves, let me check if Gaskin owns or leases a vehicle that fits our evidence."

"We also need to find out what was formerly on the land they're developing." Skye's eyes flashed. She had a gut-deep feeling that they were on the brink of figuring it all out.

Justin tapped Skye on the shoulder and said, "I can do that."

She relayed his message to Wally.

"Tell Justin that he's still on the clock as a consultant," Wally instructed. "And he needs to e-mail the info to me as soon as he finds it."

"Got it." Skye gripped the receiver. "Call me back as soon as you know anything."

When she disconnected, Justin whirled on her. "Why didn't the police check to see if this guy owned an Escalade to begin with?"

"Since he lives in Chicago, it wouldn't have been within the parameters of Martinez's search." Skye described how a vehicle investigation worked; then, feeling a little defensive, she added, "And he was never a suspect because we had no idea that Yvonne's death was tied to her ex-husband's company. Not to mention the two times Wally and I saw him, he was driving a Honda."

Justin grunted and turned back to the laptop, clearly not satisfied with her explanation.

As Skye raised her brows at Frannie, who shrugged, the phone rang. She snatched the receiver from its base and, seeing Wally's name on the caller ID, demanded, "Does Gaskin own a 2006 white Escalade?"

"Yes. The Civic belongs to his son."

"I knew it." Skye pumped her fist in the air. "What now?"

"I just called Osborn's secretary—she gave me her cell number in case I needed to reach her away from the office—and she told me that Gaskin's been driving the Honda since the day after Christmas."

"Which matches our timeline."

"Now we have to figure out where he stashed the Cadillac." Wally's voice was grim. "Because of all the TV crime shows, he probably thinks it's a lot easier to find a hit-and-run vehicle than it really is, so he wouldn't park it in a public garage."

"And he lives in the city, so I'm guessing it has to be at a job site."

"Or wherever his company stores their construction equipment." Wally paused. "I've sent Quirk and Martinez to pick up Gaskin for questioning, and as soon as I can get a warrant, I'll assign Anthony and whoever else is available to go check all of his business's sites and facilities."

"You're going into the station, aren't you?" Skye's stomach tightened. Would he be late for their wedding or even, God forbid, miss it altogether?

"I have to." Wally's tone was cautious. "But I promise to be at the church on time. I'd never stand you up."

"I know." Skye forced a cheerful note into her voice. "In about forty-five minutes I'm leaving the house to have my hair and makeup done at Vince's salon, but I'll have my cell with me. Keep me updated."

"Will do. Love you." Wally hung up, clearly eager to get to the PD.

While Skye and Frannie fixed breakfast, Justin surfed the Web, hunting for information about the Lawnton site's previous occupant. When Skye slid a plate of bacon and eggs in front of him, he mumbled his thanks and ate without taking his eyes off the monitor.

Skye and Frannie talked about the day's schedule until Justin shouted, "Found it!"

Peering over his shoulder, Skye and Frannie both demanded, "What?"

"Gaskin's development is on land that used to have a facility that made porcelain enamel frit for steel." Justin tapped the screen. "The plant was in operation from 1917 through 1978. The metals utilized in making the porcelain contained lead, nickel, cobalt, and chromium, which are all potentially toxic. And the structure that housed the factory had asbestos insulation."

"Oh, my." Skye pointed to the last paragraph on the monitor. "It says here that the process's waste products and the asbestos taken out of the building when it was torn down were discarded on the northwest corner of the property. That's where the playground is going in."

"All those kids exposed day after day to carcinogens." Frannie shuddered. "I wonder if Mr. Osborn knew what his partner was up to."

"I'm sure that's a question we'll be asking Gaskin

when we interview him." Skye checked her watch. It was time to forget about the investigation and think about her wedding. She said to Justin, "I need to get over to Vince's right now. Can you make sure Wally sees this info?"

"I've already e-mailed it to him, along with Mrs. Osborn's files." Justin closed the laptop and headed for the door. "I'll see you at the church."

"Two thirty sharp. Don't be late." Skye turned to Frannie. "You need to be at the salon at ten."

"Trixie and Loretta are picking me up at a quarter to." Frannie patted Skye's shoulder. "Just relax. We've got your back."

Ten minutes later, Skye walked into her brother's shop, and he immediately went to work on her hair. Once Vince had finished coaxing her natural curls into a cascade of ringlets down her back with a few tendrils surrounding her face, he secured her Swarovski crystal tiara to the crown of her head, then turned her over to the cosmetician he'd hired to do the bridal party's makeup.

Due to a little gentle persuasion on his wife's part, Vince had recently expanded his business and employed two additional hairdressers, so when Trixie, Loretta, and Frannie arrived, all three could be styled simultaneously.

It was nearly noon by the time they were all coiffed and made-up, so they headed to May's, dropping Skye's car at her place on the way. Skye breathed a sigh of relief when she walked into her folks' house and saw that all the Christmas decorations had been put away.

Skye and her mom shared a teary embrace, and May sobbed, "I can't believe my baby is getting married. I've dreamed of this day since you were born."

"Really, Mrs. D?" Frannie asked, a note of astonishment in her voice. "You literally started planning this wedding as soon as you went into labor?"

"Yes. I certainly did." May narrowed her eyes at Frannie, daring the young woman to dispute her statement. When Frannie was silent, May said to the group, "I fixed you a bite to eat. You'd better sit right down because the photographer is due in an hour."

Skye had butterflies in her stomach, but she knew better than to refuse lunch. It was never a good idea to rile May, especially not today of all days. Besides, dinner wouldn't be served at the reception until seven, and she didn't want her stomach to growl during the ceremony.

While everyone else chatted and ate May's homemade broccoli cheese soup and chicken salad croissants, it hit Skye that in three hours she'd be Mrs. Walter Boyd. Skye Denison Boyd. She smiled. It had a nice ring to it.

As soon as they were finished eating, May shooed them into Skye's old bedroom, where their wedding finery had been stashed. Trixie and Frannie quickly put on their dresses, and Loretta struggled into hers—Skye swore her sister-in-law had gotten even bigger since last night when she'd seen her at the rehearsal.

While her attendants were changing, Skye shed her tracksuit, blessing the article she'd read that suggested wearing a top that opened down the front and didn't have to be taken off over her freshly styled hair. Then she exchanged her bra for a strapless bustier and slipped on her stockings and a long petticoat.

Gesturing to her gown, she said, "I think I'm going to need help getting into this thing."

Frannie lifted the dress from where it hung from the top of the door, unzipped it, and spread the full white charmeuse satin skirt so Skye could step into it. Once she was in the center, she slid on the long sleeves and tugged the off-the-shoulder décolletage into place.

Sucking in, Skye said, "Okay, do me up." If the dress wouldn't fasten, she would so regret eating the tower of chocolate last night.

Frannie grabbed both sides of the material and pulled them together; then Trixie took hold of the tab and inched the zipper upward. Once it was closed, Skye let out a relieved sigh. It was a little tight, but she could still breathe.

Loretta adjusted the marabou-trimmed neckline and stepped back.

"How do I look?" Skye asked.

At that moment, May appeared in the doorway dressed in an ecru beaded-taffeta sheath. She sighed. "Like a princess." She hugged Skye and whispered in her ear, "Honey, remember to enjoy the little things because when you look back at your life, you realize that they were really the big things."

"Thanks, Mom." Skye blinked back tears. "I will."

May sniffed, then announced, "The photographer's here."

The photographer snapped pictures of Skye gazing into the mirror, being rezipped into her gown, and putting on her shoes, then herded them into the living room.

As he was arranging them all into an elaborate pose on the sofa, Frannie whispered to Skye, "Have you heard from Wally yet about the case?"

"What about it?" May's head snapped up and swiveled in her daughter's direction.

"Uh . . ." Skye stalled.

"Don't make me call the PD." May waved her finger in Skye's face.

Recognizing the futility of trying to keep the information concerning the break in the case from her mother, Skye explained the morning's events and Wally's work at the station. May's expression went from curious, to dismayed, to horrified. She collapsed against Frannie and grabbed her chest, moaning.

Afraid her mother was about to have a nervous breakdown, Skye hastily added, "Wally promised he'd be at the church on time and I trust him."

May took a deep breath, visibly composed herself, and said, "Then I do, too."

Skye hugged her mom, and while the photographer pondered his next shot, she said, "Would someone go grab my purse for me?"

Frannie fetched the handbag and Skye checked her

cell. Wally had left a voice mail. "We just got the warrant to search the construction company's properties and Gaskin's residence. No one answered the doorbell at his house, but now we can legally gain entry. So far, Quirk and Martinez haven't been able to locate our suspect, but they'll keep trying. I'm headed home to change. Dad, Quentin, Vince, Justin, and your father are already there. See you soon."

Skye relayed Wally's message to her mother, who was reassured to hear that Wally had left the PD and was home getting dressed. Once May's stress had been alleviated, Skye and her attendants posed for a couple more photos.

Finally, the photographer gathered up his equipment and announced, "I'm going over to the groom's to take some pictures of him and his guys getting ready."

With the photographer on his way, Skye took a minute to thank her bridesmaids and to give them their gifts—ruby-and-pearl pendants. At two thirty, they piled into the limo that was waiting in the driveway—a much more modest version than the one Carson had provided the night before—and left for the church.

As they were driven the short distance to the ceremony, Skye silently recited the old rhyme. She had her something old—Grandma Leofanti's bracelet; something new—her gown; something borrowed—May's handkerchief; and something blue—the bow on her garter. She was all set.

The parking lot was full when they arrived, and Skye smiled in relief when she saw Vince's Jeep. He'd been the one in charge of transporting the groom. She and her attendants slipped into the side entrance, hurriedly ducking into a small room at the back.

The florist waiting in the anteroom pinned a corsage of crimson amaryllis blossoms and Hypericum berries on Skye's mother; then May went around front, where Uncle Charlie would escort her to her seat. A similar corsage had been given to Skye's grandmother, whom May would join in the front pew.

Next, the florist handed Trixie, Frannie, and Loretta domed nosegays of white hydrangeas with long, red satin streamers gathered at the ends in soft ruffles. Skye's bouquet consisted of tiny pinecones tipped in glitter, forming a halo around scarlet roses and baby's breath ringed with white marabou.

Almost immediately, Father Burns knocked and asked if everyone was ready. When they said yes, he instructed the bridesmaids to line up and told Skye that he'd send her father in to her.

Skye heard the music change and pictured Frannie walking toward the altar, followed by Loretta, then Trixie. Soon it would be her turn. She fingered the necklace that Wally had presented to her after the rehearsal dinner. The two swirling ribbons—one lined with shimmering baguette-cut diamonds and the other with glittering round diamonds, forming an X—matched the earrings he had given her for Christmas. She marveled at how lucky she was. It amazed her that her very ordinary life had turned into such a magical love story.

Before Skye could get nervous, Jed opened the door, tugged at his tuxedo shirt collar, and said, "Guess this is it."

Skye took his arm and they moved into position at the end of the aisle. When Pachelbel's Canon in D started, she looked at her dad and asked, "All set?"

He squeezed her hand, then said, his voice husky, "You know I like Wally, and I think you're good together, but if you're not sure, I'll walk out with you right now. Don't worry about your ma being mad. I'll take care of her."

"I'm sure, Dad." Skye blinked back her own tears. That was the longest speech she'd ever heard from her taciturn father. "I love Wally with all my heart. And I'm positive that he's the man I want to spend the rest of my life with."

Jed kissed her cheek and grinned. "Then let's get 'er done."

As Skye walked down the aisle, all she could see was

Wally. In his Class A uniform, he was strikingly hand-some. The three gold stars on the epaulet of his jacket glinted in the light that streamed through the stained-glass windows. Catching her breath, she stared in awe. Wally truly was her prince. His crisp black hair, chocolate brown eyes, and rugged profile were something out of a fairy tale.

Wally's expression when he stepped forward and took Skye's hand was one of both love and devotion. Skye knew that this man would never let her down. Her heart was beating so loudly, she barely heard her parents' response to the priest's question of who gives this woman to be married.

The rest was a blur until Father Burns asked, "Walter and Skye, have you come here freely and without reser-vation to give yourselves to each other in marriage?"

Wally and Skye gazed into each other's eyes and said, "I do."

They also affirmed the priest's next two questions: Will you honor each other as man and wife for the rest of your lives, and will you accept children lovingly from God and bring them up according to the law of Christ and his Church?

Then Father Burns said, "Since it is your intention to enter into marriage, join your right hands, and declare your consent before God and his Church."

Although many priests did not allow the bride and groom to write their own vows, Father Burns had permit-ted Skye and Wally to do so as long as they included the traditional Catholic wording as well.

In a steady voice, Wally said, "I, Walter Boyd, take you, Skye Denison, to be my wife. I promise to be true to you in good times and in bad, in sickness and in health. I will love you and honor you all the days of my life." He smiled tenderly and continued. "I promise to always en-courage you. Whatever may come, I will create dreams with you and live every day in love with you. This is my solemn pledge."

Hoping she could get through her vows without crying, Skye answered, "I, Skye Denison, take you, Walter Boyd, to be my husband. I promise to be true to you in good times and in bad, in sickness and in health. I will love you and honor you all the days of my life." She took a deep breath. "I give you my heart and my dreams. From this day forward, I swear to nourish your mind, comfort your spirit, delight in your joy, and share in your sorrow. I will love you and hold you close for the rest of our lives."

Next, Father Burns blessed the rings and gave them to Skye and Wally to exchange. Once the rings were on their fingers, the priest said, "You may now kiss your bride."

Wally took Skye in his arms, and as his lips touched hers, it felt as if her very world trembled. The kiss lingered until the priest cleared his throat and they finally drew apart. During the remainder of the Mass, Skye thought of the path that she'd taken to find Wally and become his bride. It hadn't been an easy trek, but it had been worth every step to be where she was now.

Finally, the recessional music started to play and Skye took Wally's arm. Walking down the aisle as husband and wife, she thanked God for where her journey had led her.

CHAPTER 25

Throw the Book At

As the last couple went through the receiving line, Skye felt Wally's cell start to vibrate. They'd been standing close together, but she stepped away and pointed below his belt. "Is that your phone or are you just happy we're married?"

Wally gathered her into his arms, kissing her thoroughly. When they came up for air, he said, "What do you think, darlin'?"

"I think you better answer that thing before it shakes right out of your pocket." She poked his thigh. "It's probably about the case."

"Are you sure you don't mind?"

"I want Yvonne's killer caught as much as you do." She lifted one shoulder. "At least we got through the ceremony before they called you."

"Not quite." Wally grinned. "Didn't you feel the phone vibrating during the 'you may kiss the bride' part?"

"Now you tell me." Skye shook her head. "And I thought it was you rocking my world."

"I'll rock your world, all right. Just wait until we're alone," Wally growled; then, when the phone started pulsating again, he sighed, flipped it open, and said, "Yeah?"

Skye, cuddling close to Wally, heard Quirk say, "We have Gaskin in custody. We should be at the station in less than half an hour. Once Martinez and I gained entry to his house with the warrant, we found him hiding in the closet."

"Has he said anything?"

"After we read him his rights, he just kept screaming something about it not being his fault." Quirk's tone reeked of disgust. "And since I don't speak moron, I couldn't make out what he meant by that."

"How about the search?"

"The guy has huge gambling debts." Quirk snickered. "Gaskin was probably hiding from the sharks as much as from us."

"Any word on his Escalade?"

"Our guys found it in the construction company's Naperville equipment barn." Quirk sounded like he was reading from his notebook. "There was bumper and fender damage consistent with forcing a car off the road and wood slivers that are similar to the bridge's railing. The seat was adjusted to Gaskin's height and there was dried blood on the steering wheel."

"Send someone over to the crime lab with the Escalade ASAP and tell the supervisor this is an emergency. They need to call a couple of techs in and process the vehicle right away." Wally frowned. "It's crucial that we know if the wood matches the bridge and the blood matches the suspect before we question him."

"Will do." Quirk's salute could be heard in his voice. "Anything else, Chief?"

"Let Gaskin cool his heels. I'll talk to you when you get to the PD."

Wally put the phone in his pocket and turned to Skye. "I'm really sorry. I know you'll be upset, but I need to interrogate Gaskin before we leave for our honeymoon."

"I knew who you were and what your values were before I agreed to marry you." Skye raised an eyebrow. "Besides, I want to be there for his questioning, too." She tapped her foot. "I want you to take me for better or worse, not for granted."

"Never for granted. I promise." Wally put his hand over his heart. "Any idea of *when* the best time would be for us to go talk to him?"

"How long can you hold Gaskin without charging him?"

"Twenty-four hours."

"What time do we need to leave Scumble River tomorrow?"

"Let's see." Wally wrinkled his forehead. "Our flight will take three hours. We have to be at our destination by three p.m. our time in order to catch our transportation for the next leg of the trip. Dad has offered to drop us off on his way to Texas, so we should leave town no later than nine a.m. That would put us at the airport by ten thirty. Security for private flights is a lot quicker than commercial, which means the plane will be able to leave by eleven. That would put us where we need to be by two and gives us some breathing room in case of any delays."

"Then, since we're spending the night at the house, we could talk to Gaskin in the morning. If we plan on being at the station by six a.m., we'd have three hours. And by morning you'll probably have the wood and blood results from the crime lab." Skye looked at Wally. "What do you think?"

"I think we won't get much sleep tonight."

Skye leaned closed and whispered into his ear, "I hadn't planned on it anyway."

Their embrace was interrupted by the photographer, who herded them toward the altar. During the planning phase, he had informed Skye that the pictures at the church would take about an hour. With that in mind, she had arranged for cocktails and appetizers to be served to their guests at the Country Mansion from five until six thirty.

The photographer took the group shots first, then allowed everyone else to leave for the reception while he finished up with Skye and Wally. The wedding party was waiting for them in the banquet hall's foyer when they arrived, and as soon as they stepped through the door, Skye knew something was wrong. Her mother's face was red and Jed had his head down and his hands in his pockets.

The moment May spotted Skye, she hurried over and shrieked, "Everything's ruined! The Dooziers are already drunk, and Simon showed up with that flashy blond stripper from the bachelor party. I can't believe he had the nerve to crash your wedding."

"The Dooziers will be fine." Skye crossed her fingers, then said to Vince, "Can you keep an eye on them?"

"Sure." Vince squeezed Skye's shoulder. "I'll ask the cousins' husbands to help me."

"Great." She smiled at her brother, then said to May, "Simon didn't crash."

Skye turned to Wally and explained what Simon had done for Justin and what Frannie had said about his reasons for wanting to come to the wedding.

Wally nodded his understanding and asked, "Can you squeeze him and Emmy in at Bunny and Spike's table?"

"That's a terrific idea. The reception coordinator said the tables could hold ten, but I had her set them for eight since I hate being crowded at events like this." Skye hugged him, both for his helpful suggestion and his understanding about her motive for inviting Simon. "Trixie, can you take care of that?"

"No problem." Trixie hitched up her dress and dashed into the banquet hall.

"You're not going in until everyone's seated." May thrust out her bottom lip. "I don't want people watching the chairs being arranged instead of you."

"Sure." Skye hugged her mom. "But let's line up so we're ready."

Trixie was back in a few minutes and reported that all the guests were seated and she'd cued the DJ. Each member of the wedding party's entrance was broadcast until only the bride and groom were left.

When the DJ announced, "And introducing Mr. and Mrs. Walter Boyd," everyone cheered.

Skye and Wally waved at their friends and family as they walked to the head table, and she noticed her uncle Dante seated with his wife. She had wondered if he'd attend, because of both his trip to the hospital and his anger over the thwarting of his incinerator scheme, but he looked healthy and was as close to smiling as he ever got.

The food was delicious and Skye was surprised to find that she was hungry. She'd chosen the baked Cornish hen glazed with orange-ginger, and Wally had selected the butterflied steak wrapped in smoked bacon. While they ate, she gazed around the beautifully decorated space. The two walls of windows that overlooked the gardens and Dwight's historic windmill were the perfect frame for the rest of the room.

Skye was relieved that the Dooziers appeared to be behaving themselves. The bar was closed during the dinner hour, which would give them a chance to sober up. As she smiled and waved at Earl, she tried to figure out what he was wearing.

He had on black plastic glasses that looked like the goggles that the kids wore to play virtual reality games. But since the Dooziers already lived in an alternate dimension, what would he need with those?

At least Earl didn't have on his usual camouflage sweatpants. Instead, he wore a chartreuse satin leisure suit. And Glenda's considerable endowments were only half hanging out of her pink pleather bustier. The black hot pants, fishnet stockings, and go-go boots were a bit much, but the waist-length platinum blond wig with the big red velvet bow was the pièce de résistance.

After dinner, it seemed to Skye that time went by too quickly. It felt as if the reception had barely begun when the cake was being wheeled to the center of the room to be cut. Tom Riley had done a magnificent job and the stunning red-and-white four-tiered creation elicited many *oohs* and *aahs.* Once Wally and Skye had fed each other a bite, the photographer informed Skye that she should now throw the bouquet.

As Trixie escorted Skye to the dance floor, Trixie grabbed Frannie, who had been heading in the opposite direction, and said, "You're not missing this."

"Sure." Grinning, Frannie said, "I just don't want to be the one who gets so into catching the bouquet that it looks as if she's trying for the last loaf of bread during the zombie apocalypse."

Skye laughed and was a little relieved when one of the single teachers nabbed the flowers. Frannie really was too young to think about getting married.

The garter toss was next. Anthony caught the lacy, blue satin loop, blushed, and immediately glanced at his date, Judy Martin. Afterward, while Wally and Anthony were surrounded by their friends, Skye slipped outside to cool off. As she had feared, the heavy bridal gown was too hot for the mild weather.

As she stepped through the exit, Simon caught the door and said, "Thank you for inviting me."

"You're more than welcome." Skye smiled fondly at him. In appearance, Simon was the direct opposite of Wally. Although both men were tall, Simon was lean rather than muscular, with stylishly cut auburn hair and golden hazel eyes. "I'm just sorry it was so last-minute. I would have sent you an invitation if I'd had any idea you wanted to attend."

"I understand." Simon leaned against the building and stared at the sidewalk. "Anyway, Emmy is having a great time, and I appreciate the chance to show everyone that there are no hard feelings between you and me."

"I'm glad that you've accepted we aren't a good match." She patted his arm. "And I'm really happy that you've found someone else."

Simon straightened and shoved his hands into his pants pockets; then he lifted his gaze to hers and said, "I didn't give up on you because I don't care anymore but because I realized that you didn't."

Before Skye could think of a reply, he turned and walked back inside. She followed him; then, still pondering his last statement, Skye looked for her new husband. Simon always had been enigmatic, but that was no longer her problem.

When Skye reached Wally's side, he was watching the Dooziers dance. Or at least she thought that's what they were doing. It looked a little like a cross between the Macarena and the Hokey Pokey. Glenda, MeMa, and Bambi were lined up with Earl, Junior, and Cletus facing them.

MeMa, the family's octogenarian—or maybe nonagenarian—matriarch, was wearing leopard-print harem pants with a mesh crop top. And as she flipped her hands up and down to the music, the clearly visible black bra underneath her shirt bobbed up and down, too. Skye was half afraid the old woman was going to knock herself out with one of her boobs.

Bambi, Earl's thirteen-year-old daughter, had on what Skye thought might be a leftover Halloween costume. The purple velvet dress had long puffy sleeves and a handkerchief hem, and at the waistline, trios of black roses were sewn to a satin ribbon. Suddenly the teenager grabbed her cousin Cletus's hands. The couple do-si-doed around the room, treating anyone who didn't get out of their way like bowling pins meant to be knocked over.

Until the Dancing Dooziers started using the other guests as targets to be eliminated, Wally and Skye had been amused by their antics, but as Cletus and Bambi attempted to pick up a seven-ten split, Skye signaled to her cousins' husbands, who moved in and escorted the duo away.

Thank goodness Earl and Glenda had left the dance floor to line up at the bar and missed their offsprings' removal. Otherwise, the couple might have felt compelled to defend the family honor and start a fight. As it was, the clan stood out like artichokes on strawberry shortcake, and the last thing Skye wanted was for anyone to get their just deserts.

Around eleven, Skye asked the DJ to announce the last set of songs, and she and Wally began to say their goodbyes. As Skye kissed her mom's cheek, she was surprised that May didn't order her to phone home during her honeymoon.

Normally, her mother would need at least a couple of calls reassuring her that Skye hadn't died in a fiery plane crash or been eaten by a rogue alligator. Figuring her mother's attention had now turned toward her grandchild's impending birth, Skye's thoughts flashed to Loretta.

Thank goodness, her bridesmaid hadn't gone into labor during the reception. Skye had been ninety-nine-percent sure that they'd have to call the paramedics to deliver the baby on the dance floor.

It took nearly half an hour to finish their goodbyes, but Skye and Wally finally made it into the limo. As they were driven toward Scumble River, Wally said, "Everything was wonderful. You did an amazing job planning our wedding."

"You know me. I overprepare, then go with the flow."

"Well, it flowed perfectly."

"It *was* nice." Skye snuggled next to him. "But that's not how I measure the success of the day. For me, the real success was the way you looked at me as I walked down the aisle."

"Darlin'," Wally murmured into her hair, "I promise that's the way I'll look at you all the rest of our lives."

Twenty minutes later, Wally carried Skye over the threshold. He had insisted on honoring the tradition, and she was relieved that he hadn't hurt his back lifting her, but she wasn't taking any more chances and insisted on walking up the stairs under her own power.

Skye had candles scattered around the room and the

CD player ready with Rod Stewart's "Tonight's the Night."

By the time she changed into an emerald green lace baby doll, Wally had lit all the candles and stripped down to a pair of black silk boxers.

When she appeared in the bedroom doorway, he pushed the CD's ON button. Slowly and seductively, his gaze slid down her body; then he took her hands and gently eased her onto the satin sheets. A ripple of excitement shot through her as he joined her, and suddenly she ached for his touch.

He slid the gown off her shoulders and down her arms, then kicked off his boxers and gathered her against his chest. Skye instinctively arched toward him, and together they found the tempo that bound their bodies together. A moan of ecstasy slipped through her lips, and she knew that she had found the man who not only unlocked her heart, but also her soul.

Morning came much too soon. As Skye woke up, she realized that she and Wally had been able to make love—several times—and Mrs. Griggs hadn't destroyed anything. In fact, there was a scattering of rose petals on the bed that Wally swore he hadn't placed there. Had Trixie been right? Was the pesky poltergeist happy now that Skye and Wally were married?

Smiling at that happy thought, Skye got dressed, and by six a.m., Wally's T-bird was loaded with their honeymoon luggage and they were on their way to the police station. The prisoner had been held overnight in the station's sole cell. It was located in the basement and rarely used, since most of the Scumble River detainees were transported to the county jail in Laurel.

Skye and Wally slipped in through the garage entrance, and Quirk had Gaskin waiting in the coffee room. Wally and Skye's goal was to accomplish the interrogation without anyone else becoming aware of their presence. The last thing they wanted was May finding out they had delayed their departure and were still in town.

Gaskin was seated at the table, the remains of his breakfast—an Egg McMuffin and hash browns—scattered in front of him. The night in jail had taken its toll on the man. His shirt was wrinkled, there was a stain on his khakis, and his thinning hair stood on end. He looked every one of his fifty-eight years.

Skye took the seat facing him and Wally leaned against the counter to the suspect's left.

Wally waited until Gaskin's claims of innocence had sputtered to a stop, then confirmed, "You've been read your rights?"

"Yeah." The stocky man sulked. "But I'm not paying any shyster lawyer to tell me what to do when I haven't done anything wrong."

"Really?" Wally took his notebook from his shirt pocket. He was dressed in his uniform and would change before leaving for the airport. "Because we know all about the contaminated land and Yvonne's threat to expose your company's fraud. We also have a witness who saw you threatening her with a crowbar on December twenty-third, just one day before she was murdered." Wally paused, then delivered the coup de grâce. "And we have your Escalade in custody."

"How . . ." Gaskin gulped, a look of panic on his face. "I mean, where did you find it? Someone took it on Christmas Eve."

"Did you report it stolen?"

"Uh." Gaskin wrinkled his brow. "I, uh, have been meaning to, but with the holidays, I was just too busy."

"Right." Wally's voice was knife-edged. "The vehicle's bumper was damaged, and we were able to get both wood and paint scrapings from it. The lab results from those samples should be back any minute. We're certain the wood will match the bridge Yvonne Osborn was forced off and the paint will match her car."

"You're saying whoever took my Cadillac killed poor Yvonne?" Gaskin's voice cracked. "Well, it wasn't me."

"The seat in the Escalade was adjusted for your height and there was blood on the steering wheel." Wally crossed his arms. "Remember being tested last night? We already know the blood in the SUV is your type, and we're running the DNA right now."

"That doesn't prove anything." Gaskin puffed his chest out. "I cut myself shaving the other day. The blood is probably from that."

"Or it's from the gash on your knee." Wally shrugged. "We have a witness who will testify that you were limping that night after the time of the murder."

"You're twisting everything." Gaskin slumped forward. "Maybe I do need a lawyer."

"Only if you want to escalate the proceedings." Wally hooked his thumb in his belt loops. "And it'll take a lot more time. I hope you don't have anything planned for the rest of the day."

"I . . . I . . ." Hank scrubbed his eyes with his fists and looked at Skye. "What do you think I should do?"

"Well, you do have a right to counsel, Hank." She reached across the table and patted his arm. "But then you won't be able to tell us your side of the story. We won't know the mitigating circumstances of the situation." She paused to let him think about what she'd said, then asked, "Do you want to call your attorney?"

"No. I guess not." Gaskin sniffed, obviously realizing he was running out of options.

"Well, you can anytime." Skye didn't want the judge to throw out his confession because Gaskin's rights hadn't been upheld. "But let me tell you what I think happened." She smiled reassuringly at him. "I think you were trying to catch up with Yvonne that night to talk to her. You were probably going too fast, so your Escalade slid on some ice and you accidently nudged her car off the road."

"Yeah. That's it." Gaskin nodded vigorously. "I just wanted to ask her for more time so we could clean up the site." He straightened and spoke faster. "But she slammed on her brakes and I hit her." He smoothed back his hair. "I tried to help her, but it was clear she was already dead and I panicked and left."

"So you admit you were behind the wheel?" Skye wanted to make sure it was clear that Gaskin had been the one driving the Escalade that forced Yvonne off the bridge.

"Yes." Gaskin nodded. "But I didn't mean to kill her."

"Buzz. Wrong answer." Wally pounced. "We have evidence that proves there was no way Yvonne's car crash was an accident."

"But—but," Hank stammered, then pointed at Skye. "But she said—"

Wally interrupted him. "The forensics can prove Yvonne was intentionally forced off the road." Wally raised a brow. "If, as you claim, you had hit her in the rear, there wouldn't be paint from your SUV on the side of the victim's vehicle."

"Hank." Skye made her voice soothing and her expression sympathetic. She needed this scumbag to confess so she could go on her honeymoon. "If you tell us what happened and show remorse, I bet the prosecutor will take the death penalty off the table."

Gaskin buried his face in his hands and refused to speak.

Wally stepped over to him and snatched his arm. He pushed up the man's sleeve and said, "I hope you have good veins. Because if you don't, they have to poke around with the needle, and all the time they're jabbing you, you're wondering, 'Is it going to be now? Am I going to die now?'"

Gaskin's head jerked up, and sensing he was about to crumble, Skye asked, "Did Neil force you to help him kill his ex-wife?"

"Sort of." Gaskin collapsed against the back of the

chair, a broken man who clearly had run out of ideas on how to deny his guilt. "Neil discovered that I had bought polluted land when he took the wrong file home. He told me that Yvonne knew and was going public unless we cleaned up the contamination and informed the buyers of what had previously been on the property." Gaskin paused. "Neil told me to take care of the problem. That he wasn't going down because I was a fool."

"So when you threatened her on the twenty-third and she ran you off with a shotgun, you felt you had no choice but to kill her?" Skye asked. "Does Neil know you were the one who ran her off the bridge?"

"I think so." Gaskin shrugged. "He told me that he was glad I had taken care of our problem." Gaskin sobbed. "I didn't want to hurt anyone. But it all just sort of got out of control. If Yvonne told the media about the contamination on our site, our company would have gone bankrupt, and I couldn't let that happen."

"Because of your gambling debts?" Skye asked.

"Yeah." Gaskin wiped his cheeks with the back of his hand. "Those guys don't mess around. It was her or me." His expression hardened. "That bitch just didn't understand. You don't mess with a man's livelihood."

Skye and Wally exchanged a disgusted look, and he wrapped up the questioning. Three hours later, Gaskin's case had been turned over to the city attorney and Skye and Wally were on their way to the airport.

As they merged onto I-55, Skye said, "I'm surprised Gaskin caved as fast as he did."

"Except for habitual criminals, most people find it hard to maintain a lie when there is so much evidence against them." Wally's smile was grim. "Besides, in my years as a cop, it's been my experience that if you act with authority, most people will tell you anything."

"I've seen that as a school psych, too." Skye was silent for a few miles, then said, "What I admire about Yvonne is that she cared so much; she couldn't look the other way even if it put her life in danger."

"Most folks are happy to do the right thing when it's easy." Wally kept his gaze on the traffic. "But when it gets hard, they usually put themselves first."

"So many people claim that principles are situational or personal, but that's just an excuse to look the other way and not hold someone accountable for their actions. Yvonne believed that doing the right thing meant caring about others as much as herself." Skye squeezed Wally's hand. "The prevalent opinion seems to be that behaving honorably makes life less enjoyable. But really, doing the right thing allows us to live in a way that fulfills us. Otherwise, it's like a diet of candy bars. Yummy while you're eating them, but they never quite satisfy your hunger and you know that something you need is missing."

"That's a hard message to get across to people." Wally wrinkled his brow. "Maybe you can convince Kathy Steele to have the *Scumble River Star* do an article honoring Yvonne as someone who took a big risk and made the ultimate sacrifice for the common good."

"That's a great idea." Skye leaned over and kissed his cheek. "It would show all those people she annoyed that she was so nitpicky about the small rules because allowing herself to overlook them would have made it easier to ignore true evil when she was faced with it."

They were silent for a few miles; then, as the traffic thinned, Wally relaxed and said, "I wonder which parent Phoebe will be like."

"I hope she's a blend of them both," Skye murmured. "That way she'd have ethics, but also a sense of survival. If Yvonne had had that, she'd be alive today."

Checking Out

Skye and Wally snuggled on the white leather sofa in the middle of his father's private jet. Carson and Quentin were in the front of the plane, seated on matching armchairs. Although Skye had flown several times in the past, this was nothing like those commercial flights.

First of all, there had been no parking problem or luggage issues. Wally had pulled his Thunderbird into an empty hangar, and their luggage had been whisked away. Security had also been much quicker, and instead of taking two hours to board, they'd walked onto the plane in less than twenty minutes.

Then there was the food. Since they'd skipped breakfast, Skye was hungry and hadn't been looking forward to a package of peanuts and a soda. She was astounded when the flight attendant offered them a luncheon menu listing coq au vin, veal Oscar, or steamed Maine lobster. She'd chosen the lobster, which came with roasted red potatoes and grilled asparagus. Dessert was chocolate mousse cake.

While they ate, she said to Wally, "So this is what your life was like before Scumble River?"

"Pretty much." He dug into his veal Oscar. They'd

both burned a lot of calories the night before. "Except it was more like that." He pointed his fork at his father poring over a stack of papers while Quentin talked on the phone.

"I didn't think you could use a cell while flying." Skye watched her new cousin as he propped the tiny black rectangle between his shoulder and ear so he could take notes as he spoke.

"Private jets have their own Internet and phone links that use either satellites or special ground stations." Wally finished his entrée and reached for his dessert.

"Oh." Skye had no idea how the top one percent lived. "I suppose that's a necessity, since most are used for business."

"And speaking of business, this is the last little bit. I promise." Wally took out his cell as "Hail to the Chief" blared from his pocket. "Yeah." He listened, then said, "Good." He listened again and shook his head. "No. You're in charge now. I don't want to hear about it unless Scumble River is attacked by a band of vampire were-wolf zombies." He paused, then added just before click-ing the phone closed, "Actually, not even then."

"Was that Quirk?"

"Yep." Wally turned his cell off and stuck it in his carry-on bag. "The lab results confirm that the paint is from the vic's car and the wood is from the bridge. Prov-ing the blood on the wheel is Gaskin's will take a couple more days, but in exchange for immunity from an acces-sory charge, Neil Osborn has agreed to testify against him."

"Sounds like an airtight case." Skye finished her cake. "But I'm still glad we got the confession."

"Me too." Wally pushed his plate away and reached for Skye. "Now we don't have to think about anything but us for the next seven days."

"A cruise!" Skye squealed. "I've always wanted to go on a cruise. I was so jealous of Trixie getting to take one."

After the CB International jet had landed in Fort Lauderdale and they'd said goodbye to Carson and Quentin, a limo had taken Skye and Wally to the port, where Wally had finally revealed his big surprise. They were honeymooning in the eastern Caribbean on the *Diamond Countess*.

"What ship is Trixie on?" Wally asked as a tuxedoed man showed them to their quarters.

"I don't know." Skye shrugged, distracted by the soaring lobby. "I don't think she ever said, or if she did, I don't remember."

"Too much wedding talk, right?" Wally teased.

"Probably." Skye's expression was sheepish. "I have been a little self-involved since we started planning it."

The man pressed the elevator UP button and announced, "Your suite is on deck seven."

"A suite!" Skye yelped. "Oh, my gosh!"

"I told you I was able to afford an upgrade because I got such a good price using your mother's tip." Wally beamed at Skye's excitement.

"My mother." Skye's voice rose.

"Yes. She told me about the special the travel agency in town was running." Wally sounded puzzled. "Remember—"

"No," Skye interrupted him. "There, on the stairs." She pointed. "Isn't that my mother?"

A book club meeting turns deadly
and romantic rivalries take center stage in
Denise Swanson's next
Devereaux's Dime Store Mystery,

Dead Between the Lines

Available in March 2014 as a paperback
and e-book.
Read on for a fun excerpt. . . .

Well, this was awkward. In my head, I could hear my grandmother Birdie yelling, "Devereaux Ann Sinclair, what have you gotten yourself into this time?" Ann wasn't my real middle name, but little details like that never stood in Gran's way when she was truly ticked off at me.

I slid a cautious glance to my left. My shop, Devereaux's Dime Store and Gift Baskets, boasted three soda fountain stools, and two of them were occupied by men who had recently kissed me silly. In the antique Bradley and Hubbard cast-iron mirror hanging behind the counter, I could see them sitting shoulder to shoulder, glaring at each other. The gilt cherub on top of the glass smirked back at them.

Being the coward that I am, I ignored the two rivals for my affection and forced my poor weekend clerk, Xylia Locke, to deal with them while I stayed firmly behind my beloved 1920s brass cash register, ringing up the purchases of the last few lingering customers. As I bagged Mr. Williams's Lucky Tiger Liquid Cream Shave, I wondered what my straitlaced employee thought of the two smoldering men in front of her, or for that matter, what her opinion was of my less than orderly life. Xylia was majoring in business administration at the local junior college, and she hated it when life—especially the emotional part—got muddled, chaotic, or messy.

Xylia liked her world to be as neat and tidy as she was, never appearing in public in anything but perfectly tailored slacks and sweater sets in muted colors. In fact, when I had first hired her, she'd offered to take a pay cut in exchange for not having to wear a sweatshirt with the store logo embroidered on the front. I'd been a little insulted that she didn't want to have my name across her chest, but I'd swallowed my pride and agreed to her proposal.

Even the small amount of money I saved on her salary was a godsend to my cash-starved bottom line. Because, while quitting my consulting job at Stramp Investments and buying the dime store had reduced my round-trip commute from two hours to fifteen minutes and cut the time I spent at work almost in half, it had also shrunk my income from six figures to nearly poverty level. So even if it bruised my ego a bit that Xylia didn't like my sweatshirt design, any way that I could keep my books in the black was okay with me.

The change in career path, aspirations, and lifestyle had all been worth it in order to be able to spend the extra time with my grandmother. When Birdie's doctor had informed me that she needed me to be around more to keep an eye on her due to her memory issues, I knew it was my turn to help her. How could I do anything less, since she had been the one who had taken me in and loved me when I had nowhere else to go and no one else who cared?

I had just turned sixteen when my father went to prison for manslaughter and possession of a controlled substance. My mother, unable to handle the shame, loss of income, and reduced social status, had dropped me on my grandmother's front porch with a fifty-dollar bill and a couple of suitcases containing all that was left of my previous life. Having disposed of her burden, Mom then headed to Cal-

ifornia to start over, leaving my grandmother and me to
face the town's condemnation by ourselves.

"Ms. Sinclair?" Xylia slipped from behind the soda
fountain and scurried over to me as I flicked off the neon
OPEN sign. It was Friday and we closed at six o'clock.

"Yes?" I had given up trying to persuade her to call
me Dev or even Devereaux. She claimed it didn't show
the degree of respect an employee should have for her
superior. Sometimes I wondered what century Xylia
thought we were living in. While I loved vintage collectibles and antiques, I had no desire to bring back the formal manners and rigid customs of days gone by.

"What about them?" Xylia glanced uneasily between
the men and the locked door. "Are they staying?"

"Apparently." They obviously had no intention of
budging from their perches. Having swiveled around to
face the store, they had crossed their arms in identical
gestures of stubborn defiance and were now glaring al-
ternately at me and at each other. Their silence was un-
nerving, and if looks could kill, both guys would be dead
and I'd be fatally wounded.

"But we have to get ready for the book club." Xylia
fingered the tiny heart-shaped birthmark on her cheek,
something she did only in times of extreme stress. "They
aren't members."

"It'll be fine." Throughout Xylia's shift, I'd noticed
that she had been even more tightly wound than usual.
Now I realized that she must be nervous about hosting
her club's meeting. It had been her idea to have it at the
dime store, and she probably felt responsible for the
event's outcome.

"We won't have enough chairs." Her voice rose. "Mr.
Quistgaard was very specific in his requirements. He'll
leave if anyone is standing. Everything will be ruined."

"We'll work it out," I assured her. "Do you know Mr.
Quistgaard?" Seating for everyone seemed an odd condition for an author to have, especially one who wasn't a
"big name." If J. K. Rowling or Nora Roberts wanted

everyone sitting, you damn well better have everyone off their feet, but Lance Quistgaard, not so much. "Did you select his book for your club?"

"Our president, Mrs. Zeigler, engages all our speakers." Xylia backed away from me, bumping into the APRIL SHOWERS BRING MAY FLOWERS display. "Usually through their Web sites."

"I see." I bent to replace an overturned red clay pot on a bag of mulch.

"Let me do that." Xylia nudged me out of the way and moved the small Victorian iron patio table a fraction of an inch to the left, then straightened the two matching chairs. "I've been meaning to fix this all afternoon." She adjusted the shepherd's hook plant hanger that was holding a basket of yellow and purple pansies a smidgen to the right.

Did I mention that my clerk was a little OCD?

As I leaned against the gas grill that the hardware store had loaned me for my display, I said, "Did you enjoy this month's book?"

"Uh." Xylia bit her lip. "I'm sure I will once I understand the poems better."

One of the men at the soda fountain cleared his throat, and Xylia flinched at the sound. She grimaced, then put her hand on my arm and pleaded, "Do something before they spoil the whole evening."

"Don't worry." I turned away so she couldn't see me roll my eyes. "They'll be gone before the author arrives." I was fairly certain neither of the men currently scrutinizing me was interested in hearing a poetry reading.

"But wh—"

"I'll handle it." I cut her off before she could hyperventilate. "My Supergirl cape is at the dry cleaner, so you'll just have to take my word for it, but I promise they'll leave before you're finished setting up."

Xylia opened her mouth to protest, but closed it when I frowned and ordered, "Go start getting the crafting alcove ready for your group."

With one last worried peek over her shoulder, Xylia headed toward the back room, where the folding tables and chairs were stored.

The minute she was out of sight, both men shot off their seats and stomped toward me. Taking a deep breath, I focused on the one who, by elbowing his competition, then cutting his opponent off at the pass, got to me first. Tall, dark, and devastating, Deputy U.S. Marshal Jake Del Vecchio had blown back into town an hour ago, plainly expecting us to pick up where we had left off and just as plainly unhappy to find another guy warming *his* stool at *my* soda fountain.

I had met Jake when he was recuperating from a line-of-duty injury at his granduncle's ranch. He had helped me clear my name when I had been accused of murdering my old boyfriend's fiancée. Then a month ago, after being declared fit for duty, he'd returned to St. Louis. And except for a brief visit and make-out session a few weeks ago, that was the last I'd seen of him.

Now, as he cupped my cheek, his words sent a sizzle down my spine. "I've been dreaming about doing this the entire time I was gone."

He leaned in for a kiss, but with his mouth inches from mine, I stepped back, and his hand dropped to his side. It had been hard to pull away. The electricity between us was enough to light up most of North America. But I knew that if I let our lips touch, I'd lose all my willpower to resist, and I couldn't allow that to happen.

In the meantime, the guy who had been sitting next to Jake had reached my side. Sleek, elegant, and aristocratic, Dr. Noah Underwood had been my high school boyfriend. Because both our mothers had been pregnant at the same time, we claimed to have known each other since the womb. The Underwoods and the Sinclairs were two of the five founding families of Shadow Bend, Missouri, our hometown, which meant while growing up we were constantly thrown together at parties, charity events, and community functions. So when Noah and I hit adolescence, it had seemed inevitable that we would become sweethearts.

For a while, we were inseparable. During that time, Noah was the most important person in my life, and I had thought I was the most important one in his. Sadly, I'd been mistaken. When we started dating, the Sinclairs and the Underwoods were social equals. But after my father's disgrace, the Sinclairs became the town pariahs, and Noah dropped me like a lit match before his reputation could go up in the same flames that had consumed my family's good name.

According to Noah, he'd had a noble reason for breaking off with me. However, even though he'd proven there was still a spark between us, I wasn't sure I believed his version of past events. And I definitely didn't trust that he wouldn't dump me or betray me again if a similar situation were to occur.

Moving with an inherent grace, Noah put both hands on my shoulders and spun me so that I was facing him. That I now had my back to Jake was probably just a bonus. Once Noah was sure he had my attention—he was a methodical kind of guy—he put his lips to my ear and whispered, "Get rid of Deputy Dawg. I've got a surprise planned for you."

"What?" His warm breath tickling my neck sent a *bibbidi-bobbidi-boo* message to my girl parts. Both of these guys could melt my panties right off my hips. "Were we supposed to get together tonight?" I knew we didn't have plans because that wasn't something I would have forgotten, but I wanted to hear his explanation.

"No." Noah's head dipped closer. "I thought it would be fun to be spontaneous."

"Possibly." I finally got control of myself and leaned away from him. "Except I have a club meeting here at seven and Gran is expecting me home after that."

"Take your hands off of her, Frat Boy." Jake muscled his way in between Noah and me.

I moved so that I was facing both guys, but when they

crowded forward, I realized that I had let them corner me. My back was against solid shelves, so I couldn't retreat, and the men had cut off any possible forward escape route.

"Hold it, fellas." I crossed my arms. "Let's maintain a little personal space here, shall we?"

Jake cocked a dark brow and gave me a badass grin, but he didn't budge, and Noah, despite looking a little sheepish, didn't give an inch, either. Frustrated, I put a hand on each of their chests and shoved. Even though Jake was brawnier, Noah had a lean strength, so it was like pushing against twin statues.

Lowering my gaze to their crotches, I threatened, "Don't make me go for the family jewels."

Jake raised his hands. "Fine." He tipped his head toward Noah. "But are you really dating this bozo?"

Noah tensed, then narrowed his slate gray eyes, shouldered his way in front of Jake, and said to me, "After not hearing from this jerk for weeks, you're not thinking of seeing him again, are you?"

Well, hell! This was truly a hot mess. I *so* didn't want to have this conversation with either of them right this minute. Mostly because I had no idea what to say. Both men were gorgeous, in utterly different ways. Mysterious versus familiar. Strikingly masculine versus classically handsome. A German shepherd versus a Russian wolfhound.

However, both had significant drawbacks as well. While the sexual chemistry between Jake and me was off the charts, he lived in St. Louis, a good five hours away. There was also the troublesome detail that he worked closely—very closely—with his ex-wife, who happened to be his team leader and thus his boss. In fact, his most recent assignment had required that they pretend to be boyfriend and girlfriend.

So, Noah had the advantage of availability, but I had a painful history with him. Jake had a clean slate, but complications.

Neither guy was a sure thing; nor was either one an

obvious choice. With all that in mind, as well as the knowledge of my many previous romantic missteps, I figured that dating either man would probably be a lesson in candy-coated misery.

What I should do was convince them that we could all be friends and keep both relationships platonic. Of course, I rarely did what I should. Still, I had to do something before they killed each other or shed someone else's blood, namely mine. I'd detested being a suspect in a murder case, but I was pretty damn sure I'd hate being a victim even more.